DEADLY CONFRONTATION

Sam held his gaze fixed ironlike on Fain's eyes. "Ready to take them now?" he asked, running his free palm back and forth across the two gun butts.

Wanting a way out, Fain looked at the other two gunmen. The looks on their faces told him they weren't backing down. He took some courage from knowing the odds were on his side.

"Oh, we'll be taking them, sure enough," said Fain with a scowl. His eyes widened. "You don't come carrying our friends' guns in here and telling lies, saying you killed them, whether you did or not—"

His words stopped short as McCool's big Russian Smith & Wesson came up from Sam's waist and made a vicious swipe across the outlaw's jaw. Fain flew backward to the floor. Montoya and Petty wasted no time snatching their guns from their holsters. But it did them no good. Before either gun aimed or fired, both the Russian Smith & Wesson and Sam's own Colt fired at once.

"One _____"

_____ Horseman

"Cott_____ works becau_____ e fill his books._____ ___ *Magazine*

TWISTED HILLS

Ralph Cotton

A SIGNET BOOK

SIGNET
Published by the Penguin Group
Penguin Group (USA) LLC, 375 Hudson Street,
New York, New York 10014

USA | Canada | UK | Ireland | Australia | New Zealand | India | South Africa | China
penguin.com
A Penguin Random House Company

First published by Signet, an imprint of New American Library,
a division of Penguin Group (USA) LLC

First Printing, February 2014

Ⓟ REGISTERED TRADEMARK—MARCA REGISTRADA

ISBN 978-0-451-46591-7

Printed in the United States of America
10   9   8   7   6   5   4   3   2   1

For Mary Lynn, of course . . .

PART 1

Chapter 1

———◆———

The Badlands, Arizona Territory

Under a blazing desert sun, Arizona Ranger Sam Burrack slid two warm and spent cartridge shells from his bone-handled Colt and replaced them with fresh rounds from his gun belt. A thin sliver of smoke still curled in the gun's cylinder. He closed the Colt's loading gate and held the gun upright as he looked all around the rocky, desolate desert floor. A mile out, trail dust rose and drifted across a stretch of flatlands reaching toward the border.

"Looks like your pal Pres Kelso decided it's time to clear out of here," he said down to the wounded outlaw lying beneath the sole of his left boot.

"Preston Kelso . . . was never my *pal*, Ranger," the wounded man, Curtis Rudabell, replied in a pained and halting voice. "I only rode . . . with him this one time. He's a . . . son of a bitch. . . ."

So it was Pres Kelso . . . , Sam ascertained to himself. That was what he'd wanted to know. Looking at the outlaw's bloody chest, realizing Rudabell wasn't going anywhere, the Ranger lifted his boot off his shoulder. He stooped down beside him, picked up the smoking revolver sitting at Rudabell's side and held it in his free hand. He picked up a tobacco pouch made from a bull's scrotum, with Rudabell's initials carved on it. He tipped up the brim of his pearl gray sombrero and took a long breath. Twenty yards off lay the horse Rudabell had ridden to death.

"Feel free to take anything of mine you might need," Rudabell said with bitter sarcasm.

"Obliged," Sam said, his own sarcasm more veiled. As he spoke, he shoved the tobacco pouch behind his gun belt. He felt a few coins down inside the bag mixed with some chopped tobacco.

"Sons of Mother Nancy . . . I'm left for dead . . . ," Rudabell muttered under his failing breath. "Blast Kelso's eyes. . . ."

"I could have told you he's a runner," Sam said.

Rudabell clutched his bleeding chest.

"Yeah . . . but you *didn't* tell me, did you?" the outlaw said bitterly, his voice weakening as he spoke. He stared at his gun in the Ranger's hand. "Tell the truth. . . . I nearly got you, didn't I, Ranger?"

"To tell the truth, Curtis," the Ranger said quietly, "no, you didn't. Fact is, you didn't even come close." He looked all around again, feeling the scalding heat of the sun pressing hard on his shoulders through his shirt, his riding duster. "Can I get you something . . . some water?" he asked.

Rudabell gave him a sour look. "Got any . . . whiskey?" he asked.

"Not a drop," Sam said.

"That . . . figures," said the dying outlaw. He reflected for a second, then said, "You reckon . . . there'll be whiskey aplenty in hell?"

"Never gave it much thought, Curtis," the Ranger said. "Seems like a tough place to go drinking." He stayed patient.

"I bet I've . . . drank in worse," Rudabell commented.

"Where's Pres headed in old Mex?" the Ranger asked. He knew the odds were long on the outlaw telling him anything, but it was worth a try.

"He's headed . . . to Cold Water, Ranger," Rudabell offered without hesitation.

"Agua Fría," the Ranger said.

"Yeah . . . that's right, Agua Fría," said Rudabell. He gave a deep, wheezing chuckle, his teeth smeared red with blood. "I hope you bust out and . . . follow him there."

"I intend to," Sam said, wanting to get as much information as he could from Rudabell before he died. "Why do you hope I follow him there?"

Rudabell didn't answer, his eyes drifting shut. Sam shook the outlaw by his shoulder.

"You'll see," said Rudabell, his eyes managing to re-open and focus on the Ranger. "My kind of people . . . have taken over Agua Fría." He gave a waning grin; his eyes closed again. "Ranger, guess what . . . ," he whispered. He managed to grip Sam's forearm, as if to hold on and keep from sliding off the edge of the earth.

"What?" the Ranger replied, letting him hold on, feeling his grip diminish with each passing second.

"There *is* whiskey in hell . . . I see it, plain as day . . . ," Rudabell said. He let out a breath, which stopped short and left his mouth agape.

Lucky you, Sam thought wryly.

He shook his head, reached out, touched the barrel of Rudabell's gun beneath the outlaw's beard-stubbled chin and tipped his gaping mouth shut. A trickle of blood seeped from the corner of Rudabell's lips and ran down his cheek toward his ear.

Sam stood up and looked off at the trail of dust roiling in the distance, seeing it disappear over a low rise of rocky ground. Lowering his Colt into its holster, he took off his sombrero and ran his fingers back through his damp hair. He shoved Rudabell's Smith & Wesson down behind his gun belt. On the ground lay a set of saddlebags stuffed with cash from the Clifton-American Mining Project.

Since he'd retrieved the money, he reasoned, maybe this was a good time to pull back and do some thinking.

For the past year, he'd heard of various thieves and killers taking refuge in and around the town of Agua Fría. It was time he checked things out there. Under the Matamoros Agreement, the Mexican government gave U.S. lawmen limited rights to cross the border in pursuit of felons in flight from American justice. But after what he'd just heard from Curtis Rudabell, which was nothing less than a dare, he wasn't going to follow Pres Kelso there. Not today.

He'd head there later—maybe a week, maybe longer. And when he did go to Agua Fría, he wasn't going to be wearing a badge. *Huh-uh.* He got the feeling that wearing a badge would be the same as wearing a bull's-eye on his chest. He looked himself up and down, the pearl gray sombrero hanging in hand, the long duster. He looked over at his Appaloosa stallion, Black Pot; then he gazed back down at Curtis Rudabell.

"Obliged for the warning, Curtis," he said to the dead outlaw. He stooped enough to grip Rudabell by his shirt collar and drag him off toward a pile of rocks.

Preston Kelso rode hard and straight, nonstop, until he reached the shelter of a rocky hill line. He wasn't sure if he had yet crossed the border, but when he swung his sweat-streaked bay around and looked back through the billowing dust, he saw no sign of being followed. *What the hell—?* Only a vast and empty stretch of desert floor lay behind him. Nothing moved on the arid rocky ground, save for the black shadow of a hawk circling high overhead.

"Ha," he chuffed to himself in surprise. So much for all the brave and relentless lawmen along the border.

He smiled to himself; but then his smile fell away quickly, as his fear subsided and his memory sharpened.

The money . . . !

He turned quickly in his saddle and looked down at his bay's sweaty dirt-streaked rump.

Damn it to hell! He let out a breath in exasperation, realizing Rudabell had been carrying the money—not just some of the money, but all of the money.

"Damn it to hell!" he repeated, this time out loud, looking back again in the direction of the place where he and Rudabell had had the running shootout with a lone lawman. "Curtis, you lousy dog," he murmured, "if you don't show up with that money, you'd better be deader than a cedar stump when I find you."

He jerked the bay's reins, turning the horse hard-handed, as if it were to blame. He slapped the long ends of the reins to the winded animal's side and spurred it forward at a run. The bay chuffed hard in protest, but shot forward, resuming the same fast pace beneath the scorching desert sun.

"You fall dead on me, cayuse," he warned, "and I'll eat your tenders and leave your carcass for the night feeders."

He gave a dark laugh and pushed the tired animal a full hour farther until they reached a water hole at the base of a low rocky hill line. After both horse and rider had drunk their fill, Kelso started to step up into his saddle when he heard the chilling sound of a snake rattling its warning from a pile of rocks less than five feet away. Instead of swinging the already frightened bay away from the sound, he instinctively turned, snatched his Colt up from its holster and fired into the rocks, blindly. The bullet ricocheted three times off the rocks, whined back toward Kelso's head and zipped past the bay's ear.

The horse, badly spooked by the sound of the snake followed by the blast of the Colt and the whining bullet, reared in panic and jerked free of Kelso's grip.

"Whoa!" Kelso shouted. But the bay bolted fast, its reins sliding through Kelso's hand before he could stop it.

Seeing the bay bounding away from the water hole and the hillside, out across the desert floor he'd just crossed, Kelso swung his smoking Colt up in anger. He fired two wild shots at the fleeing animal before he stopped himself and let his smoking Colt slump at his side.

"You're going to let me down too," he shouted at the animal, walking forward, seeing the bay slow to a halt less than a hundred yards away. The bay turned quarterwise to him and stared back, its head lowered, its reins hanging to the ground. Kelso saw the horse scrape a front hoof on the rocky, sandy ground.

"Stay right there, you flea-bitten bag of bones," he murmured to himself. "I will beat you god-awful fierce." Even as he spoke, he closed the distance between himself and the bay with his left hand held out, as if offering it some sort of treat. The bay turned its stance a little more toward him, its muzzle pushed out in curiosity. A hot breeze lifted its dusty mane.

"Thatta boy," Kelso said, easing forward the last fifteen feet, his Colt still hanging in his right hand. He knew how much he needed the horse to get across mile after mile of rocky hills and long stretches of desert between here and Agua Fría. "Easy, now, ol' pal of mine," he whispered, taking the last few steps. "You know I wouldn't hurt you for the world."

The horse stood still, blowing and staring at him until Kelso got close enough to reach out for the dangling reins. But just as he made a grab for the reins, the bay spun sharply, bolted off twenty yards, stopped again and seemed to jeer at him.

"You lousy son of a—" Kelso gritted his teeth, jerked his Colt up and fired again before he could stop himself.

Because he was weakened and winded, the impact of the shot knocked him off his feet. As the bay turned and loped away from the sound of the shot, Kelso staggered to his feet and bolted after it, weaving, screaming, cursing both the horse and himself. He fired another wild reckless round as he ran. Again the gun's impact knocked him to the ground.

For a half mile the bay continued to play its mindless stop-and-go game with him. Kelso, falling with every shot fired, was gasping for breath and so engrossed in catching the horse, he neither saw nor heard the four unshod Indian ponies and their riders bound up behind him and sit watching him curiously from forty feet away. Still cursing the bay, Kelso staggered in place, winded and sweat-soaked, his mind bordering between sunstroke and hysteria.

"I've . . . got . . . you . . . now . . . ," he said, his breath heaving in his chest. He shoved fresh rounds into his Colt with shaking hands while the horse stood fifteen feet away, scraping its hoof on the arid sandy ground. "You . . . rotten . . . dirty . . . no-good . . ." Kelso panted and wheezed and struggled to catch his breath as he finished reloading, lifted the heavy revolver with both hands and took aim.

On one of the Indian ponies behind him, a young Apache brave named Luka looked at an older warrior, Wallace Bad Man Gomez.

"This one shoots at his own horse . . . ?" Luca whispered sidelong to the older warrior.

Without taking his dark eyes off the staggering,

cursing white man in front of them, Gomez nodded and laid his hand on the stock of an old short-barreled flint-lock rifle lying across his lap.

"I have seen them do even worse," he replied, refer-ring to his days as a scout for the U.S. Cavalry's desert campaign. He stared intently at the staggering, cursing white man. "And they wonder why we want to kill them."

The others grunted in agreement.

Kelso, with his revolver cocked and ready, finally steadied himself and smiled a dry lip-cracking smile.

"I've got you now, you run-off son of a bitch," he mur-mured to himself. He started to squeeze the trigger; but he stopped and clenched both hands tight on the gun butt as a searing pain sliced through his back. The Colt's bar-rel tipped upward and fired a blue-orange streak into the sky. Kelso staggered in place but remained upright. His eyes widened as he saw an arrow shaft suddenly stick-ling out of his chest, its chiseled stone point smeared red with his blood. His left hand turned loose of his Colt and felt the tip of the arrowhead as if to make sure it was real.

Oh no! Damn it! Kelso said to himself. No sooner had he realized that an arrow was stuck through him than another bloody arrowhead appeared beside the first as if to reinforce his findings. "All day it's . . . been like this . . . ," he gasped to himself. Behind him he heard his bay's hooves pounding away across the desert flatland.

Son of a bitch . . .

He turned to face the four Apaches, his gun still up in his right hand, but weaving unsteadily. One of the arrows through his back had sliced one of his wide suspender straps. The strap flew loose so fast it caused the other strap to fall off his shoulder. As he'd turned, his low-slung gun belt and loose trousers fell down around his boots. He faced the Apache in his dirty long johns as a third arrow whistled in and sliced deep into his chest.

Kelso grunted with the impact of the arrow; his Colt fell from his hand. Scrambling, he managed to stoop down for the gun as he saw one of the Indians come charging toward him. He grabbed the gun and stood just in time to see pony and rider streak past him in a roil of sand. He felt a strong hand lift his hair, hat and all, atop his head, and in the next second, the rider was gone, swinging his pony in a short, tight circle, letting out a war whoop.

Kelso turned and stared, feeling a dark, sharp burning across the top of his exposed head. He caught a glimpse of his hat brim fluttering to the ground a few feet away.

"Oh . . . my God," he said, his gun hand falling to his side, dropping the Colt to the ground. "I've been ruint." He stared in disbelief at the young warrior whooping and shouting, waving the crown of Kelso's hat back and forth in his hand—Kelso's hair and bloody skin hanging beneath it. Staring at his own stringy hair clasped in the warrior's hand, Kelso sank straight down to his knees; then he flopped forward onto his face in the hot, sandy dirt.

As the Apache sat their horses above Kelso, the older warrior, Gomez, saw one of the young warriors raise a battered French Gruen rifle to his shoulder and take aim on the center of Kelso's bloody back. He held up a hand toward the warrior, stopping him.

"Let this fool's shots be the last ones heard," he said. He shook his head in disgust. "Even his horse deserts him." He looked all around as he turned his horse and gestured for the others to do the same. The young warrior, Luka, held Kelso's bloody scalp and stringy hair out for the others to see.

"A good day for one of us is a good day for all of us," he said proudly. The warriors and their horses fell in alongside Gomez and rode away abreast, out across the flatlands.

In the ensuing silence, two hours passed before Kelso opened his bleary eyes at the feel of the horse's hot, wet muzzle nudging the side of his neck. A layer of dust had gathered on the top of his raw, bloody skull. In a weakened state, as he tried to push himself up from the ground, he felt the dried blood and the points of the two ground-stuck arrows reluctant to turn him loose. Yet, as his memory returned to him through a fiery painful haze, he managed to struggle upward onto his haunches and look at the bay, who stood staring at him.

"I'll kill you . . . for this . . . ," he said painfully, reaching all around on the dirt for his Colt.

The bay only chuffed and blew and shook out its mane, as if taunting the man for the sudden loss of his hair. Kelso, realizing the Apaches had taken both his handgun and rifle, gave a deep sigh and pulled himself up on the bay's front leg and leaned against its side. The horse stood quietly.

"I don't know . . . what else can . . . befall a man . . . ," he groaned, seeing the brim of his hat and its sliced-off crown lying in the dirt at his feet. He stooped, picked up the brim and pulled it carefully down over his raw-scalped head, drawing the string taut under his chin. He crawled up the horse's side. "I'm killing you . . . first chance I get," he whispered to the bay. Righting himself in his saddle as best he could with arrows still sticking through him, he managed to turn the horse and ride away.

Chapter 2

———

The Hooke Brothers, Charlie Ray and Hazerat, sat atop their horses looking down on the flatlands from a high rock ledge in the direction of the gunfire they had heard an hour earlier. Shadows of cactus and rock spurs stretched in the evening sunlight. With a long brass-trimmed naval telescope to his eye, Hazerat Hooke studied the single horse trudging along at a slow pace on the distant desert floor. The worn-out animal walked half-hidden by a low mound of rock that had spilled off the hillside over the years and formed up like a jetty in an ocean of sand.

"Whatever all the shooting was, looks like it only left one survivor," he said sidelong to his brother seated beside him.

Charlie Ray Hooke sat slumped in his saddle, his wrists crossed on his saddle horn. He gazed off down at his gloved hands, not attempting to see through the wavering desert heat.

"One survivor . . . ," he said in a tone of disgust. "What is he, an Injun or a beaner?" he asked with disinterest.

"Neither one," said Hazerat with a half sigh. "All we

got coming here is a horse—a half-dead one at that."
He lowered the telescope from his eye and handed it
sidelong to his brother.

"A horse, huh?" Charlie said, taking the telescope,
raising it to his eye. "All that shooting, I expect the rider
is somewhere back there, dead in the dirt." He paused,
then said idly, watching the tired horse trudge along, the
rock wall growing shorter as it neared the end of it,
"Wonder what the shooting was over."

"Nothing worth riding back to look at," said Hazerat.

"Hard as it is crossing this furnace, I ain't taking a step
backward for nothing or nobody," said Charlie. "We're
close enough to Agua Fría, I want to ride on in tonight.
Come morning I hope to be drunker than a blind rooster."

"Yeah, me too," said Hazerat, reconsidering the matter. "I've seen enough Mexican desert to last me a good
while—"

"Uh-oh, we've got more," Charlie interrupted, seeing the lone horse walk past the end of the rock wall.
Behind the tired horse, he saw a rider being dragged
along in the rocky dirt, his boot stuck inside the horse's
stirrup. The unconscious man slid easily over the rocky
floor like a limp rag.

Hazerat tilted his head back and squinted into the
evening sun glare.

"What have we got?" he asked, tapping his brother's
side, holding his hand for the telescope, which Charlie
made no effort to give him.

"He's dragging some poor pilgrim behind him,"
Charlie said.

"Hey, let me see, damn it," said Hazerat, tapping his brother's side a little harder. "Is he dead or what?"

Charlie studied the man being dragged, seeing the short arrow stubs sticking out of his chest. Black dried blood covered the hapless man's chest. More black dried blood covered his face below the sliced-off hat brim still held in place by its taut drawstring.

"If he ain't dead, he's wishing he was," said Charlie. He lowered the telescope and passed it to Hazerat. "Looks like he's been kilt and scalped."

"Tough knuckles," Hazerat replied, taking the telescope and raising it to his eye again. He studied the horse and body behind it closer. "But better him than us."

"I'm guessing that whatever is in this fool's pocket ain't worth riding down for," said Charlie Hooke. "But since we're riding down anyway . . ." He let his words trail, turned his horse away and nudged it toward the narrow path leading down to the flatlands.

"Didn't you just say you wasn't taking a step back for nothing or nobody?" said Hazerat.

"I'm not," said Charlie, his horse walking on down the narrow trail.

Hazerat cursed under his breath. He collapsed the telescope and shoved it inside his buckskin shirt. Turning his horse behind his brother, he caught up with him ten yards down the trail.

"Still," Charlie said as Hazerat drew up behind him, "I hate thinking he might be carrying a few coins, and we missed a chance at closing our hands around them."

"You might have a point, Brother Charlie," said Hazerat. He gazed off in the direction of the lone horse.

"We're not riding back, but I expect we can draw up, rest in some shade down there," said Charlie.

"And riffle this fool's pockets when he gets here." Hazerat finished his older brother's words for him. He gave a stiff, parched grin.

"Watch out for whoever stuck the arrows through him," Charlie cautioned, the two looking in the direction of the rising stir of dust on the desert floor.

At the base of the steep hill trail, the two gunmen nudged their tired horses into the long evening shade behind a goliath land-stuck boulder and stepped down from their saddles. They seated themselves on two smaller rocks and sat sipping warm water from their canteens until at length the lone horse trudged into sight. After a few more minutes, they stood up and dusted the seats of their trousers as the horse continued trudging past them.

"Right on time," Hazerat said, capping his canteen.

The two moved out of the shade and stepped in front of the laboring horse.

"Whoa, now. . . ." Charlie took the dust-covered animal by its bridle and raised its dangling reins from the dirt as it came to a staggering halt.

Hazerat stepped back to the body trailing from the horse's stirrup. He cocked his head curiously and walked alongside as Charlie led the horse into the shade of the boulder.

"This fool looks familiar, don't you think?" he commented.

Charlie turned loose of the horse's bridle and shoved its probing dust-caked muzzle away from his canteen.

He stepped back and stood beside his brother, looking down.

"I'll say he does," said Charlie. "That's ol' Preston Kelso—it *was* anyway," he added.

"Jesus, I nearly didn't recognize him, his topknot skinned to the bone," said Hazerat. He swallowed a tightness in his throat. He looked up from the battered, blood-caked face and gazed back into the wavering heat, as if expecting trouble to be not far behind a man like Preston Kelso. "What do you suppose he was doing out here?"

Charlie stared flatly at his younger brother.

"He's a thief, Hazerat, just like us," he said.

"I know *that,* Charlie Ray," Hazerat said. He looked the tired horse over, seeing no saddlebags. "Whatever he was doing, it looks like there was no money in it."

The two stooped down over Kelso. They studied the black blood at the base of the arrows sticking up from his chest.

"Maybe he took to hunting the 'paches," Hazerat further speculated.

"That would explain his hairstyle," Charlie offered. He cocked his head back and forth, looking at Kelso from varied angles. As he spoke, he took a hold of one of the broken arrow shafts and started to pull it up from Kelso's chest.

"Poor bastard," Hazerat said with a wince. He reached out and squeezed each of Kelso's trouser pockets, feeling for any money or valuables. "We're lucky we didn't run into the same bunch."

As the arrow shaft began to pull free of the congealed

blood, a shriek came from Kelso's dust-caked lips, and his body jerked and trembled like a man stricken by a sharp bolt of lightning. Both gunmen reeled back on their haunches, startled by the sudden outburst. Hazerat's hands jerked away from Kelso's trouser pockets.

"He's *alive!*" said Charlie, stunned. His hands sprang away from the arrow shaft.

The two stared as Kelso slowly took in a thin breath and opened his dust-coated eyes.

"Preston," Charlie ventured, "can you hear me?"

"Who's . . . there?" Kelso asked weakly, as if answering a door.

"It's the Hookes," said Charlie. "Hazerat and Charlie Ray. We didn't do this to you."

"Water . . . ," said Kelso. His eyes skimmed over the canteen in Charlie's hand.

But Charlie tightened his grip on his canteen. He looked at Hazerat and said to Kelso, "I'm nearly out, Preston. Hazerat here will oblige you, though."

"*Me?*" said Hazerat. He clutched his canteen to his chest. "Hell, I've got less than you, Charlie."

"Water . . . ," Kelso repeated.

"I apologize for my brother Hazerat's *uncouthness,*" said Charlie, giving Hazerat a dark stare. "If I had water to spare, I'd give you some right off. But I'm down myself." He pushed up his hat brim. "Truth of it is, you're looking none too spry. And this is no country to be wasting water on a dying man."

"I understand . . . ," Kelso groaned. He closed his eyes as if in resignation to his fate. "I was . . . headed for Agua Fría. . . ."

"So are we, as fate would have it," said Charlie. "We aim to go to work for Raymond Segert. Hope to go to work for him, that is."

Kelso fell silent for a moment, then reopened his eyes and took a deeper breath.

"Tell . . . Segert I hid the money . . . before they killed me," he whispered. His eyes closed again.

"We'll tell him for you, Preston," Hazerat put in. "We'll tell whatever you want us to—"

Hazerat shut up as Charlie stiff-armed him on his shoulder.

"We'll need to tell him *where* you hid it, Preston," Charlie cut in. "Knowing ol' *Segar*, he'll be asking *where,* sure enough. Don't you think?" He and Hazerat gave each other a look.

"Too dry . . . to talk," Kelso murmured. He closed his eyes and fell silent.

The Hookes stared at each other, Charlie with a harsh cold expression toward his younger brother.

"You heard him, Hazerat," he said. "Give him some water."

Hazerat hugged his canteen to his chest. "Damn it, Charlie, you've got as much to spare as I have. Why am I the one on the spot here?"

"Give the man some water, Hazerat," Charlie demanded. "What kind of selfish turd are you?"

Hazerat bit his lip in anger. But he uncapped his canteen as he did so.

"All right, there," he growled. He poured a measured trickle of warm water into his cupped hand and held it down to Kelso's parched, cracked lips. "I'm giving him a little of mine. Now you give him some of yours. That's as fair as I know how to cut it."

Without taking his hard stare off Hazerat, Charlie uncapped his canteen, leaned close to his brother and whispered near his ear.

"Stop being an ass about this, Hazerat," he said. "Didn't you hear him say he hid some money back there?" He gestured a nod toward the endless desert hills.

"Yeah, I heard him," Hazerat replied grudgingly.

"Okay, then, help me out here, brother Hazerat," said Charlie under his breath.

Hazerat made a sour expression, but he reached over, raised Kelso's scalped head and held the canteen over to his lips.

"Come on, Preston, drink up, ol' pard. What's mine is yours," he said.

"Atta boy," Charlie said. "When you get through watering him, free his foot out of that stirrup." He reached over and gave his brother a slap on his shoulder.

"Free his foot?" said Hazerat.

"Yeah, free his foot," said Charlie, "unless you're planning on dragging him all over the desert that way."

"I wonder why it is you can't free his foot, Charlie," Hazerat said, "since I'm doing all the rest here."

Charlie shook his head, but he stepped over, untangled Kelso's boot from the stirrup and let his leg fall to the ground with a thump.

"There," said Charlie in a put-out tone. "Now get him watered and let's clear out of here before the 'paches stick a few arrows in us too. We're sitting ducks out here." He nodded toward a hill line standing obscured by the wavering heat in the southwest. "There's a water hole no more than seventeen, eighteen miles. If we ride the night we can be there come morning. Take cover in the rocks."

"I'm game," said Hazerat. He gazed warily back and forth across the desert floor. "What about sticking him in the saddle?" He nodded down at Kelso. "Like as not, it'll kill him."

"We have to stick him in the saddle anyway," Charlie said. "I don't see as we have much choice." He stared at Kelso's scalped head, his arrow-punctured chest. "Anybody lives through all this, I can't see a saddle killing him."

"They should have left him a gun and a bullet to kill himself with," said Hazerat. "Damn 'paches. . . ."

At the first streak of dawn in the eastern sky, the Hooke brothers had stepped down from their saddles, their canteen straps over their shoulders. They had eased Kelso down between them. Instead of his falling like deadweight as they had expected him too, both Charlie and Hazerat were surprised that the scalped and wounded man staggered on his feet, trying to support himself.

"Watch . . . my arrows, boys," Kelso murmured. The arrow stubs looked black and sore sticking out from his chest.

"Holy Joseph! You're still alive, Preston!" said Hazerat, one of Kelso's limp arms looped over his shoulder, his other arm looped over Charlie's.

"Hell yes . . . I'm alive . . . ," Kelso snarled weakly. "Help me . . . over to the water."

Charlie and Hazerat looked at each other, but did as they were told. At the water's edge, they seated him on a rock. Kelso motioned at the canteen hanging from Hazerat's shoulder. Hazerat stepped over to the water, uncapped the canteen and sank it and watched it gurgle and fill.

Stopping beside Kelso, Charlie studied Kelso's raw, bloody skull.

"We both thought you'd be gone off to hell by now, Preston, truth be told," he said.

"Truth be told . . . I could give . . . a blue damn less what you thought," Kelso replied. He reached for the canteen as Hazerat brought it to him. Helping him hold it, Hazerat raised it to Kelso's parched, cracked lips and let him drink. Beside them the three horses lined up along the water's edge and lowered their muzzles into water cooled by the passing night. Charlie reached over, cupped some water into his hand and wiped it onto his dust-caked face.

"Glad to see you're feeling better, Preston," he said.

"I'm glad . . . that you're glad," Kelso grumbled sourly, lowering the canteen with Hazerat's help. Water ran down his blood-caked chin and dripped red-black down his chest. "Now, give me . . . a gun," he demanded, snapping his weak fingers toward Hazerat.

"Wait!" said Charlie, seeing his brother obediently lift a spare Colt from behind his gun belt. But it was too late. Hazerat handed the Colt to Kelso, who took it and let the weight of it pull his hand down into his lap. His hand stayed around the gun butt; his thumb lay deftly over the hammer.

"Wait . . . for what?" said Kelso, his voice still weak but sounding stronger. He leered at Charlie. "If the 'paches show up again . . . you need all the guns . . . you've got."

Charlie looked at the gun in his lap, unsure if Kelso could raise and fire it, but not wanting to find out on himself.

"You're right, Preston," he said. "I was just thinking, in your shape and all . . ."

"Let's get this straight," said Kelso. He wiped his wrist across his mouth, wincing at the pain in his cracked lips. "What you want . . . is the money I hid. That's all that's . . . standing between me and the end of your gun barrel."

"Preston, I don't know how you can say—"

Kelso cut his protest short. "Because that's what I'd be thinking . . . were it the other way around," he said. He looked up at Hazerat. "Ain't that so, Hazerat?" he asked.

"I can't say we haven't thought about the money—" Hazerat started.

"Hell yes, it's so," the wounded, scalped gunman answered for him, cutting him off. Kelso struggled to his feet and stood shakily. But he managed to raise the Colt in his right hand and wave it back forth menacingly. "Get me to Agua Fría . . . ," he said in a strained voice. "If I live . . . I'll split the money with yas. If I die . . . you get nothing."

The Hookes looked at each other.

"How do we know we can trust you?" Charlie asked flatly.

"You don't," Kelso replied. "But it's the only hand you're holding."

"What about Segert?" Hazerat said. "Is he going to stand for you sharing money that's partly his?"

"He's got no choice," said Kelso. He coughed as he spoke and had to sit back down. A thin trickle of fresh red blood seeped down from around an arrow stub. "Especially when you . . . both tell him you saw those thieving 'paches ride off with the money. . . ." His words ended in a deep pained-racked cough.

"We didn't see them do that," said Hazerat with a puzzled look.

Kelso rolled his eyes from Hazerat to Charlie. "Is he always like this?" he said, wheezing, but with his thumb still over the gun hammer.

Hazerat looked more puzzled. "Like what? All's I said is we didn't see—"

"Shut up, Hazerat," Charlie said. "We both saw them take off with the money—saw them clear as day." He stared steadily at Hazerat; so did Kelso, even as he coughed and wiped blood from his lips.

"Aw, yeah, that's right. We did," Hazerat said, finally getting it. A grin lit his face. "Them damn thieving 'paches," he said for the second time.

Chapter 3

———

Ranger Barracks, Nogales Badlands Outpost

A week had passed since the Ranger had arrived at the Badlands Outpost. Now it was time to get back on the trail. He had spoken with his Captain, Morgan Yates, about Agua Fría, and wasn't surprised to hear that the Mexican government was as curious as the Rangers about the place. Captain Yates was aware of the recent upsurge of American thieves and killers taking refuge there. The local law, the *rurales,* had caved in to outlaw leaders, either by use of intimidation or by the weight of the U.S. dollar. *Yes,* Captain Yates had agreed, it was time to send someone in, see what was going on there. . . .

In the dim light of an oil lantern, Sam took off his boots, his riding duster and his silver-gray sombrero. He placed the items inside a wooden storage locker and pulled out a set of clothes that had been stored there for over a year waiting to be used should the proper occasion arise.

And now that occasion is at hand, he told himself,

closely inspecting the clothes, the boots, in the dim circle of lantern light.

He put on a dark gray shirt that unlike his own shirt bore no pinholes or the faded imprint of his six-pointed badge, which he'd removed from his old shirt and shoved down into his trouser pocket for the time being. The collarless shirt had been boiled free of a wide bloodstain and its bullet hole darned flawlessly. Over the clean shirt, he put on a California-style three-button tan corduroy coat with weathered dark leather trim around the sleeves and lapel.

He buttoned the upper two buttons of the coat and left the lower one open to accommodate his sidearms and afford him more comfort in the saddle. He replaced his sombrero with a wide flat-brimmed range hat that lay on a wooden bench beside him. Sitting, he exchanged his calf-high boots for a pair of taller Spanish boots with Chihuahua seven rowel spurs attached to them. Worn silver-tooled conchos adorned the leather spur straps.

Stylish . . .

He crossed a boot atop his knee, flipped the spur with his finger and watched the rowels spin.

Maybe *too* stylish for his taste, he thought. But then he reminded himself that for this job he wasn't Ranger Sam Burrack, he was another man altogether—the kind of man who wore an extra cross-draw holster and liked silver conchos on his spurs.

A gunman bandito, a desperado. . . . He gave a slight chuff at the irony of it. *You, of all people . . . ,* a voice chided inside him.

He stood up. Through an open rear window he saw the big restless dun he'd chosen from the livery corral. The dun stood in the pale moonlight hitched to a post in the alley behind the barracks, trail-ready and waiting for him. He saw it lift its muzzle, probe the hot dusty air and shake out its mane as if in anticipation. He'd chosen the big dun for many reasons, not the least of which was the fact that the horse bore no brand, no markings of any kind—perfect for working undercover, he'd told himself.

Undercover . . .

He looked out at the dun, then at the flat-brimmed range hat. He didn't like working without a badge. There was an element of deception to it that ran against the grain of his nature. He had tried to live his life in a straightforward manner, open and honest to a fault. He preferred walking up to a man, identifying himself, and telling the man flat-out what he was accused of and what was about to happen to him. "Make your choice," he would say with calm finality. And so it would go. That was the way he saw the law to be best served.

As a rule, he usually carried a list of names of the men he hunted. Once he found them, he gave them a choice. They could lay down their weapons and turn themselves in, or they could buck the odds at killing him and once more staying a few steps ahead of the law. These were tough, wild, desperate men, who for the most part liked their odds at killing him. But so far he'd always managed to kill them first. As he thought about it, he pictured their faces staring up at the sky, their boot soles exposed to him as he walked forward, his Colt smoking in his hand.

He kept no running count of how many men he'd arrested as opposed to how many he'd left lying dead in the street; he marked their names off his list and moved on to the next one. It couldn't get more honest and simple than that. Yet he knew there were times when undercover work had to be done, and like all Territory Rangers he did whatever the particulars of a certain job called for to the best of his ability. He picked up his plain leather gun belt and looked it over.

In this case the job involved taking off the badge and putting on a whole other identity. There was trouble a-brewing in Agua Fría. Curtis Rudabell couldn't have made it any plainer. "It's my kind of people running Agua Fría," he'd said.

So be it, Sam told himself. He swung the two-inch-wide gun belt around his waist, buckled it, adjusted it and picked up a second ivory-handled Colt and slid it down butt forward into a cross-draw holster he'd added onto the left side of his gun belt. He tied the right holster down to his thigh, straightened and stamped the big boots down firmer onto his feet. It wasn't the first time he'd worked undercover; it wouldn't be his last.

He reached down to the glowing lantern and trimmed the wick low. He had measured enough fuel to keep the lantern burning for as long as an hour after he left, rather than have anyone see the lantern light go out all at once. This was how a man covered for himself when he wanted his comings and goings to be obscure. *Get used to it,* he reminded himself.

In the dimmer shadowy light he picked up a set of saddlebags sitting on the floor at his feet and swung them up over his shoulder. He picked up his Winchester repeating rifle, which was leaning against the wall and walked out the open back door and stepped down to the post where the big dun stood staring at him in the pale purple darkness. The horse stamped a restless hoof and shook out its mane.

"I expect you're ready to go?" the Ranger asked quietly, swinging the saddlebags from his shoulder onto the dun's back. He tied the bags down behind a California-style saddle he'd taken from the livery tack room. As if in reply to him, the dun jerked its head against its tied reins. The Ranger shoved his rifle down into the saddle boot, untied the reins and swung up atop the dun.

Slipping out of town like a thief in the night, he told himself, backing the restless animal onto the narrow alleyway.

He turned the animal toward the black shadows of a backstreet that would lead him to the border trail. For a moment he stared out through a gray-red haze of dust looming in the distance between the earth and the starlit sky. Taking a breath as if to settle himself for what lay ahead, he touched his boots to the dun's sides.

"Let's be off, then," he said quietly, feeling the horse jerk forward beneath him and down along the alleyway into a long gantlet of greater darkness. "We've got a long ride ahead of us."

The dun carried him forward at an easy gallop, the sound of its hooves falling flat and muffled in the dirt behind them. In the blind darkness the Ranger had no

sighted path to follow, only a narrow slice of purple sky
carved along the upper edges of rooflines above the
blackness surrounding him and the horse. At the end of
that corridor of purple sky, a three-quarter moon lay
silver-white amid a thin veil of passing cloud. The
Ranger rode into the moon until the blacker shadows
fell behind him and the distant hills of Mexico stood up
slowly like great beings arisen from sleep.

When he reined left onto the trail toward the border,
the Ranger let the reins slacken in his hand; and he
let the dun set its own pace in the soft cooling night,
liking the feel of the horse's strong, easy gait. When the
lingering howl of a wolf resounded off in the night, the
Ranger noted the horse's senses quicken, yet he felt
no fear, no hesitation, no break in the rise and fall of
hooves.

"We're going to get along just fine," he said down to
the dun, patting a gloved hand on the horse's withers.
He upped the horse's pace with a touch of his bootheels.
And they rode on.

Twice in the night the Ranger had stopped along the
rocky border trail. During his first stop, he had rested
and watered the dun at a narrow stream of runoff water
snaking down from a stone basin seated atop a low hillside. Approaching the runoff, Sam had seen red eyes
rise from a black starlit mirror of water and level at
him, unblinking, from the other side of the stream.
Then he'd seen the eyes vanish in the darkness as the
dun rode closer.

When he'd finished watering and resting himself and the dun, he'd ridden on, looking back at length and seeing the red eyes reappear in his wake. He did not stop again until the first streak of silver-gold morning light mantled the far horizon.

Atop a low rise of sand and layered stone, he spotted deep wheel tracks of a wagon that had swung up from the floor sometime in the night and rolled along the cusp of a low-sloping hillside. He noted that the hooves of only one horse lay between the wheel tracks, and these hooves were to the wagon's left—the sign that one horse had been put upon to pull a two-horse rig.

A heavily loaded wagon at that, he further noted, judging the depth of the wheel tracks.

He stepped down from the California saddle and walked along between the wagon tracks, leading the dun for the next half hour as morning swelled above the distant edge of the earth behind him. He had no doubt that the wagon would come into sight, and when it did, he saw it now sat farther back down the sandy hillside, tipped dangerously to one side.

A peddler's wagon, he decided, looking closer in the thin morning light. A single gaunt, white-faced roan stood to one side, its muzzle down, probing in vain for any trace of graze in the rocky sand.

When Sam was within thirty feet of the wagon, he stopped again and stared at the blackness of an open rear door.

"*Hola* the wagon," he called out, reminding himself right away that he was not Arizona Territory Ranger

Sam Burrack. He was only one more lone rider—some gunman risen from the black desert night.

"Do not come any closer," a woman's voice called out from the black open door. "I am not alone here."

Sam caught the slightest accent in her voice and tried to identify it. Romanian? Polish? Russian? He didn't know. But he did know she was alone. Of course she was alone, he thought. Why else would she even mention it?

His first impulse was to ask her if something was wrong, if she needed his help. But he reminded himself again that he was not the Ranger. He was a man who couldn't care less what happened to anybody except himself out on this desert crossing. As much as he disliked doing it, he took a breath and looked back and forth.

"Suit yourself," he called out to the open door.

He gave a tug on the reins in his hand and started forward, the dun plodding right behind him. Veering slightly, he started walking wide of the wagon and its gaunt roan. As he drew diagonally closer, he saw the horse lift its sand-crusted muzzle and stare toward him and the dun. He saw hunger in the horse's dark eyes.

"Wait," the woman's voice called out to him before he got past the wagon, the gaunt roan.

All right . . .

The Ranger stopped, almost relieved. He still didn't speak; he only stood watching as a dark-haired young woman stepped down from inside the wagon and stood staring at him, her right hand pressed close to her long gingham skirt. Sam had seen this position enough to know that she held something there, a revolver, a short shotgun, some sort of weapon.

"We—" She halted and corrected herself. "That is, *I* cannot move my wagon down the hillside. It has started to tip. It will fall over," she said, sounding both embarrassed and worried. "Can you please help us, *por favor,* mister—*señor*?"

Sam heard her stiff clumsy attempt at Spanish.

"I'm not Mexican," he said. "I speak English." He kept his voice firm but not unfriendly.

"Oh, I see," the woman said.

Again, the trace of an accent—ever so slight. She kept her hand pressed against her skirt, watching as Sam stepped forward toward her.

He looked her up and down, then shifted his gaze to the side of the wagon as he walked closer. Weathered remnants of unreadable letters adorned its side.

"What's wrong with the wagon?" he asked.

"We—I mean, *I* started back down to the trail, but I turned too much at once and the wagon started tipping. Now I cannot move it in any way that does not make it tip even worse. Can you help me?"

Sam looked the wagon over and only nodded as he walked. He could see that his walking closer made her uncomfortable. Yet he didn't stop until he stood ten feet away.

"First thing, let's make clear if you're a *We* or an *I*," he said flatly. "I like knowing how many people I'm talking to."

"I am not alone. My father is inside," she said. She

looked frightened and took an instinctive step backward toward the rear wagon door.

"I will not be taken advantage of," she said, her voice turning shaky. "I warn you."

Sam looked at the wagon door, not believing her.

"Father or not, if I was going to take advantage of you, we wouldn't be talking right now," he said, giving his tone a hard edge. He stepped past her and alongside the tilted wagon, inspecting it. Whatever she had pressed to her skirt, it wasn't a gun, he figured, or else she would have raised it toward him along with her warning.

"Oh," she said, seeming to understand his logic. She followed along behind him and the dun, her first few steps reluctant, then becoming less so as she spoke. "I have been told many bad things about those who ride this desert crossing."

"Is that a fact?" Sam said, tossing the matter aside as he looked at the dangerously leaning peddler's wagon. "If that's a pigsticker you're holding, you need to put it away. It'll take the three of us to straighten this rig."

He stopped and turned, catching a glimpse of pale bare thigh at the second she lowered her raised skirt over the knife in its hidden leather sheath.

Who . . . Sam forced himself not to look away as he would ordinarily do as a matter of good manners. As she straightened her skirt down into place, he noted again what a strikingly beautiful woman this was standing before him. No wonder she was worried. Sam wished for a second that he had his badge on just to rest her fears.

She hurriedly stepped forward and drew his attention to the leaning wagon.

"You are right. It will take you and me *both*," she said. "My father cannot help us." She quickly passed over the matter. "What must we do?"

Sam looked at her.

"Why can't he?" he asked.

She only shrugged and didn't answer. She didn't look at him, only at the wagon.

Seeing she wasn't going to answer, he let it go.

"Do you have a rope?" he asked.

"Yes, I have one inside," she said, gesturing toward the open door. "I will get it." She paused, appearing concerned that he might try to follow her inside. "You wait here. My father must not be disturbed."

Sam watched as she backed to the door and only half turned and entered without taking her eyes off him. He waited, listening to the sound of her rummaging for a rope. After a moment, he stepped forward and up into the dark doorway and became immediately stricken by the smell of death coming from a bunk bed hanging on chains against the side wall.

Seeing him, the woman ran forward, the tilted wagon swaying dangerously beneath them, and tried to shove him backward from the wagon.

"Get out of here!" she screamed. "You must not be here!"

But the Ranger stood firm, balancing himself on the uneven floor. He caught her by her wrists and held her in place. He glanced at a blanket-wrapped figure lying on the bed. The top-heavy wagon creaked and swayed sideways, then stopped and sat at the same deep angle.

"Take it easy, ma'am," he said, noting the unstable wagon. He held her wrists firmly until she finally began to settle, realizing he wasn't going to turn her loose otherwise. He felt her give in and almost collapse against him.

Her voice weakened to a whimper of pain and fear. "I won't allow you to—"

"Shhh," he said, cutting her off. "I'm not going to hurt you," he said. "Is that your father?"

She didn't answer. Instead she nodded.

"You realize he's dead, don't you?" he offered, his tone turning softer, consolatory.

"No!" she said, shaking her head. But then she caught herself as reality came to her. "Yes—I mean, I don't know. . . ."

"Yes, he's dead, ma'am," Sam said in a firmer tone. "He's been dead awhile, and we need to bury him." He paused, then added, "Do you understand me? He needs to be buried." He didn't want to mention that the smell would soon summon buzzards, and any other carrion scavengers on the desert floor.

She stood silent for a moment, staring at the small blanketed figure. "Yes," she said finally, at the end of a sigh. "I know he must be buried."

"Yes, ma'am, he must," Sam said gently. As he spoke he looked all around inside the wagon, at heavy iron cooking utensils stacked all the way to the wagon's roof—pots and pans, iron skillets, Dutch ovens, iron kettles as large as a witch's cauldron. Heavy peddler's items, he noted to himself—items that would have to be unloaded if they were going to move this wagon without turning it over sidelong down the sandy hillside.

Chapter 4

The Ranger and the woman spent over an hour lowering the top half of the heavy cooking utensils to the floor of the peddler's wagon to better center the weight. Many of the items they unloaded and stacked in the sand on the hillside. For the time being Sam laid the blanketed body of the woman's father on the sand beside the stacked items. Sam noted a clear difference in the steadiness of the wagon once the load was rearranged. As they'd lowered the items still inside the wagon, they had deliberately loaded most of it onto the high side of the wagon floor, giving the wagon more resistance to tipping over.

"This will have to do," Sam said finally, standing back in the hot desert sun, seeing that the wagon still had a sharp lean to it. The woman stood beside him as he stooped and picked up the rope she had rummaged from inside the wagon. She watched him uncoil the rope and check its condition and judge its strength.

"How will we do this?" she asked, following him as he took the end of the rope to the high side of the tilted wagon.

"First," Sam said, "I'm tying this to the wagon, up high." He stepped up on the side of the wagon carefully and tied the rope around an iron cargo rail. "I'm going to steady the wagon with this rope. We're going to walk it down to the flats."

"Am I going to drive the wagon while you steady it?" she asked, sounding worried.

"No, that's too dangerous," Sam said. He stepped back down and uncoiled the rope as he walked to where the dun stood near the gaunt wagon horse. He dropped the remaining coil of rope beside the dun. The woman stayed right beside him.

"What, then?" she asked, following him to the wagon horse.

Cupping his hand beneath the horse's soft, sandy chin, he walked it to the front of the wagon as he spoke.

"I'm going to hitch this fellow to the high side. I want you to walk him forward. Keep him at a long angle all the way down. Don't stop until the wagon is sitting level, down on the flats."

"And you're going to hold it with the rope?" she asked, sounding doubtful.

"As best I can," Sam said. "If you see me losing it and it starts falling over, don't try to stop it, get out of the way."

"But—but what about Andre?" she said, gesturing at the wagon horse as Sam hitched it to the right side of the wagon.

"Andre . . . ?" Sam brushed sand from the horse's muzzle and patted the side of its head. "Well, Andre will have to take his chances." He turned to the woman.

"The only other choice is to leave the wagon behind and ride Andre out of here."

"But my belongings, all of my father's business goods, are inside it," she said, looking the tilted wagon up and down.

"I understand," Sam said. He stopped hitching the horse and stood looking at her.

She stood looking at the horse for a moment, then turned to the Ranger.

"All right, it must be done," she said with finality.

Sam nodded and turned back to the horse. He spoke as if consoling the horse.

"Don't worry, *Andre*," he said. "I'm hitching you in a way you shouldn't get tangled if the wagon falls over. Get this wagon down there in one piece, I'll see if I have some grain for you."

The roan raised its white face with red freckles to him.

The woman watched how he handled the horse. She saw a firm gentleness in his hands, his touch. She heard the same quality in his words. She watched him finish with Andre and turn to give her the long wagon reins.

"Here we go, ma'am," he said.

"My name is Lilith," she said, taking the reins.

Sam nodded.

"All right," he said. "Here we go, Lilith."

"It is the name of Adam's first wife," she added. "Adam, from the Bible . . . ?" she said.

"I see," Sam said quietly. "I didn't know he'd been previously married."

"Oh yes," she said, arranging the reins as she spoke. "It's a long story."

"I bet it is," Sam said. He stopped and picked up the rope at his feet and stepped away to get a long, steady grip on the wagon.

"And what is your name?" she called out to him. "What may I call you?"

Sam looked back at her as he walked out any slack in the length of rope. He hesitated for a moment before answering.

"Joe," he said finally. "Just call me Joe."

"Joe what?" she asked as he continued walking out the rope.

He stopped again and looked back at her.

"Joe's enough," he said. This was what he didn't like about working without a badge—the deception, he reminded himself. The way he had to treat people. "Let's get this wagon down there, Lilith," he said. "That's the main thing."

The woman looked a little embarrassed, he thought, as she turned away and stood with the wagon reins in her hand. She quickly gathered and coiled the long reins and left a three-foot length between her and the horse. She looked up at the Ranger.

"Tell me when you're ready, *Joe*," she said.

Standing thirty feet up the hillside with the end of the rope in his hands, Sam braced both feet into the rocky sand and leaned his body against the weight of the tilted wagon. At this uphill angle he could feel his weight making a difference against the wagon.

"Take the horse forward," he called down to the woman.

The woman took a step and gave a tug on the reins. The horse lurched forward and put its back into getting the wagon wheels turning once again in the sand. Sam stood braced and moved along parallel down the hillside, keeping himself leaning against the tilted wagon. As the wagon began to move forward, it slowly leveled in the sand. Sam felt it grow steadier through the rope in his hand. As he moved along with the slow wagon, the dun came forward and followed behind him.

"This is going to work," he whispered to himself. Yet he kept the rope drawn taut, not taking any chances as the wagon crept forward, less tilted, at a safe shallow angle toward the flatlands below.

As the woman led the peddler's wagon forward, keeping her eyes on both the horse and wagon, from Sam's vantage point on the hillside above the flatlands he spotted three riders come into sight out of the wavering morning heat. As the riders moved closer, he saw a man on foot trotting along in front of them. Sensing trouble, he knew that all he could do was keep the wagon moving at the same slow pace and hope he and the woman reached the level desert floor before the riders caught up to them.

Fortunately the riders were still over a hundred yards away as the wagon rolled onto the flatland and the woman collapsed in relief against the horse's skinny neck and embraced the animal.

"We made it," she cried out, almost sobbing with relief. "Thank goodness, we have made it."

But the Ranger had no time to stop and congratulate himself. As soon as he saw the wagon was safe, he dropped the rope and stepped back to the dun, who stood six feet behind him. He slid his Winchester rifle from the saddle and levered up a round.

"Get inside the wagon, ma'am," he said, sidestepping down the sandy hillside to where Lilith stood with her arms still around Andre's neck. Having not yet seen the approaching riders, she stared at the Ranger with a puzzled look.

"What's wrong?" she asked.

Sam gestured toward the dust rising and roiling behind the horse's hooves. "Riders coming," he said.

As she looked toward the riders, Sam saw fear come into the woman's dark eyes.

"Might be nothing, ma'am," he said to keep her calm. "But get inside, just in case."

As she moved toward the rear door of the wagon, she kept staring toward the approaching riders. They were more clearly in sight now as if the gait of their dusty horses had parted the wavering heat. In front of the riders Sam could see a rope looping to the ground between one of the riders and a young Indian running barefoot, his hands tied behind his back.

The woman saw the Indian too. She stopped before reaching for the wagon door.

"They have a prisoner," she said, hesitating. "Maybe they are lawmen?"

"Maybe," Sam said, not having time to discuss the matter. "Please get in the wagon. We'll find out soon enough.

She dropped the reins to the wagon horse and hurried to the wagon door as the riders slowed their horses and proceeded forward. Sam watched the Indian slow to a trot and stagger a bit as the contingent rode right up to within fifteen feet of him before coming to a halt.

"Looks like you had trouble with the hillside, stranger," the man in the lead said, a rope running from his hand to the Indian's neck. He gave a greasy grin through a tangled sand-filled beard.

Before Sam could offer a reply, the men nearest the lead rider gave an equally humorless grin.

"Must be he's new to these parts, Roden," he said. "A tenderfoot, I'm guessing." He gave Sam a smug grin. His eyes went across the unloaded items and the blanket-wrapped body lying in the sand up along the dusty hillside.

Sam didn't bother to explain or reply. He saw scalps hanging in a bunch around the lead rider's saddle horn. Recognizing a bullying attitude in the making, he cocked the Winchester in his hands.

"Ride on," he said firmly.

"Whoa, now," said the lead rider, Bo Roden. "No need to be inhospitable, stranger."

"*Inhospitable* was you riding right up here without helloing the wagon," Sam said. He leveled the Winchester. "Now ride on."

"Hold on, mister," said Roden, his hands raised chest high in a show of peace. "That was wrong and rude of us, I admit. I'm Bo Roden. This is Ollie McCool. We've got a man gut-shot here and likely to die on us if we don't take care of him fast." Beside him the other man raised his hands too. They parted their horses enough for Sam to see the third man drooped low in his saddle, his lap and lower belly covered with blood.

"It looks like you should have stopped before now," Sam said.

"That's true too," said Roden. "But here we are, and there he is, damn near bled out already. Can we lay him down here? Maybe get some binding cloth from you?" As he spoke, Sam saw the young Indian sink to his knees, his lips cracked and bloody.

"Get him down, take care of him," Sam said. "I'll see about some cloth. He sidestepped to the dun with his rifle still leveled. He took down a canteen and pitched it to the young Indian. The Indian stared at the canteen, then at him. Then he jerked the canteen up, opened it and started drinking deeply.

"Damn it, fellow, the Injun can't have water!" said the second rider. He started to jump his horse forward. But Sam's cocked rifle stopped him. "We've got a bet how far he goes before he dies of thirst!" the man said.

"Bet's off," Sam said. He looked at the young Apache and gave him a nod to continue. Then he looked back at the riders. To the second rider he said, "If I'm going have to shoot you, let's go on and get it done."

"Wait! Don't shoot!" the second rider said.

The lead rider gave a dark cackling laugh as the second rider backed his horse away warily.

"Ollie, this man does not like your style," he said. "Maybe you best cool your heels. I believe he'd shoot a man for little reason."

"You're right. I will," Sam said. "Now, get your

wounded man down and tend to him. Then clear out of here."

On the shaded side of the peddler's wagon, Sam stood with his rifle in hand and watched as the two scalp hunters probed deep into the screaming wounded man's belly with a long skinning knife and dug out a rifle bullet. The dun and the wagon horse, Andre, stood at the rear edge of the wagon and watched stony-eyed. Inside the wagon the woman sat huddled in a corner, her hands over her ears.

When the bullet was out, the two scalp hunters saw the wounded man collapse into silence. Roden slapped his docile face back and forth.

"Alvin, wake up, you son of a bitch," he shouted at the limp bloody figure. "Don't you die, not after all we've done for you!"

"You're wasting your breath, Roden. He's already done it," Ollie McCool said. He stood and wiped his bloody hands on a cloth and stepped over to the Ranger while Bo Roden stood up and gave the dead man an angry kick to the ribs.

"You was always weak." Roden sneered down at the corpse.

"Well, that's that," said McCool. Dismissing his dead comrade, he stared at Sam. "Right now I'd kill and skin an Alabama preacher for a drink of whiskey," he said.

"I have no whiskey," Sam said curtly.

"Why don't I just step inside and look around for myself?" McCool said.

"Stay out of the wagon," Sam said, sidestepping in between McCool and the rear wagon door.

McCool stopped, but he gave a sly grin.

"What's wrong? You afraid the woman in there ain't safe around the likes of scalp hunters?"

Sam only stared at him without reply.

"Oh, I know there's a woman in there, mister," said McCool. "I saw her no sooner than we broke the horizon. So don't try to tell me there's not." He sniffed the air. "I can smell a woman's hair farther than a tracking hound."

Sam still only stared.

"Whoever is in there is no concern of yours," he said. "Now back off." He kept the rifle aimed, ready to fire.

"Leave it alone, Ollie. You're pushing your luck," Bo Roden warned McCool over his shoulder.

"I don't like being lied to," McCool said, staring into Sam's face, working his courage up. "I *believe* he's got whiskey, and *I know damn well* there's a woman inside this gypsy rig—"

The ranger's rifle butt snapped around and slammed into his ribs before he got his words finished. McCool grunted, dropped to his knees bowed at the waist and fell over onto his side. Sam stood holding the downed man's gun, a battered nickel-plated revolver that he had slipped from his holster as he fell.

Roden stopped what he was doing and stared, his hand wanting to go for his holstered black-handled Colt, but stopping under the Ranger's cold gaze.

"Touch it, I'll kill you," Sam said to Roden. He held

the Winchester one-handed as he shoved McCool's pistol behind his gun belt. McCool groaned and grunted with his hands clasped to his sternum.

Roden raised his hand away from his gun butt. Sam stayed fixed in place, ready to squeeze the Winchester's trigger.

"I—I can't breathe," McCool rasped in the sand.

"Then don't," Sam said sharply. To Roden he said, "Get your man bandaged and get out of here. This one is bent on making me kill him." He gestured toward McCool on the ground.

"He's an ass. I could have told you as much," said Roden. "We're leaving. Just give me a minute to finish here."

"Damn it to hell, Roden!" McCool said, suddenly catching his breath, staring at ground level beneath the wagon. "The Injun's gone!" He began struggling to his feet, still clasping his sternum.

"The hell . . . ?" said Roden, standing quickly, hurrying around the wagon to where they had tied their horses and the young Apache on the other side. "He's gone! Horses, rifles and all!" He turned a complete circle, enraged, bewildered, his arms spread wide. "I knew better than to leave him out of sight!" He stooped and picked up the rope that had bound the Apache's wrists behind him. The rope was chewed through.

McCool said in a strained voice, "He slipped the rope under him, got it in front and gnawed through it like a rat. Damn rope-chewing varmint." He flung the short length of rope away.

The Ranger stood in silence, staring out across the desert flatland, seeing hoofprints of the three horses leading out toward a stand of rocky hills without so much as a rise of dust. While the two scalp hunters stood a few feet in front of him staring out across the desert floor, Sam stepped forward, lifted Roden's pistol from his holster and stepped back. He was ready when Roden and McCool turned to face him.

"He's even got our bounty scalps we've been collecting!" Roden said, staring at Sam. "You've got to give us loan of these horses to catch him! We'll bring them back."

"Not a chance," Sam said.

"I ain't *asking*. We're taking the horses," Roden said. He started to turn surly, his gun hand ready to draw until he spotted his revolver in Sam's hand, McCool's gun shoved down behind his belt.

"You're not taking anything," Sam said. "You are unarmed and afoot. Better watch your manners."

"Mister, you've got to help us," Roden said, his attitude softening quickly as Sam's words sank in. "We'll pay you, soon as we get them scalps back and get them turned in for bounty."

"Your scalps and horses are long gone," Sam said. "You can forget about them."

"All because you gave that sneaking bastard some water," said Ollie McCool. "Caused him to get his strength back."

"Shut up, Ollie," said Roden, realizing that sticking close to the wagon was their only way out of here. To Sam he said, "Mister, we made a mistake stopping here.

We should have let Alvin there die and left him baking in the sun." He spread his hands. "What can you do to help us out?"

"You can walk on the shaded side of the wagon. I've got water enough for us to all make it to Agua Fría. If that don't suit you, you can start walking out on your own."

The two men looked at each other, then back at Sam.

"That's all I've got for you . . . ," Sam said. "Take it or leave it."

"We'll take it, mister," Roden said. He let out a breath in resolve. "And we're obliged to you."

As the three spoke, the rear wagon door opened slowly and Lilith stepped down and pitched two shovels to the ground.

The two only glanced at the shovels. Then their eyes went to the woman and seemed to stick there. Without a word, Lilith stepped back into the wagon and shut the door quietly.

"Lord God Almighty . . . ," whispered McCool. The two stared at the closed wagon door.

Sam wasn't about to let their interest dwell on the woman. "Pick up a shovel and start digging a grave. The sooner this one's underground, the sooner we'll get the wagon loaded and head for Agua Fría."

Chapter 5

When the dead was buried and the peddler's wagon reloaded, the group followed a low, worn trail across the flatlands toward a distant hill line that rolled upward and spread layer upon layer until it vanished from sight. The Ranger drove the wagon, the woman sitting beside him, his dun hitched to the rear. To make up for lost daylight, they traveled on after dark and made no camp until well past midnight. Seeing Roden and McCool scouring around in the purple moonlight for scraps of wood, Sam walked over to them, his rifle in the crook of his arm, their guns still stuck down behind his belt.

"You're not starting a fire," he said. "We don't need to show your escaped prisoner where we are. He might decide to come back for these other two horses."

"I wish he would try," Roden said. "It would give us a chance to get back our scalps and supplies."

"If I thought it would bring him back, I'd build a fire that would light the whole desert," McCool said with a dark chuckle. "You don't know the 'pache, fellow—leastwise not like Roden and I do. Right, Roden?"

"Right," said Roden. "The Injun is long gone. We don't need to worry about him."

Seeing no use in trying to reason with either of the scalp hunters, Sam simply repeated, "No fires," and started to walk back to the wagon where he had hitched the two horses to the side out of the moonlight and laid his blanket down between them.

The two men groused back and forth under their breath. Finally Roden called out, "Can we at least smoke some tobacco? I've got some curly cigars I've been carrying for over two weeks. You're welcome to one yourself."

Sam shook his head and sighed to himself.

"No smoking either," he said. "Unless you want to get far enough away from here that nobody will see your fire and follow it to the wagon."

"If anybody wanted to find the wagon, there's a long set of wheel tracks all the way from the hillside where you damn near turned it over," said McCool, defiantly.

Sam wasn't going to bother telling them it wasn't him who had almost toppled the wagon.

"I want no fire of no kind," he said, sliding down between the two horses. Inside the wagon the woman had spread a blanket on the bunk bed and gone to sleep.

"I'm smoking me a damn cigar before I turn in, and that's the long and short of it," said McCool. He fumbled through his clothes for a tin of matches.

In the moonlight the sound of Sam's Winchester cocking broke the quiet night. McCool froze with a match in his hand ready to strike.

"All right, damn it!" Roden called out to Sam. He snatched the match out of McCool's hand. "We'll walk off a ways and smoke. Surely you have no objections to that."

"Suit yourself," Sam said, "but your guns are staying here for safekeeping."

"We need those guns," Roden said. "What if something comes out upon us in the night?"

"That's a good question," Sam said. "Good night, gentlemen."

"Gentlemen my ass," Roden cursed. He snatched up one of the two spare moth-eaten blankets the woman had rummaged from inside the wagon for them. "Come on, Ollie. Let's take these blankets and make our own camp."

"We leave an hour before daylight," Sam called out quietly as the two turned and walked away.

Seventy yards from the wagon, Roden and McCool sat down side by side on a low flat rock in the purple moonlight. McCool struck one of the long wooden matches along the side of the tin, held the flame to his black cigar and puffed on it as he spoke.

"For two Mexican pesos I'd kill this greenhorn in his sleep," he said. "What kind of man fears a half-starved Injun? Especially one who's seen what we done to his pals." He blew a stream of smoke as he held the flaring match sidelong for Roden to use. "Making us walk all this way just to smoke a cigar . . . ," he grumbled.

Roden puffed his cigar to life and blew out the match.

"I'm glad we did, though," he said. "This gives us some time to talk about how we're going to do it."

"Do what?" said McCool.

"Kill this man in his sleep, Ollie, like you just said," Roden replied.

"That was just talk," said McCool. "He's got our guns, don't forget." He puffed on the cigar and blew a stream of smoke up at the starlit sky.

"I ain't forgot, Ollie," said Roden. "But I ain't forgot all the trade goods we loaded into the peddler's wagon either." He puffed on his cigar. "I did sort of a running count on how much all that stuff would be worth if a man hauled it somewhere and sold it."

"Yeah . . . ?" McCool stopped smoking and turned his attention to his partner. "What did you make it to be?"

"I'd say a hundred dollars, easy enough," he said. "That's not counting the wagon itself, and that skinny horse." He blew on the end of his cigar as he speculated. "I figure it helps make up what scalp money we lost—puts us back in the game, so to speak."

"Just how do you figure we'd do it without any weapons?" McCool asked.

"Catch him dozing off guard in the night and beat him into the ground," said Roden. "Once he's down, we'll take his rifle. We'll take our guns from his belt and finish him off."

They sat in silence for a few seconds while McCool worked it out in his mind.

"What about the woman?" he asked.

"I knew you'd get around to her," Roden said with a dark chuckle.

"Ever since I smelled her I ain't been able to think of nothing else," said McCool. "So, what about her?"

"We'll have to kill her too, Ollie," said Roden. "She'd tell the *federales* what we done, first thing, you can bet on it."

Ollie studied the matter, staring at the haze of cigar smoke streaking up across the purple sky.

"We wouldn't have to kill her right away, though, would we?" he asked finally.

"No . . . *hell* no," said Roden. "We can put it off some— kill her later, before we ride into Agua Fría. There's no need in being uncivilized about this." He shrugged and drew on his cigar. "We can take our time."

"Then I'm all for it," said McCool, "the sooner, the better." He puffed on his cigar, then gave a little cough and a grunt and fell silent.

"How about this, then?" said Roden after a quiet moment of contemplation. "You take the woman all to yourself . . . I get the man's dun."

After a moment when McCool didn't answer, Roden looked at him in the moonlight.

"If that don't suit you, how about this?" he said. He started to unveil another option, but before he could he saw McCool lean forward and collapse onto his face.

"What the . . . ?" He started to stand up, but a strong bare arm crooked around his face from behind. The arm twisted his face in one direction while a long blade sliced deep in the opposite direction across his exposed throat.

From behind the rock where the scalp hunters had

sat, two dark wispy figures stepped around as silent as ghosts and stood looking down at the bodies.

The older warrior, Wallace Gomez, stooped down and picked up Roden's cigar. He examined it in the moonlight, then took a puff. As he puffed, he held his head lowered and shielded the cigar's glowing tip toward his chest with his cupped hand.

The young warrior, Luka, stooped and picked up the other cigar and puffed on it in the same manner.

Gomez said in a whisper, "By killing these two you have saved the life of the man who gave you water."

"Yes, I heard them," Luka whispered. "They were going to kill him."

"Him *and* the peddler woman," Gomez pointed out.

"Yes, I heard this," said Luka. He gazed off in the direction of the wagon.

"Does this make you and the white man *pony for pony*?" Gomez asked.

Luka didn't answer right away.

"We have killed the scalp takers," Gomez said. "Will that be enough for you?"

Still no answer from Luka.

"You have killed the men who killed our warriors, and you have saved the life of the man who gave you water," Gomez said. "You have made a good day."

"I know," said Luka. "But I can never kill enough white men to fill me." He stood gazing off in the direction toward the wagon.

"I know that hunger all too well," Gomez said. "Only in the long passing of time have I been able to step back from killing them."

"I will call him out onto the desert floor," said Luka. "If he comes out, I will kill him."

"A test, eh?" said Gomez.

"Yes, I will test him," said Luka. He looked down at the cigar glowing softly in his hand. "I'll let the night decide if this man's courage will get him killed, or if his wisdom will keep him alive."

The Ranger only allowed himself to doze a few minutes at a time. At some point, when he felt he was going too far, he managed to catch himself and pull himself back from the deeper edge of sleep before getting too close. With the wagon horse on one side and the dun on the other, he liked to think he was borrowing their keener senses. Under these circumstances he could think of nothing on two legs or four that was going to catch him unaware. Yet, while he lay leaning back against the wagon wheel, it was he rather than the animals who spotted the glow of the cigars moving across the desert floor toward him in the night.

His first impulse was to call out, quietly but firmly, and tell the scalp hunters to stub out the cigars. But something stopped him. Instead he raised himself into a crouch and sat huddled between the horses, his Winchester up, ready to press it to his shoulder and take aim if need be. And he froze in place, silent, watching, as he saw the cigars stop in the night. The two fiery red glows stood there, suspended in the dark night air, as if searching for him—wanting him to see them? They wanted him to call out to them—to rise from his spot beside the wagon and come to them . . . ?

Not a chance. . . .

But why? he asked himself. What sort of trick did the scalp hunters have planned for him? He had expected them to make a move on him at any moment. Was this it? If it was, he had news for them. He wasn't falling for it. Silently he lowered himself onto his belly and lay prone on his blanket, staring at the glowing cigars down his rifle sights. He would stay right here—keep them in his sights until dawn if need be.

But he didn't have to wait long. Before the Winchester grew heavy in his poised grip, he lowered the rifle in front of him and kept it resting on the ground, near his shoulder. After only a moment the cigars went black in the night.

What now? he asked himself.

On either side of him the horses stood sleeping. He lay in complete silence, waiting out the remainder of the night until the purple veil of darkness turned silvery and a mantle of sunlight seeped up over the eastern horizon.

Soon he heard the woman's footsteps in the wagon behind him; then a thin sliver of lantern light spread out flat from a crack along the edge of a shuttered window. Sam moved out of the sliver of light and stood up beside the dun, whose eyes were open and who inched away in order to give him room.

Sam patted the dun's rump and walked to the rear door of the wagon. With a soft knock, he stood waiting, looking back over his shoulder across the changing darkness of the desert floor until the woman raised the iron bolt and opened the door quietly from inside.

He slipped into the soft light and closed the door behind him. The woman stood staring at him, holding a kindling hatchet down her side, pressed against her thigh in the folds of her cotton nightgown.

"The hunters have been gone most of the night," he said, barely above a whisper.

"Maybe they've left, on their own?" she asked, sounding hopeful.

"Maybe," Sam said, doubting it. "But I best go see for sure. He glanced at the hatchet. "We'll be leaving when I get back." Then he looked back at her in the shadowy light.

She only nodded. Her dark hair draped her cheeks; she faced him as if peeping out from inside a small tent.

"Drop the bolt on the door," he said in afterthought, although he knew he wouldn't have had to say it.

Again she only nodded. And she moved forward as he opened the door just enough to slip through it, as if to keep the lantern light from escaping.

Sam heard the iron bolt lower into place as he stepped away from the wagon. With his rifle cocked and ready in hand, he walked away quietly in the sand. Ten yards from the wagon he crouched and touched his fingertips to the boot prints left by the scalp hunters as they had walked away from the camp. Once he'd found their prints, he had no difficulty following them in the grainy morning light.

When he came to the point where the boot prints continued on, but the faintest print of moccasins appeared in their midst coming from the opposite direction, he froze.

For a moment he crouched and looked all around in the deathlike silence of the desert floor. When he stood up warily, he backtracked the moccasins a few yards and found hoofprints standing in the sand where the animals had been left while the two moccasin wearers had slipped forward.

He stood for a moment, reconstructing through the tracks of both man and animal what sudden and decisive fate might have been held in store for him had he come out from his hiding place between the two horses to investigate the cigars burning in the night.

Straightening, rifle in hand, he moved forward, stepping diagonally away from the prints and following them upward onto a low rise of sand, preparing himself for what he might find there. Yet, accustomed as he was to the violent death he had witnessed man bestow upon man, he also knew that preparation for such a finding was always inadequate. When the Apache had a hand in it, and it was orchestrated out of vengeance, well . . .

As he neared the top of the low rise in the first ray of sunlight, he pictured the young warrior, the look on his face as he'd raised the canteen with his tied hands. Sam found another set of moccasin tracks that led up behind a low flat rock. With a look back and forth in the grainy morning light, he moved forward, stepped up onto the rock and stopped suddenly with a jolt, like that of a man who had walked into an unseen wall.

"Holy God . . . ," he whispered to himself, staring down at the maimed and mangled bodies of the two scalp hunters—*or what's left of them,* he told himself.

He cradled his Winchester across his knee and stooped

down and looked away from the carnage, out across the waking desert floor. At least Roden and McCool had died first, he reasoned, or else he would have heard their screams throughout the night. So much for the scalp hunters. What about him and the woman? Why had they been spared?

The water . . . ? he asked himself. Had a simple act of humanity spared his life? Yet, as he pondered the matter, he thought about the cigars burning in the night. He couldn't rule that out. But whatever that was about last night, they hadn't been luring him out to talk about the weather.

He stood and took a deep breath of morning air. They were gone now, he decided, but their handiwork of the night before left a warning that only a fool would refuse to heed. This was a reminder, a staggering reminder. No matter the game at hand, no matter what flag waved above this hot, desolate inferno, this was *their* land. Here at the blood level, he knew it always would be.

Above him in the thin grainy light, he saw the first of what he knew would soon be an army of buzzards coming to claim what the violent night had bequeathed to them. The large scavenger swept into sight out of a silvery mist in a wide lowering circle.

They're all yours. . . .

Turning, he stepped off the rock and walked back along the last tracks the scalp hunters would ever make on the face of this dry, merciless land.

Chapter 6

Agua Fría
The Twisted Hills, Blood Mountain Range

The Hooke brothers gazed out their second-floor hotel room window overlooking the tile streets below. The main street of Agua Fría rose from the desert floor, wound through rock and canyon, crossed a swift, narrow river and came to a halt at the front porch of Banco Nacional. The bank, a large white adobe, stone and timber structure, displayed a Mexican flag hanging above its polished double doors. On either side of the doors stood a canon aimed out along the street as if confronting the world at large.

"I'd feel a lot better if we were fixing to rob ol' Banco Nacional down there," Charlie said. He stared at the flag, and at the bank respectively, malice a-brew in his dark bloodshot eyes as he dunked a boiled egg halfway into a bowl of fiery red pepper sauce. He continued to stare at the bank as he bit the egg in half. He washed the fiery egg down with a long swig of mescal from a huge earthen jug cloaked in basket-woven corn husks. He raised the jug with both hands. His face turned red-blue before he let out a hiss, caught his breath and spoke in a stiff tone.

"Segert would kill us pine-box dead if we robbed that bank," Hazerat said, standing beside him. "He made it clear to keep our hands off it."

"If this was a free country, he couldn't tell a man what to rob and what not to," said Charlie. "That's what makes a fellow long for America in spite of all her faults."

Hazerat gave him a strange, confused look.

"I guess," he said.

"Besides, he's apt to kill us anyway," said Charlie. "The way I make it, we've been made fools of by that hairless maggot-headed Kelso." With that he took another swig of mescal and let out a tightened breath.

Hazerat nodded a drunken acknowledgment. He looked back and forth along the street below and spat a tough piece of goat gristle down onto the brim of a wide straw sombrero passing on the stone sidewalk below. When the sombrero's owner looked up at the hotel window, Hazerat gave him a threatening sneer and hurled a rib bone down at him.

"What are you looking at?" he growled down like a vicious dog. The Mexican diverted his gaze and hurried on along the street.

"Are you listening to me here, Hazerat?" Charlie asked, giving his brother a gig with his elbow.

"Yeah, what did you say?" Hazerat said sidelong, still staring down at the passing Mexican.

Charlie just looked at him.

"*What did I say?* Damn it, I'm talking about how Kelso lied to us and led us on," he said.

"I know that," Hazerat said. He reached over for the jug of mescal. "But there ain't much we can do about it now. We've stepped out and lied for him too. Now if Segert finds out we lied about seeing Injuns ride off with the money bag, he'll kill us, no two ways about it."

Charlie handed him the jug, then grimaced thinking about the spot they were in.

"We shouldn't have lied for him," Hazerat offered.

"Shouldn't, wouldn't, couldn't," said Charlie. "It's too late for all that. We done the deed." He shook his head in regret. "What's bad is we don't even know if there ever was any damn money bag to begin with," he added. "Now we've gone and told Segert we saw Injuns take it." He shook his head in regret. "What the hell was we thinking doing that?"

"I don't know," said Hazerat. "Looking back, we should have forced him to take us to it first."

"He wasn't giving it up," said Charlie. "He knew as well as a dog has whiskers that we would have killed him and taken the money."

"Looking back," said Hazerat, "we should have stuck something sharp in his ear and wiggled it around some—made him take us to the money first."

Charlie considered it as he turned from the window and picked up his gun belt from a chair back. He strapped it around his waist and tied the holster down to his thigh.

"We might yet do that," he said. "A sharp stick in the ear might be just what it takes to pull this thing around for us."

"I say just kill him and stop fooling around," said

Hazerat, also strapping on his gun belt. "As long as he's alive, there's a risk of him telling Segert we lied."

"What would he do that for?" Charlie asked. He picked up his hat and set it atop his head.

"I do not know," said Hazerat, feeling his mescal. "I do not know why anybody does anything they do." He turned, picked up the earthen jug, took a deep swig and shivered all over as the fiery liquid went down. "I do know that whatever they do, it all stops once you put enough bullets in them."

The two walked out of the hotel room and down the hall to the rickety stairs.

Lowering his voice on their way down the stairs to the small lobby, Charlie said, "We don't want to rush to kill him, though, just in case there is money hidden out there."

Hazerat nodded.

"I'm going along with whatever you say, Charlie," he said from behind a hot belch of mescal.

Leaving the hotel, the two walked in a half-drunken silence down the clay-tiled sidewalk to an ancient church sitting back off the main street behind a low adobe wall. Inside the wall, on the path to the side door of an infirmary, a big skinny hound stood up and started to bark. Yet, looking the pair of gunman up and down, the dog appeared to change his mind and slunk away into the shadows.

As the two walked into the infirmary, a young priest stood up from where he'd sat on a wooden stool fanning Preston Kelso's pain-wrenched face. His jaw tightened as he took note of the huge jug hanging in Charlie's hand by its woven husk handle. Yet, without a word, he set the fan on the stool and excused himself with a silent nod.

"How's our pard feeling today?" Charlie Hooke asked Kelso, the two stopping at the foot of Kelso's bed.

"How the hell do you think I feel today?" Kelso growled. "Look at me." He gestured his eyes upward toward a cloth headband circling his skull above his ears. "I've got worms eating me alive." Inside the bandage, a bed of writhing gray-white fly maggots were feeding on puss and dead putrid skin.

The Hookes looked at the grisly scene and managed to keep themselves from wincing.

"Jesus," Hazerat whispered under his breath.

"I brought you some fresh agave squeezings. Maybe it'll help take your mind off it a little," said Charlie, holding the huge jug out of sight behind him. He swung it around and held it up with both hands for Kelso to see.

"*Mescal!* Thank you, *Jesus*," Kelso said gratefully as the two moved around from the foot to the side of his bed. His eyes softened a little.

Charlie said, "We figured if you had this—"

"Get it open," Kelso growled, cutting him off. He reached out for the jug before Charlie had it uncapped.

Charlie looked around at a wicker nightstand beside the bed.

"Where's your cup?" he asked.

"Damn a cup. I don't have one," said Kelso. "Give it here," he demanded.

Charlie handed him the huge jug and the two watched him turn it up with both hands and take a long guzzling drink. When he lowered the jug an inch and wheezed and choked, Charlie reached out to help him set it down. But Kelso gave a warning growl, pulled it away from Charlie's hands and raised it to his lips again.

As Kelso took another drink, Charlie cautioned him, saying, "You might want to go a little slower on that jug, Preston. I had the ol' fellow who makes that stuff punch it up with an extra bag of peyote cactus powder."

"I don't give a damn if he punched it up with a bag of snake droppings," Kelso said in a strained voice. "I've got a head full of worms I'm dealing with here." He held the jug away from Charlie and rested it on his mattress beside him.

"We brought it to share with you, Preston," said Charlie. "You don't want to drink the whole thing by yourself."

"The hell I don't," said Kelso. "Reach your fingers out for it again, you'll pull back some stubs." His left hand went under the pillow behind his shoulders and came back wielding a big rusty Colt Dragoon he'd talked the young priest, Father Octavia, into bringing him.

"Whoa! Hang on, Preston," said Hazerat. "It's yours, the whole jug of it!"

"I *know* it is," Kelso said with certainty. "Now clear out of here. I'm not telling you nothing, if that's what you thought."

"Easy, Preston," Charlie said. "The truth is, we did hope maybe you'd tell us about the *you know what*." He glanced around as if to make sure they weren't being overheard.

"I'm not telling you a damn thing today," Preston

said, his red-rimmed eyes already taking on the swirl-ing effect of the strong peyote-laced mescal. "You come back tomorrow, bring me some more of this stuff. Soon as these worms quit eating my head, maybe I'll tell you. Maybe I'll even send you to get it and bring it back here, if you can do it without Segert finding out." He paused for a second, seeing if they fell for his ruse. "Well, can you?" he demanded.

The Hooke brothers looked at each other.

"We can, Preston," said Charlie. "You can count on it."

Kelso nodded his bandaged head.

"I'm going to keep that in mind," he said. He let the big Dragoon fall to the bed at his side. He looked at the jug of mescal with admiration. "This stuff has got the strangest bite to it I've ever seen." His eyes were already a-swirl. He turned them back to the Hookes. "Bring me another jug tomorrow. Now get the hell out of here."

The Hookes looked at each other again. Charlie ges-tured toward the jug and said to Kelso, "Preston, you need to show some caution drinking this stuff—"

"Let's go, Charlie," said Hazerat, cutting his brother off. "He knows how to drink without you telling him." He pulled Charlie away by his arm.

"Damn right I do," said Kelso as the two turned and left the infirmary.

The young priest reappeared and gave them a sour look as they passed him on the stone sidewalk leading toward the front wall. As soon as the priest was out of listening range, Hazerat spoke to his brother in a lowered voice.

"You didn't tell me about the peyote powder," he said.

"I meant to," said Charlie.

"*Meant to* ain't going to help a damn bit while I'm howling at the moon and grinding my teeth down," said Hazerat. "I'm already feeling it take on a strange turn." He squeezed his cheeks and twisted his lips back and forth. There's parts of me I can no long feel."

"You're letting it spook you, Hazerat," said Charlie. "I've drank as much of it as you have. Look at me, I'm good as gold."

"You think you are, but you're not," Hazerat said, his own voice sounding distant and strange, like the twang of a plucked guitar string. "Why did you do something like that anyway, and me not knowing?" he asked, still feeling himself over here and there for numbness.

"I only intended him to drink a cupful," said Charlie, "just to loosen him up, get him talking freely. I never counted on him taking the whole damn jug from us."

"Well, he's done it," said Hazerat. "Now there's no telling what he's apt to do. Let's hope all that punched-up mescal don't turn him wilder than a rat on a hot griddle."

"Speaking of rats," said Charlie, "look who's coming here." The two stood in a deepening mescal stupor, watching a gunman walk toward them from the direction of the hotel.

"Look how long his legs are," said Hazerat in amazement, watching the gunman's boots appear to rise unusually high in the air with each approaching step.

"You two come with me," said the gunman, spotting the Hooke brothers leering at him. "Segert said bring you to see him most quick."

The two stood staring.

"Is he speaking Chinese?" Hazerat asked.

"He could be, far as I can tell," Charlie speculated.

The half-Chinese gunman, Jon Ho, stood off to the side in Raymond Segert's office. Having delivered the Hooke brothers as he'd been instructed, he stood quietly, listening without appearing to be listening—something he was good at. As he stood *not* appearing to listen, his dark sharp eyes remained fixed and blank, staring straight ahead as the Hookes stood in front of the powerfully built former Arkansan rebel leader.

"So, the two of you were on your way here when you came upon Kelso under attack," Segert said, having heard their concocted story three days earlier.

"That's the gist of it, Mr. Segert," Charlie Ray said, the mescal making his tongue feel too large for his mouth. His words sounded clipped and awkward.

Jon Ho stood as still as a statue. He knew the Hookes had scrambled their brains on mescal earlier. He'd smelled it on them. When they had gone to the hitch rail before riding out here, Charlie Ray had stepped up onto the wrong horse, twice. Hazerat had fumbled around like a blind man until he'd gotten his reins sorted out. Maybe the five-mile ride here had sobered them a little, Ho thought.

But what did he care? he reminded himself. Gunmen like the Hooke brothers were a dime a dozen—Preston Kelso too, for that matter.

"You saved Kelso's life," Segert said to the Hookes.

"I can't see him living through all this if you hadn't found him when you did and brought him to Agua Fría."

The Hookes just stared.

"And now you're here, you've rested a few days," he added, "and you want to ride for me. . . ." His eyes drifted from Charlie Ray to Hazerat.

"We'd be pleased," Hazerat said thickly.

Segert nodded and lifted a cigar from an ornate silver Mexican ashtray on his desk. He put it in his mouth and reflected for a moment.

"We talked some the other day, but let me make sure I understand how this went," he said. "You heard gunshots. You rode toward the sound, found Kelso shot full of arrows, scalped, fighting for his life. . . ." He drew on the cigar and blew out a stream. "Helped him chase those motherless savages off, and saw them ride away with saddlebags full of money—*my money*," he added with a dark, heated look. "And that's about it?"

"Except . . . ," said Charlie Ray. His words trailed.

"Except what?" said Segert.

"Except we didn't know it was money in the bags," he finished.

"Of course not," said Segert. "How would you have known?"

"We didn't," Hazerat put in.

Segert just looked at him.

"He knows that, Hazerat," Charlie reminded his brother.

Segert looked back and forth between the two as he drew on his cigar again.

"It happens I am short of men right now," he said. "I can use a couple of men who aren't afraid to take what they want from this life, and not afraid to cross the border to get it."

"You know us," Charlie said, implying friendship with a man he had only met twice before in his life and then merely in passing. "The border's just a line in the sand to us."

"Yeah, I know it is," Segert said, letting Charlie's implication stand. "I'm putting the two of you with Jon Ho here." He gestured a nod toward Ho. "How does that sound to you, Ho?"

Ho gave an ever so slight nod. The Hooke brothers stood staring at him.

"Ho here takes some getting used to, fellows," Segert said as he leaned back and propped a well-shined boot on the desktop. "Any problem taking orders from a half-breed?"

The Hookes shook their heads no.

"Ho is not all that big, but he's wiry, fast and deadly as a rattlesnake," said Segert. "You have never seen a man fight like he does. Knife, gun, fists, you name it." He paused, then raised his cigar in his scissored fingers for emphasis. "Do not cross him. He'll kill you quicker than the plague. Right, Ho?" he said.

"Damn right," Ho said flatly. He stared coldly at the Hookes through black shiny eyes.

Looking back at the Hookes, Segert said, "We're getting ready to make a big run. So be ready to do some killing when the time comes. Meanwhile, if Ho tells you to jump, don't even ask *how high*, just jump as high as you can and figure that's what he meant." As he spoke, he caught a glimpse of a peddler's wagon roll into sight along the trail past his sprawling hacienda. "Any questions?" he asked the Hookes. Before they could respond, he said, "Good. Now go with Ho. He'll take you around, help you meet some of our men."

"Yes, sir," the Hookes said as one.

But as they started to turn and walk away, Segert stopped them.

"Be advised, if I find out anything you or Kelso is telling is a lie, Ho here is going to kill all three of you," he said matter-of-factly. He gave them a short, tight grin and a brush of his hand, dismissing them.

Chapter 7

————

At a trail fork along the final stretch of miles to Agua Fría, Sam stopped beside the peddler's wagon as Lilith reined the rig over to the side and sat staring ahead. Lilith appeared to be deciding something. Seeing the seriousness in her dark eyes, the Ranger sat quietly for a moment.

"Is everything all right, ma'am?" he asked after her hesitant silence.

"We are in *Colinas Torcidas*—the Twisted Hills. I will be turning off here," she said, still not facing him. "I live up this trail on the other side of the Agua Fría." She nodded along the fork in the trail.

"If you're afraid of Apaches, I can accompany you on home," he offered. "I don't have to be in Aqua Fria any particular time."

"No, please go, Joe," she said, still staring away from him. "You have been a great help to me, and I thank you for your kindness. But now you must go on to Agua Fría, and I must go home."

"If that's what you want," Sam said, not about to impose himself. He had to admit, it would be easier showing up in Aqua Fria on his own—just a hill country drifter like any other gunman on the run.

"Yes, it is what I want," she said. Then her demeanor seemed to soften and she turned his eyes to him. "I know the kind of men who go to Agua Fría these days. I know that you are an outlaw, perhaps a man wanted by the law—"

"Whoa, Lilith," Sam said, cutting her off. "You don't know anything about me. As far as me going to Agua Fría is concerned, it's a business matter, nothing else." He had to be careful. He didn't like her having a bad opinion of him. But he certainly wasn't going to tell her what he was and why he was really here.

"A business matter?" She stared at him skeptically. "And what business are you in, Joe?" she asked.

Sam gave a shrug.

"I'm a speculator," he said. "You know . . . tools, hardware, this and that." He offered her a smile, knowing she wasn't buying his answer.

Her look said she wasn't going to swap questions with him.

"Anyway, what's wrong with Agua Fría?" Sam asked, searching for any information she might have.

She continued her critical gaze. Finally she let out a breath and shook her head slightly.

"It has been overrun by outlaws, Joe," she said, still looking dubiously at him. "As if you didn't already know."

"No, ma'am, I had no idea," Sam said. "Overrun how?"

"Are you trying to make a fool of me, Joe?" she asked him tightly, her hands clenched on the wagon reins.

"No, ma'am, I had no idea about any of this," Sam said in a serious tone. "I really do want to know." He paused, then said, "If you want to tell me, that is."

Lilith sighed as if reaching a resolve with herself.

"Even though I think you are an outlaw, I have seen good in you, the way you helped me, the way you buried my father and were careful and kind to Andre."

Sam only watched her expectantly, neither confirming nor denying himself as an outlaw.

Lilith looked around the rocky land surrounding them, as if making sure no one was in listening range.

"There are two gangs of outlaws fighting to see who's going to run Agua Fría," she said quietly. "There's Bell Madson and his cutthroats, and there's the Segerts. The Segerts are run by a Southern rebel leader named Raymond Segert. Madson and Segert are leaders of dangerous men. Decent people fear and avoid them. Maybe you've heard of these men?"

Sam shrugged, his wrists crossed on his saddle horn.

"The names aren't familiar," he said, even though he recognized them both. "But I'll remember them, and try not to cross their paths while I'm here."

She gazed coolly at him.

"Even if you are not an outlaw, I don't think you are the kind of man who will avoid these men," she said.

"I'll do my best to," Sam said flatly.

"I hope you do," Lilith said. "And I hope I am wrong about you. It is hard to have faith in anyone in times such as these."

Sam watched her lift the wagon reins in her hands, preparing to turn Andre onto the narrow fork trail.

"I understand," he said sincerely as she gave a deft touch of the reins to the roan's back, putting him forward. He wished he had something more to offer her, something to restore her faith. But he had nothing, not now at least, he reminded himself, watching the wagon make its turn and sway gently back and forth. He sat watching until the rig rolled out of sight around a turn in the trail.

All right, that was as good as he could've played it, he told himself, turning the dun toward Agua Fría. It was best that she went on home. He'd done what any man should do, he'd helped her. Something even an outlaw, even a hardcase like himself, might've done. He was back on the job now. He didn't want to show up with a woman and a peddler's wagon in tow.

On the outskirts of Agua Fría, Sam rode the dun at a walk along a rutted dirt street littered with bottles, empty cartridge cases and other debris. On one side of the street, a sow lay in a thick puddle of muddy water, three piglets sleeping at her teats. Flies danced and hovered. A sour stench lay above the street like a heavy blanket. Nearby, a thin goat standing at the corner of an alleyway bleated at the dun until horse and rider had passed by. Then it tweaked its ears and turned its attention to the sow and piglets.

Out in front of a sagging half-tent, half-adobe cantina, Sam veered the dun to a hitch rail and stepped down under the gaze of three desert-bitten gunmen leaning against the front of the cantina. One of the men, a tall, lanky Mexican, held a big bone-handled bowie knife. As

Sam carried his rifle and headed for the dirt-striped curtain that served as a front door, the Mexican stared at him blankly and jammed the knife deep into the adobe, leaving it standing there.

Beside the tall Mexican, one of the gunmen gigged him a little with his elbow as Sam walked past them into the cantina.

"Did you see what I just saw, Carlos?"

"Maybe so," said the Mexican, Carlos Montoya, staring after Sam into the dark shade of the cantina. "What did you see?" Even in the shadowy cantina, Montoya saw men at the bar make room for the stranger and his Winchester.

"I saw a man carrying Bo Roden's black Colt in his waist," said the gunman, a swarthy Texan scalp hunter named Hugh Petty. "I saw all the notches along the butt."

"You sure enough did," said the third man, Vincent Fain. "I saw Ollie McCool's big shiny Russian too. Ollie worshipped that Smith and Wesson more than I thought was natural."

"There's a lot about Ollie I never thought was natural," said Petty, staring into the shadowy cantina. "What do you suppose happened?"

The three stood looking in, Fain holding the dirty curtain to one side.

"For some stranger to be carrying Ollie's revolver, I'd have to say Ollie is dead. Most likely Roden too."

"This is what I say as well," said Montoya. "They are not men who give up their guns easily. Especially not Roden's Colt."

"Being dead would explain why they haven't shown up," Fain added quietly.

The other two just looked at him.

"Well, *it does*," Fain said defensively. He turned the curtain loose and let it fall back in place. "All's I'm saying is we've been waiting here for them going on a week, and they haven't shown up yet."

"That doesn't mean they're dead," said Petty.

"It doesn't mean they're not," said Montoya.

"Follow me, amigos," said Fain, sounding annoyed by the two. He fanned the dusty curtain aside, walked into the cantina and went straight to where Sam stood at a makeshift plank and barrel bar, a mug of frothing beer standing in front of him.

Sam saw the drinkers along the bar move away as light came in from the open curtain. In a brand-new mirror that four Mexicans were in the midst of hanging behind the bar, he saw the three men enter and walk toward him. He raised the frothy mug to his lips and took a drink. He turned quickly, facing the three as they stopped less than six feet from him.

"Close enough, hombres," he said flatly, bringing the three to a sudden halt. "What can I do for you?" His big Colt had streaked up out of his holster as he'd turned. He held it cocked and aimed at Fain's chest.

Fain's eyes widened at the sight. Montoya and Petty froze. Their hands stopped near their holstered sidearms, but made no attempt to grab them.

Fain found the courage to speak, but his boldness had subsided under the gaze of the open gun bore.

"Those shooting irons in your belt belong to a couple

of associates of ours, stranger," he said. "I want to know why you're carrying them."

"These two guns?" Sam said, deliberately putting the demanding gunman off. He placed his free hand atop the butts of the two guns in his belt.

"Yeah, those two guns," said Fain, impatient, getting bolder again. "What other guns would I mean?"

Sam shrugged. The two dead scalp hunters' guns standing behind his belt had drawn just the sort of attention he'd thought they would.

"I have no idea," he replied casually. Lowering his Colt an inch, he said, "You want them?" He hadn't intended to ride in meek and unnoticed. He'd come here to shake things up. This was a good way to start.

Seeing Sam's Colt lower, Fain noted the other two gunmen stepping up on either side of him. Growing even bolder, he gave them a sidelong glance and a smug grin.

"Stranger," he said to Sam, "if we want them, we'll take them. First I want to know what you're doing with them."

Drinkers who had shied away from the bar stood listening, watching intently. Behind the bar the Mexican workers had stopped hanging the new mirror. Metal wall hooks were in place, but the long mirror leaned against the wall, resting atop four tall stools.

"Your friends had no more use for them," Sam said calmly, letting the three take it any way they wanted to.

"Mister," said Petty, "we're getting tired of your attitude. We've been waiting for Bo Roden and Ollie McCool for over a week. Don't give us short answers when we ask—"

"They're not coming," Sam said with finality. He just stared at the three.

"Meaning what, 'They're not coming'?" said Fain. "That somebody killed them?"

"Yep," Sam said.

The three looked surprised, but only for a second.

"Another of his damn short answers," said Petty with an angry expression. "For two cents I'd—"

"Apaches killed them," Sam said, cutting Petty off. "They were running a young warrior, betting how far he could go before he dropped. He managed to get away, stole their horses, rifles, everything they had. They camped with me overnight. The Apaches came back and killed them both before morning."

"Why didn't they kill you?" said Fain.

"Because I have a pleasant disposition," Sam said wryly.

"The hell you say," said Petty, cutting him off. "No damn Apache born could catch those hombres unawares. I don't believe you."

"So you're calling me a liar," Sam said quietly.

"I might be at that," said Petty, poised like a dog with its hackles up.

"All right, then," Sam said flatly. "I killed them. You like that better?"

"No, I don't. I don't believe that either," Petty said. "Leastwise, you didn't kill them in a fair fight."

"Both of them?" Fain said to Sam, sounding impressed in spite of trying hard not to.

"Yep, both of them," said Sam. He laid his free palm on Roden's black-handled Colt. "First this one." He placed his hand on the Colt. "And then this one." He moved his hand to the nickel-plated Russian Smith & Wesson. "One shot each . . . *in the heart*," he said, taking his time, letting it sink in.

"I don't know that I believe him either, Petty," said Fain. To Sam he said, "Those ol' boys were pretty damn fast, stranger. I've seen them both handle some damn tough hombres—"

"One shot each . . . *in the heart*," Sam repeated, slowly, deliberately. He held his gaze fixed ironlike on Fain's eyes. "Ready to take them now?" he asked, running his free palm back and forth across the two gun butts.

Wanting a way out, Fain looked at the other two gunmen. The expressions on their faces told him they weren't backing down. He took some courage from knowing the odds were on his side.

"Oh, we'll take them, sure enough," said Fain with a scowl. His eyes widened. "You don't carry our friends' guns in here and tell lies, saying you killed them, whether you did or not—"

His words stopped short as McCool's big Russian Smith & Wesson came up from Sam's waist and made a vicious swipe across the outlaw's jaw. Fain flew backward to the floor. Montoya and Petty wasted no time snatching their guns from their holsters. But it did them no good. Before either gun aimed or fired, both the Russian Smith & Wesson and Sam's own Colt fired at once.

A blast of orange-blue gunfire streaked in the shadowy cantina. Both gunmen took a bullet. Petty, a smaller man, caught a deadly shot in his chest. He flipped backward and smacked the dirty clay-tiled floor facedown. The tall Mexican only staggered backward two steps and got off one wild shot. A third bullet, this one from Sam's Colt, slammed Montoya hard in his shoulder before he could get his footing steadied. He went backward to the floor as his gun made another shot. This time his bullet flew wildly into the ceiling rafters, struck a nail head, sang out with a large spark and ricocheted.

Behind the bar the big mirror cracked loudly, shattered into a large spiderweb around the bullet hole and fell in shards as the Mexican workers fled for cover.

Seeing that both gunmen were out of the fight, Sam kicked Montoya's gun across the tile floor. He stepped over to Fain, who had struggled onto his knees and reached for his gun while blood trickled from the bloody welt Sam had laid across his cheek.

"Ple-please, mister . . . ," Fain groaned, his hand slumping, letting his gun fall from it. Sam cocked his smoking Colt an inch from his forehead.

"I shot your pals Roden and McCool for making threats they couldn't keep," he said down to Fain. "Where does that put you?"

"We—we weren't all that good a friends," Fain said in a shaky voice. "I didn't mean any threats, I swear I didn't."

"That's what I figured," Sam said. He let the hammer down on his Colt and took a step back. Montoya had struggled to his knees and begun pushing himself to his feet, gripping his shoulder wound.

"Get this one up and get out of my sight," Sam said,

letting his Colt hang loosely in his hand. He shoved the shiny Smith & Wesson back down in his waist and patted it and the black-handled Colt. "Come get these guns anytime you're feeling edgy."

"What about our guns, *señor*?" said Montoya.

"Leave them," Sam said. "The bartender will hold them for you until you pay for the mirror." He reached down and slid Fain's gun from its holster and pitched it atop the bar with a loud thump.

Montoya looked at the bare wall behind the bar where the workers had returned and stood staring down at a pile of broken glass. Without another word, Montoya nodded and turned to Fain.

Sam stood at the bar watching the tall Mexican with two bullets in him help Fain up onto his feet. The two staggered toward the front curtain as a hand reached out and pulled the curtain aside for them.

Sam heard the crunching footsteps from the far end of the bar and turned and saw a raggedly-dressed American with a long beard and a sagging slouch hat standing with his arms spread looking down at the shards of mirror glass.

"Son of a bitch!" he said. "I didn't even get this one hung before they broke it." Smoke curled from a short cigar in the corner of his mouth.

While Sam stood staring at him, a Mexican worker rose from clearing a path through the broken glass. He looked at Sam, then at the ragged American.

"Señor Graft," he said. "This man has kept the scalp hunters' guns to pay for the mirror." He turned to Sam and said, "This is Señor Graft, the owner of this, the Trato Justo Cantina."

"Reuben Grafton," said the owner. "I'm called *Graft* around here." He looked Sam up and down from behind his smoky cigar.

"The Fair Deal . . . ," Sam translated, instead of introducing himself. He glanced around the dusty cantina, seeing a worn and battered faro table in a far corner. Two more game tables sat along the back wall.

Graft raised a bushy eyebrow toward him.

"Anything wrong with the name *Trato Justo*, pilgrim?" he asked, his eyes moving to Sam's Winchester lying on the bar top.

"Not that I know of," Sam said. "I just got here."

Graft relaxed a little, seeing one of his Mexican workers carrying the other two discarded guns to the bar. The worker laid Montoya's and Petty's guns down beside Fain's.

"I suppose I ought to say *obliged*," he said, looking down at all three guns on the bar top. "This might be a first, somebody offering to pay for a mirror." He appraised the guns. "These won't do it, but it's a start."

Sam heard the crunch of glass as Graft stepped forward and leaned his palms on the bar top.

"What's your name, hombre?" he asked cordially enough. "What brings you to Agua Fría?" He was eyeing the front door like a man expecting bad news any minute.

"I come here looking for work," Sam said. "I got tired of eating jackrabbit and rattlesnake." He deliberately didn't give a name.

Graft looked at the three guns on the bar and the blood on the tile floor. He stared at two men carrying the body of Petty out through the dusty front curtain.

"If this is the kind of work you do, I venture you'll never go hungry around here," he said. "What do we call you?" he asked, already seeing this hard-eyed stranger wasn't giving his name up easily.

"Jones will do," Sam said evenly, almost grudgingly.

"All right, *Jones* it is," said Graft. He gave a slight grin around his short cigar. "I've met lots of your kin-folk since I've been in ol' Mex."

"I bet you have," Sam said. "Joneses are everywhere."

Chapter 8

As Sam and Reuben Grafton stood talking at the bar, a rough hand pulled the door curtain to one side. Four gunmen filed inside and looked all around at the blood on the floor. From behind the bar top, Graft waved them forward. Moments earlier the four had heard the shots and started walking to the cantina to investigate. Out front they had seen the body of Petty being carried along the street, a skinny pup running along, licking at dripping blood behind them. They'd seen the two wounded scalp hunters staggering away leaning against each other.

"No problem here, fellows." Graft waved them forward. "But come on over anyway. Let Rolo get you all a bottle of whiskey—on the house, of course, my treat."

The men walked toward the bar, eyeing Sam on their way.

"It sounded busy over here for this time of day, Graft," said the leader, Daryl Dolan, a dusty-faced gunman wearing leather wrist cuffs heavily studded with silver conchos. Dirty yellow hair hung to his shoulders. His right hand rested on the butt of a Remington Army conversion. "How's that new mirror coming along?" He looked at the gray bare wall behind the bar. "Can't see who's coming in behind you without it," he added.

"It's broke all to hell, Daryl," Graft said, waving the matter aside. "It might have been cracked to begin with."

"We heard gunplay over here," Dolan said, looking all around.

"Oh, we had a scuffle for sure, but it's all in the past now," Graft added. Sam noted the cantina owner trying to play the shooting down all of a sudden. "Jones here and I were just talking about it."

"What happened, *Jones*?" Dolan asked Sam, staring coldly at him.

Sam didn't answer right away. Instead he reached around and lifted his beer mug, as if to first take a sip before answering.

Daryl's face tightened. But before he could say anything to Sam, Graft cut in.

"Jones here didn't start the trouble," he said quickly, "but he took the scalp hunters' guns for payment against my new mirror."

"You mean Fain and them? Those scalp hunters?" said Dolan. He looked Sam up and down. "You took their guns—killed the one we saw being carried away?"

"I did," Sam said flatly. "Hope they weren't friends of yours."

"Ha," said Dolan, "that mangy bunch? They don't have *friends* here. They just have some folks who don't hate them as bad as others."

The three men behind him gave a dark chuckle.

"I heard Petty was fast with a gun—talked to my boss

some about riding with us." Dolan gave a faint grin. "I expect he wouldn't have lasted long, if he went down that easy."

"Fast didn't help him much," said Graft. "Jones here didn't let him get his gun skint before he nailed him."

"Is that right, Jones?" said Dolan. "You didn't let him get his gun drawn?"

"It didn't seem like a good idea to," said Sam.

Behind Dolan, the three gunmen gave a slight chuckle at Sam's words. But a sharp glance from Dolan quieted them.

Dolan looked him up and down again. He rubbed his chin in contemplation.

"I'm just speculating, Jones," he said, "wondering how fast you are."

Sam replied coolly, "Never waste time *wondering* when you can find out in a second flat." As he spoke he leaned back against the bar with his forearms up along the edge. His beer mug hung from his left hand; his right hand rested an inch from his Winchester.

All four of the gunmen fell silent.

Dolan gave a puzzled look while Sam's words sank in. Then his face took on a confused smile.

"Fellows, I believe *Jones* just told me to *arm up* or shut up," he said.

Sam just stared at him.

"New bottle here, fellows," Graft said eagerly.

A bottle of rye appeared on the bar top and a string of glasses spread alongside it. The bottle cork made a soft pop in Rolo the bartender's hands.

"What do you want us to do, Daryl, shoot holes in

him?" a young gunman named Clyde Burke asked, stepping up beside the lead man.

Staring hard at Sam, Dolan gave a chuff. His smile turned less confused and more genuine.

"Naw, Burke. A man can get shot anytime," he said over his shoulder. "I'm going to have a drink." He said to Sam, "Jones, you always wear your bark so tight?"

When Sam didn't answer, Graft cut in, seeing a chance to stop any further bloodshed or broken glass.

"He says he's here because he's tired of eating jackrabbit and rattlesnake," he said.

"So, you come looking for *gun* work?" Dolan asked Sam.

"Is there any other kind?" Sam said.

"Is there any other kind?" Dolan repeated with a chuckle. "If there is, I never considered it." He let out a breath and said, "Can you loosen your bark enough to have a drink?"

"I already have," Sam said. He breathed easier. He set his beer mug down from his left hand and let his right hand fall away from his Winchester.

"That's good," said Dolan. "Because it happens that you've come to the right place. We are the only outfit around here who's hiring for gun work."

"I heard there's another outfit," Sam said, turning to the bar.

"Then you heard wrong," said Dolan. He motioned for the other men to line along the bar. He stepped in beside Sam. "We're with Bell Madson. Ever heard of him?"

Sam gave a shrug that said he hadn't.

"He used go by the name *Red* Madson. Some called him *Texas Red* Madson, him being from Texas." He looked at Sam.

Again Sam only shrugged.

"Well, it doesn't matter," said Dolan. "You're new around here. You'll hear of him soon enough."

The others all watched as Rolo filled shot glasses and slid one in front of each man, including Sam and Graft. The cantina owner smiled in relief and stepped back, shot glass in hand, as two workers came through shoveling broken mirror shards from the floor behind the bar. He tipped his shot glass toward Dolan in thanks.

Dolan nodded at Sam's shot glass of whiskey.

"Drink up, Jones," he said. "It's always good to meet a man who knows his way around a shooting iron." He gave a thin smile. "To be honest, you gave a hell of an account of yourself—three on one, you killed one, wounded one and put the hurt on a third. Those damn scalp hunters. Here's to shooting the stinking sons a' bitches." He raised his shot glass as if in a toast of denouncement.

"My pleasure," Sam said, lifting his shot glass.

"See?" Graft grinned. "There was really no trouble here." But the gunmen appeared not to hear him.

As the empty shot glasses came back down onto the bar and Rolo started refilling them, the front curtain pulled to one side and harsh sunlight slanted in across the tile floor. On Dolan's other side, Clyde Burke spoke under his breath.

"Look who just showed up, Daryl," he said.

"I bet I already know," Dolan said. He turned sidelong

to the bar, as did the others. "Well, well, if it ain't Ray Segert's *boys*," he said to the new arrivals. "You didn't need to show up. We've got this covered." Then he turned to the cantina owner. "Graft, set these boys up some *sassafras* tea, on me."

"Dolan's right, fellows," Graft called out. "There's no trouble here."

The four men slowed on their way to the other end of the bar.

"I'll sassafras his ass," a gunman named Dusty Phelps growled under his breath to the man, Max Udall, standing beside him. He started to make a sudden turn toward Dolan. The men at the bar tensed, as did the four newly arrived gunmen.

"Hold your spit, Dusty," the lead man, Max Udall, demanded, stepping almost in between Phelps and Dolan. He gave Daryl Dolan a sharp snarl of a grin. "It's just Daryl's inhospitable way of being hospitable." He spoke directly to Daryl. "I see nobody's yet carved out your tongue and used it for a door hinge."

"You own a knife, Max. Come show us how it's done," Dolan returned, his hand poised deftly at his gun butt.

But Max Udall nodded his men on toward the far end of the bar, drinkers pushing aside, making room for them. Some drinkers had already slipped out of the cantina and gone on their way.

"Not today, Dolan," Udall said, walking on. "We only come to see what the shooting's about. Hope none of yas got rowdy and lost any toes."

Dolan looked down at his boots. "Still got enough toes to stick a boot up your—"

"Gentlemen, gentlemen! Welcome, one and all," Graft cut in, hoping to stop any trouble before the men got past the stage of hurling insults from their lips and started blasting bullets from their guns.

"What *was* the shooting about, Graft?" Udall asked the nervous cantina owner as he and his men lined along the far end of the bar. Graft hurried down to them behind the bar, crunching glass underfoot on his way.

"Those stinking scalp hunters, Petty, Fain and the Mex, came in here goading my new customer down there," said Graft, sweeping a hand toward Sam's end of the bar. "He put the *slam* on them, sure enough," he said, grinning.

"Is that a fact?" said Udall. He eyed Sam from the far end of the bar.

"It is a fact," said Graft. "He killed one, wounded one and left the third one carrying a ten-pound knot on his jaw."

Udall didn't comment as he appraised Sam over the edge of his raised shot glass of rye. But beside him, Dusty Phelps only half raised his shot glass and stared coldly at Sam as he spoke to Udall and Graft.

"He must be *real* tough," he said sarcastically. To his pals along the bar he said, "What about it, hombres? Should I be *frightened* here?"

A young, heavily muscled Kansas gunman named Mickey Galla downed his shot of rye and spoke in a whiskey-strained voice.

"Only if you was faint of heart to begin with," he said. "He ain't much or he wouldn't be drinking with Madson's crow bait."

Dolan and the other Madson men bristled at Galla's

words, even though the young gunman's attention and stare was centered steadily on Sam.

"Easy, Mick," said Udall. "You're hurting everybody's feelings. I'd like to drink here without having to get blood all over me for a change."

"Please, fellows, no gunplay today," Graft pleaded, seeing the atmosphere turn volatile all over again.

"I see no need for gunplay," said Mickey Galla, swelling out his chest and his thick upper arms. "I'll walk down and give him a hard smack if you want me to—see if anything rattles inside his noggin." As he spoke, he lifted his rifle and laid it up on the bar top. He began rolling up his shirtsleeves.

Sam watched coolly.

"Hold up, Mick," said Udall to the burly gunman, still eyeing Sam. He could tell that the stranger at the far end of the bar didn't scare easily.

"What's your new customer's name, Graft?" he asked the cantina owner, even though his eyes and Sam's were fixed on each other's.

"*Jones* is what he goes by," said Graft in a shaky voice, a shaky grin to match. "I told him, 'My my, Mr. Jones, I sure have met lots of your kinfolk in old Mexico.'" His grin widened and twitched. "It was just a little joke on my part," he concluded. "Get it? There's so many Joneses—"

"Shut up, Graft," said Udall, still staring at Sam. He turned his gaze slowly to Graft. "Why don't you go find yourself a deep dirty hole and stick your fingers down in it?"

"Yeah, real deep," Galla added.

Graft slinked back a step.

Sam continued to stare coolly, unshaken. His hand rested on the bar near his Winchester.

"Jones, this is Mickey Galla," Udall said, gesturing toward the huge muscle-bound gunman.

"Mr. Galla to you," Galla said to Sam.

"Mick likes picking heavy stuff up over his head. Does it for hours," Udall said proudly. "What do you do, *Jones*?" he asked, for the first time speaking directly to Sam.

"Says he's looking for gun work," Graft cut in before Sam could offer a reply. "I told him, as good as he is, he won't—"

"Graft, shut the living hell up!" said Udall, slamming his shot glass onto the bar top so hard it splintered and exploded in every direction. Turning to Mickey Galla, Udall said, "Mick, if he opens his mouth again, grab his throat and jerk him up out of his boots."

"Will do," said Galla. He gave Graft a hard, hateful stare. Graft hurried away, back to the other end of the bar to refill Dolan and his pals' glasses.

"I asked you *what you do, Jones*," said Udall again to Sam.

"I heard you," Sam replied.

Udall and his men stared in anticipation. So did Dolan and his pals.

After a tight silence, Udall cocked his head slightly at Sam.

"Well?" he asked Sam.

"Well, what?" Sam said.

"He's messing with you, Max," Galla growled. He shoved himself back from the bar and walked quick-step toward Sam, his sleeves rolled up his thick forearms. "I bet I have to smack him one." As he drew closer, Dolan's men parted, letting him through. They watched, eager to see what the newcomer had going for him.

"The man asked what you do, stranger," Galla demanded, advancing on Sam like a stalking bull. "He won't ask again—"

His words were cut short as Sam's right hand clasped around the small of the rifle stock and jammed it butt first into the big gunman's face. Nose cartilage crunched; blood flew. Galla's upper half jolted to a halt; his lower half skidded forward on his bootheels. Before he hit the tile floor, Sam's Winchester swung around in a wide arc and slammed sidelong into the big gunman's head.

At the far end of the bar, Udall and the other Segert men made a move for their guns. But Sam snapped the rifle to his shoulder. Cocking it, he aimed it straight at Udall.

Dolan's men had turned from the bar, their hands grasping their own guns and stopping there, waiting, watching. Behind the bar Graft froze, his eyes widened. He wore the same shaky grin, as if he would be stuck with it for life.

"Like he told you, hombre," Sam said quietly to Max Udall, "I do gun work. Any more questions?"

The cantina stood tense, silent. After a moment, Udall raised a hand slowly and gestured for his men to ease down. They did, a little.

"No, Jones," Udall said in a calm tone. "I think you've answered clear enough." He sat staring for a moment longer, then gave a chuff, glancing at Mickey Galla on the tile floor. Then he gave a chuckle and shook his head.

Along the bar, his men settled and laughed themselves. "Somebody go throw water on Mickey," he said quietly. "See if we need to stand him up or tie him out on a board."

His men laughed at his dark humor. Two of them walked to where Galla lay stretched out, nose crushed and already swelling beneath a mask of blood. At the other end of the bar, Daryl Dolan turned a sidelong glance to his men and eased them down as well.

"Gun work, huh?" Udall said to Sam.

"Gun work," Sam reaffirmed, lowering his Winchester back onto the bar but keeping his hand on the stock.

"Now that we know *clearly* what you do," said Udall, his eyes moving over Dolan and the rest of Madson's men as he spoke, "the question is, who do you do it for?"

"We were just discussing that when you came in, Udall," Dolan said. "I already told him he's got a job with Madson."

"Yeah, but did you say for how much?" said Udall.

"We were just getting there," said Dolan. "So go on back to your rye, let us talk business over here."

"You should have got there sooner," said Udall. He turned his gaze to Sam. "If you're looking for the best pay with the best outfit, that would be us, Jones," he said. "Our men all live longer than Madson's for some reason—healthier, I guess."

"Don't push your luck, Udall," Dolan cautioned. "That's something that can change any minute."

Graft looked back and forth between Dolan and Udall.

Jesus . . . ! Here they go again! he told himself. He

gave Sam a pleading look, as if asking him to do something before they started all over.

"I just got here today," Sam said. "I didn't know work was so plentiful." He let his hand move away from his rifle. On the floor, Mickey Galla groaned as one of the two men took a pitcher of water from Rolo, who had hurried out from behind the bar and handed it to them.

"Like I was telling you, Jones," said Dolan, "there's us, and there's them. Madson and Segert used to be pards. But not anymore. Now they'd like each other dead. So you best pick a side and stand there."

"I hate to agree with Daryl Dolan on anything," said Udall, "but he's telling you right. Stick around here doing gun work, you'll have to work for either Segert or Madson."

Sam watched the gunman throw the water onto Galla's bloody face. Galla groaned more and rolled his big head from one side to the other. Sam looked back and forth between the two opposing factions at the bar. In the exchange of threats and arguing between the two groups, the rest of the day drinkers had vanished like ghosts. All except Sam.

All right, you're here, on the job . . . , he reminded himself. He'd made a good start for himself.

"I see a third possibility," he said.

"Yeah, what's that?" Udall asked, him and Dolan both watching Sam closely.

"I might decide to go into business for myself," Sam said.

"You'd better think it over, Jones," said Udall. "You don't want to get off on the wrong side here. It'd be bad for your health." He set his shot glass down on the bar, and he and his men backed away, ready to turn toward the door.

"Damn right, you'd best give it some serious thought," Dolan said to Sam. He and his men set down their shot glasses as well. He gave Sam a dark stare.

"I already am," Sam said, his hand resting near his Winchester.

Chapter 9

No sooner had both groups of gunmen left the Trato Justo Cantina than Graft let out a sigh of relief that left him slumped over the bar. Elbows on the bar top, he buried his face in both hands for a moment and shook his lowered head.

"For God sakes, Jones," he said to Sam. "You don't take on a trifling attitude with men like these—especially not in their own damn stomping grounds." He raised his face from his hands and stared at Sam. "I hope you realize how lucky you are to be alive."

Sam took his trail gloves from behind his belt, pulled them on and walked the few feet down-bar to where Graft stood on the other side. Graft watched him pick up an uncorked bottle of rye standing on the bar and fill a shot glass. Sam pushed the drink over in front of Graft with his gloved hand.

"Have one, barkeep, *on me*," he said to Graft. "You earned it, juggling all those hardcases at once."

"Hell, I don't mind if I do," said Graft, swiping up the shot glass. "Have one yourself, *on you*," he said, nodding at the bottle in Sam's gloved hand.

"Obliged, but no, thanks," Sam said.

"What? You've stopped drinking on me, after all the trouble you stirred up here?" said Graft.

"No offense, but I do most of my drinking alone, somewhere quiet," said Sam. As a rule he didn't drink a lot of whiskey; he knew this wouldn't be a good time to start.

"Alone? *Ha*," said Graft. "Suit yourself." He drained the shot glass in one gulp and set it down firmly. "My observation from this side of the bar," he said in a whiskey-strained voice, "is that a man who drinks alone long enough starts to wonder how it feels to blow his own brains out."

"My observation from *this side* of the bar," Sam returned, "is that a man pushing against two opposing forces winds up getting himself crushed between them."

"Well, *my my!*" Graft feigned a surprised look. He gestured a hand about his empty cantina where black blood still stained the floor tiles. "All this, and you're a *man of science* too?"

"Only in self-defense," Sam said. He reached out with the bottle and refilled Graft's shot glass. Rolo, the bartender, appeared out of a rear supply room with a mop and a wooden bucket full of water. Sam and Graft saw him carry the bucket to the bloodstains and set it down. "You started it with your remark about suicide," he added.

"Yeah, I suppose I asked for that, questioning a man's drinking habits," Graft said with a sigh. He picked up his fresh drink and swished it around a little. "I don't know why I'm telling you this, Jones," he said, "but you're looking at a whipped man here. Since these two outfits have taken themselves a slice of Agua Fría, a businessman on his own, like me, ain't got a chance."

"Both sides are squeezing you," Sam ventured.

"You can't imagine," said Graft. "It was bad enough when they was all one gang, Madson and Segert both running it. Now that they've split into two gangs, it cost me and everybody else twice as much. You saw how both sides flocked here like vultures when they heard gunshots. End of the month Crazy Ray Segert and Bell Madson will both show up with their greedy hands out—charging me for having their men keep the peace. Most times it's their men causing the trouble to begin with." His face held his bitter expression. "Soon as they got settled in good and their ranks grew, they all took to bullying the *rurales* out of town—got them all too scared to move against them."

Sam nodded, then poured Graft another glass of whiskey.

"Once the *rurales* were too afraid to uphold the law, Segert and Madson got in with the *federales*," Sam said as if finishing the story for him. "Told them not to worry, they had enough guns and manpower to uphold the law in Agua Fría. The *federales* took them up on it, because . . . well . . . " He shrugged. "That's what *federales* do."

"Sounds like you've heard this song before, Jones," said Graft.

Playing his role as a hardcase, Sam said, "I've heard it, I've sung it." He stared intently at Graft. "Haven't played it for a while, but I remember all the words."

"Then what the hell am I confiding in you for?"

Graft said. "Making those scalp hunters pay for my mirror doesn't make you any different than these other ham-handed sons a'—"

"Watch your language, Graft," Sam said, cutting him off. "You don't want to call me a name you'll regret. I'm the one who can get you off the spot you're on here."

Graft eyed him.

"Oh . . . ?" he said. "How's that?" He sat with his hand wrapped around his fresh glass of whiskey, feeling the strength of it calming his chest, easing the jitters that the two groups of gunmen had stirred in his guts.

"Set me up a table in the front corner there. I'll keep down trouble long as I'm here."

"Oh?" said Graft. "Are you doing this for your health? Or what is it you get for it?"

Sam gave a shrug.

"A third," he said. "It's probably less than you're paying these vultures. I'll keep down the trouble. You won't need these men."

"A partner, for a *third*!" said Graft. "No damn way." He shook his head vigorously. "Besides, you've already come near giving me one a' them *heart attacks* I've been reading about. I don't think I have the constitution it would take to be your partner."

"Suit yourself," Sam said mildly. "I made the offer—you turned it down. I'll decide which one of these outfits to work for and throw in with them. Maybe I'll be the one who comes here to collect." He stepped sideways, picked up his Winchester from atop the bar and turned and walked toward the door.

"Damn it," said Graft. "Wait up, Jones. What's your hurry?"

Sam stopped and looked back at him.

"Come on back," Graft said. "I want to hear what kind of game you're talking about here."

Sam didn't walk back right away. Instead he stood still and gave Graft a dead-serious look. "Call it *no-peep* poker," he said. "I won't turn over my cards until I see the pot's right."

Graft considered it, then said, "All right"—giving in a little—"I'll make the pot right."

"A third," Sam said firmly.

"A third it is," Graft said, "but only if you get Segert and Madson out of my pocket, and *keep* them out."

Sam walked slowly back toward the bar.

"How do I explain a new partner to Segert and Madson?" said Graft as Sam laid his Winchester back up on the bar.

"You won't. I'm a *silent* partner," Sam said. "Nobody's going to know except you and me. I'll keep down any trouble that flares up here in the Fair Deal, and you'll tell me all about Agua Fría, what goes on here and who makes it happen." Sam would have struck up such an exchange for free just to have someone keep him abreast of the town's comings and goings. But he knew that Graft would suspect a gunman working for free.

"We've got a deal," said Graft. "But why are you so interested in Agua Fría and the gunmen running it?"

"I want to know all there is to know about these two gangs," Sam said. "They're neither one going to like hearing that you don't need them to keep down trouble."

Graft nodded; it made sense.

"I'll tell you anything I know about them, or anything new I hear," he said. He thought about matters for a moment. "Holy Joseph," he added. "I hope you're not about to get us killed."

"I'm hoping that myself, *partner*," said Sam. He leaned an elbow on the bar. "Tell me all about Crazy Ray Segert and Bell Madson. What's their game?"

Moments later, when the drinking crowd began to venture back into the Fair Deal, Reuben Grafton turned the bar over to Rolo. For the next hour and a half, he and Sam continued their discussion in the stockroom over Graft's battered wormwood desk. Most of what Graft told Sam came as no surprise, but it was good to know that the two gangs he intended to shut down were the ones responsible for the recent string of robberies and murders that had taken place along the border.

As Sam listened, he recalled the words of the dying outlaw, Curtis Rudabell, when he'd said, *"My kind of people . . . have taken over Agua Fría."*

And here it is, Sam reminded himself, hearing Graft give him the barkeeper's-eye view of the two thriving outlaw gangs and the stranglehold they held on Agua Fría.

Both Segert and Madson used to be partners. Now they were two separate gangs. They robbed banks, payrolls and trains, and neither side hesitated to kill anybody who tried to stand in their way. Both gang leaders had the kind of money it took to own the *federles* in this part of the hill country, he'd told Sam. What their money couldn't buy, their gunmen could take by force.

"Their only formidable enemy this side of the border is each other, Jones," he said. He paused, watching Sam's face intently, then said, "They will kill you without batting an eye, once they see you're costing them money." As he spoke, Sam saw him growing doubtful. "What the hell?" he said, throwing up his hands. "This is loco. We'd best forget the whole idea."

"Don't get cold feet on me, Graft," Sam said.

"But they will kill you, Jones," he said. "Damn it, are you daft, man?"

"Like I told you," Sam said, "I'm tired of eating jackrabbit and rattlesnake—"

"Right, I know," said Graft, cutting him off. "And I'm sick of being squeezed dry by these jackals. Pay no attention to me. I just got a blast of cold air up my back. Go ahead, do like we said. Clean this mess up." He took a deep, calming breath. "I reckon the bright side is, if they kill you, I won't owe you nothing."

Sam gave a slight wry grin.

"That's the spirit," he said. He pushed his chair back from the desk and stood up with his Winchester in hand. "Have you heard any whisper about a robbery going bad for one of them a few weeks back?"

"Yeah," said Graft. "Word is Segert lost a couple of men to a lawman after a bank robbery, while they were coming back across the border through Nogales." He looked at Sam closely.

"One lawman?" Sam asked.

"So I heard. What's that got to do with anything?"

"Nothing," Sam said. "I just heard some talk is all—I like to know all I can about how tough these hombres are. If one lawman took two of them down . . ." He let his opinion trail.

"I hadn't thought of it that way," Graft said. He gave a slight grin. "Not only did the lawmen stop their clocks, but Apaches stole their bank money and *scalped* one." He gave a dark chuckle. "How damn tough is that?"

Preston Kelso.

"Did he die?" Sam asked, knowing that it was Rudabell, not the Apaches, who had the stolen bank money.

"Naw, he's still alive—if you call it living," Graft said. "The monks have him at their hospital. Got his arrow holes plugged up and got his head covered with worms." He winced, looking up at Sam. "Have you ever seen a maggot bonnet?"

"Can't say I have," Sam replied.

"The monks could charge money to show that poor bastard if they would. Go by and take a look," Graft said.

"I'll do that," Sam said, turning, walking toward the door.

"So, I'll see you around tonight?" said Graft.

"Yep," Sam said, stopping, opening the door. "Have Rolo set up my corner table. Any trouble flares up in the Fair Deal, I want to be the first to see it."

"You got it, *partner*," Graft said, lowering his voice a little. He sat back and relaxed as Sam stepped out and shut the door behind him.

In the infirmary, a young man in white peasant clothing came running up to the priest, his leather sandals slapping loudly on the stone-tiled floor.

"Padre Octavia, come quickly!" he shouted, seeing the priest step into sight from around a stone column in order to investigate the approaching noise. "One of the gringos has gone crazy!"

"I have told you not to use that word in my presence, Juan," said the young priest as he caught him by his thin shoulders and held him in place. He shook him as if to calm him down. "Which of the *americanos* are you talking about?"

Before the young Mexican, Juan Mera, could answer, a shrill maniacal half laugh, half scream echoed from a hallway leading to the infirmary. Following the strange hysterical shriek came the blast of a gunshot.

"The one with the gun!" Juan said as if on cue. Another shot resounded from the direction of the infirmary.

Father Octavia crossed himself quickly and squeezed the crucifix hanging from a chain around his neck.

"*Sante Madre,*" he whispered, stung by the realization it was he who had given Kelso the big Colt Dragoon. "I have done a foolish and terrible thing," he said under his breath.

"*Padre*, he is coming!" said Juan in terror, hearing the ravings of a lunatic announce himself closer along the hallway. "What must we do?"

"Run!" said the priest. "He is drunk and wild on mescal! Find Señor Segert's pistoleros and send them here quickly. This man works for Segert."

"But you, *Padre*!" Juan said, even as he turned toward the front door of the church. "What about you?" He hesitated for a moment.

"I must intercept him before he harms someone! Now go, Juan," said the priest. "I am under God's *protección*!" He gave Juan a shove.

Juan raced away and burst through the front doors into the afternoon sunlight, and into the arms of the Ranger, who had heard the gunshot as he walked along the street toward the hotel.

"Señor, señor! Help us!" cried Juan Mera. "A wounded gringo has gone mad and is shooting at us!"

Another shot resounded, followed by a loud crash of broken glass. Sam gave the man a shove away from him and hurried to the open church door.

Inside the church the priest saw Sam come with his gun drawn and ready. He pointed him toward a broken side window.

"He leaped through it!" said the priest. "He is out there!"

Sam backed out of the church and ran around the side of the stone and adobe building just as a peal of crazy screaming laughter rang out, followed by another shot, then another.

Four shots . . . , Sam reminded himself, running forward with caution from cover to cover to the rear of the church. He saw a man's bare rear end disappear around the corner, white shirttails flapping in the air. He hurried forward, then stopped at the corner of the building as another shot exploded.

Five shots . . . , he thought, counting silently, and stepped forward around the corner, noting a splotch of white maggots squirming in the dirt at his feet.

"Preston Kelso," he said under his breath. "It figures."

When he looked along a narrow alleyway running behind the church, he saw the wounded outlaw standing bowed at the waist, his free hand on his knee supporting himself. Sam could hear him wheezing and coughing as he moved toward him. Kelso held the big Dragoon clutched against his heaving chest.

Kelso lifted his banded head and slung it back and forth; white maggots flew. Sam winced slightly and kept advancing.

When Kelso noticed Sam, he straightened and batted his swirling mescal-blurred eyes and tried to focus. Mumbling something as if talking to someone beside him, he raised the Dragoon with one hand and fired. The impact of the big horse pistol threw his hand high and knocked him off his feet. More maggots flew from above his white cloth headband.

That's six, Sam told himself. He began advancing quicker, his Colt out and cocked, his Winchester hanging in his other hand.

"Drop the gun," he demanded. "You're out of shots."

"Like hell I am!" Kelso screamed in a ranting, mindless voice. He struggled to his feet. "I've got plenty of reloads! Come and get them!"

"I hate thinking where you're carrying them," Sam

said half aloud. Kelso wore nothing but the wrinkled white shirt.

Kelso let out a shriek, raised the empty gun and clicked it at the Ranger. Sam knocked the big Dragoon aside. Seeing Kelso already staggering in place, Sam swept a boot sidelong and knocked his bare feet out from under him. Kelso fell to the ground. Sam clamped him down with a boot on his naked abdomen below the bandages on his chest.

"I know you! I know you!" Kelso ranted, squirming to get free from beneath the big boot.

"Shut up," Sam said, ready to swipe the Colt barrel across his head if he didn't settle down. Maggots lay scattered in the dirt like wiggling grains of rice.

"Please, *señor*, do not hurt him," Father Octavia called out, running up past Sam, kneeling over the downed outlaw. "He is a wounded man from the *enfermería*. He is out of his mind on mescal."

"I see that," Sam said. The priest held Kelso under control. Sam lifted his boot off Kelso's stomach. "Is everybody in your infirmary armed?"

"No, only him," said the priest, holding Kelso, straightening the headband that had sagged and was dripping the white larvae to the dirt. "I gave him the Dragoon. I do not know why." He shook his head. "He is a very convincing man. He convinced me to do his bidding and give him the gun." He shook his head again. "What was I thinking?"

Sam heard more boots behind him and he looked over his shoulder to see the Hookes brothers walking up. He swung his gun toward them. They stopped in their tracks and raised their hands chest high.

"*Whoa*, easy, fellow," said Charlie Ray. "We heard shooting. We come checking on our pal."

"They gave him the mescal. Only God knows what they put in it to make him so loco," the priest said.

"All right, he's got us there as far as the mescal goes," said Hazerat, the two having caught the conversation. "And he's right about ol' Preston. He can be convincing as hell when it suits him. We brought him a swig or two to ease his pain—he kept our whole damn jug."

"And it's about half peyote powder," Charlie Ray put in. "Lucky he didn't kill somebody."

The two leaned down and helped the priest pull Kelso to his feet. Kelso swooned and stumbled but managed to stay standing. His mind appeared to be spinning behind his shiny eyes.

The priest looked at Sam and gestured toward the smoking Dragoon lying in the dirt.

"Will you be so kind, *señor*?" he asked.

"Yes, go ahead. I've got it," Sam said. Stepping over, he picked up the big gun and walked along behind them, as they led the half-conscious Kelso back toward the infirmary.

"We owe you a drink, mister," Charlie Ray Hookes said to Sam over his shoulder.

Sam looked at the mumbling, mindless Kelso hanging between the three men. Maggots spilled from atop his head down the back of his shirt.

"Obliged," Sam said. "But from the looks of your pal, I think I'll pass."

The two gunmen laughed a little. Father Octavia shook

his head and stared straight ahead, seeing no humor in Sam's statement.

Sam walked on, the big Dragoon hanging in his free hand. He'd only been in Agua Fría a day, but already he felt himself making inroads among the town's less wholesome element.

PART 2

Chapter 10

The first three weeks in Agua Fría passed quickly for the Ranger. From his perch at the front corner table in the Fair Deal Cantina, he had settled a few angry flare-ups among the drinking crowd before the situations had gotten out of hand. Two saddle tramps had been carried out with welts across their heads; two of Madson's lesser gunmen had staggered out on their own, their holsters empty. But there had not been a shot fired since the ones between him and the scalp hunters. Rolo the bartender had remarked that the place had stopped smelling like burned gunpowder. Graft had ordered a replacement mirror for the wide, empty space behind the bar.

Sam had spent enough time with men in both gangs to get a pretty good idea of how things worked. Segert and Madson kept a few close gunmen on the payroll, the ones they knew they could rely on. The rest of the men were lower-level gunmen like the Hookes, who worked for Segert, or the two saddle tramps whose heads he'd thumped, who worked for Madson. But these men weren't regulars for the two gangs. These were strictly extra guns when extra guns were needed. They hung around town just waiting to be called upon for the next piece of work. Sam knew that both Segert and Madson had heard about what he'd done to the three scalp hunters.

He knew that both men realized he was here looking for gun work. He'd been noticed. Nobody knew that he and Graft had a deal between them, yet everybody did know from the first day he'd arrived at the Fair Deal that he wouldn't stand for any trouble while he was there. His groundwork had been laid, he reminded himself, sitting at his table in the front corner, his Winchester across his lap. Now it appeared he'd have to be patient—*wait to be called upon,* he told himself.

He sat considering his situation as the Hooke brothers and Preston Kelso walked through the dusty door blanket and stepped over to his table. He'd spoken and drunk some with the Hookes the past couple of weeks, but it was the first he'd seen of Kelso since the day the gunman had gone wild-eyed mad on mescal and peyote powder.

"Jones," said Charlie Ray, "might we join you? I'll stand us all a bottle of rye."

"I'm drinking beer," Sam said. "But seat yourself all the same. He gestured toward empty chairs strung around the table. The three pulled out chairs and seated themselves. Hazerat summoned a young Mexican woman named Mona Reyes, who hurried off to bring a bottle and glasses from the bar.

"How's the head?" Sam asked Kelso.

"Still raw and sore," Kelso said in a dismal tone. "I don't look for it to ever be right." He raised a large sombrero carefully from his head and set it on his lap. "Damn 'paches."

Sam saw the thick wrapping of gauze around his head from his ears up.

Sam noted the big Dragoon was gone. A slimmer, lighter Army Colt conversion rested in a cross-draw holster on Kelso's left side.

"You're the one who knocked me on my ass when I'd gone loco on the poisons these two gave me?" Kelso asked.

"No," said Sam. "But I kicked your feet out from under you, held you down until the priest came for you."

Kelso considered it for a moment, then nodded.

"Obliged," he said. "There's no telling where I might've winded up." He eyed Charlie Ray and Hazerat as the young woman stood the bottle of rye and glasses on the table.

When Charlie Ray started to reach for his pocket to pay, Sam cut in and said, "I've got this."

He pulled the bull scrotum pouch that had belonged to Curtis Rudabell from behind his belt and deliberately held it out on the table where Kelso got a good look at it. The tobacco had been removed, but the gold coins were still inside it. Sam opened it, pulled out a gold coin and let it lie on the table.

"No, sir, Jones," said Charlie Ray. "I said I'd stand this one, and I meant it. Besides, you said you're not drinking rye." He pulled out a wad of dollar bills and peeled one off and dropped it atop the table. The Mexican girl snatched it and was gone.

"Right you are," said Sam. He let Kelso watch as he

slid the coin back inside the pouch, closed the pouch and stuffed it behind his belt. This time he made sure the initials CR were turned outward, clearly visible.

With his shot glass in hand, Kelso sat staring numbly at Sam, his eyes staying on the pouch after Sam moved his hand away from it.

Charlie Ray and Hazerat took notice of Kelso's riveted interest in the pouch.

"Yo, Preston," said Charlie Ray. "Are you going to drink that rye or let it age a little longer?"

Kelso shook his head as if to clear it. Instead of answering Charlie Ray, he stared at Sam. He forced himself to stare less intently.

"So, Jones," he said to Sam, "where'd you get such a tobacco pouch as that?"

"I picked it up on my way here," Sam said casually. He just stared at Kelso, knowing the pouch had struck a nerve. "Want to see it?" he asked. Without waiting for an answer, he pulled the pouch from his belt and pitched it in front of Kelso.

"Did you sure enough?" said Kelso. "You mean at a trading post, somewhere like that?" He clasped the pouch and stared at the initials on it.

Sam could see the wheels turning in his mind.

"Huh-uh, nothing like that," Sam said. "Fact is I took it off a dead man."

Kelso went back to staring at the pouch, pieces starting to come together in his mind.

"Who do you suppose killed him?" he asked, his eyes shooting back up at Sam.

"Apache, no doubt," Sam said.

"Yeah, why do you say?" said Kelso.

"Because he was wearing the same kind of haircut you are," Sam replied, nodding at Kelso's bandaged head.

"What else was he carrying?" Kelso asked, knowing he had to play this really careful.

"Not much else," Sam said. "Why? Was he a friend of yours?"

"Yeah, I'll say he was," said Kelso. "He was riding with me when we did a job on the other side of the border. We picked up a lawman on our trail coming through Nogales. Couldn't shake him."

"Too bad," said Sam. "Looks like the Apache got to him before the law could."

"You just left him?" Kelso asked.

"Yep," Sam said. "I dragged him off the trail into some rocks. He's still there if you want to take up a shovel and ride out. It's a two-day-straight ride from here."

The Hookes looked at each other, then at Kelso.

Kelso looked at them, then back at Sam, throwing the pouch down in front of him.

"He was a good enough pal. I just might," Kelso growled. He reached down, raised his shot glass and tossed back the rye. Sam could see a puzzling wave of questions streak back and forth across his mind. Did this stranger kill Rudabell? Did he take the saddlebags of money? Did the Apaches kill him and take it? Or did Rudabell manage to hide the money under a rock before he died?

Kelso slammed the shot glass down on the tabletop and turned toward the front door. Over his shoulder he called back to the Hooke brothers, "You two come with me. We've got to talk."

The Hookes gave Sam a curious look, but Sam only shrugged. He sat back and watched as the two brothers scrambled up and hurried out through the swaying blanket behind Preston Kelso. He picked up the cork and palmed it down firmly into the bottle of rye. *That should give the three of them something to think about. . . .*

Moments later, Mona Reyes had started to pick up the bottle of rye and the shot glasses from the table when a hand pulled the blanket serving as a front door aside and light spilled in from the street. She stopped clearing the table as Daryl Dolan, Clyde Burke and Jon Ho filed in and stepped over to Sam's table.

"Leave it," Dolan said, nodding at the bottle. He looked at Sam as if for permission. Sam gave him a nod.

Dolan picked up the bottle, looked at it and swished its contents, judging the amount already consumed.

"You're one of those early drinkers, I see," he said to Sam.

Sam didn't answer. He looked at each of the three, lingering on Jon Ho, having not encountered him before.

"You're not hard to find these days," Dolan said. "I heard you sit here like you're waiting for mail."

"You never know," Sam said drily. "I could get a love letter."

Dolan chuffed and pulled the cork from the bottle of rye.

"Here's to love letters," he said. He took a swig and passed the bottle to Clyde Burke.

"I thought I got one once," Burke said, raising the bottle halfway to his lips. "Turned out, it was from a cousin of mine—said I had left her with child." He took a drink, then lowered the bottle. "I'd never even met the girl." He let out a short whiskey hiss. "She was cock-eyed as a goose. Must have figured me for some other cousin." He passed the bottle to Jon Ho. "Cousins being how they are."

Sam nodded.

"That's how stuff gets started," he said. He nodded at Jon Ho, who stood staring at him intently. "Who's your friend here?"

"This is Jon Ho," said Dolan. "He takes getting used to."

"I bet he does," said Sam, not wanting to be the first to break his cold dark stare with Jon Ho. Neither one blinked until Ho raised the bottle and took a deliberately long swig. His eyes welled as he lowered the bottle.

"Care for a chair, or are you going to drink all my whiskey standing up?" Sam asked flatly.

Jon Ho set the almost empty bottle back on the table and continued to stare. Sam looked at Dolan, avoiding Ho's venomous black eyes.

"No chair," said Dolan. "Segert sent us to get you."

"*Get* me?" Sam said coolly. He gave Dolan a tilted gaze.

"I meant *take* you to him," said Dolan. "Escort you to him."

Sam's stare didn't change.

"Jesus," said Dolan. "*Ride* with you? Show you how the hell to get there? Okay . . . ?" He looked back and forth between Burke and Ho, then at Sam. "Ease the hell up, Jones. He sent for you. You wanted *gun work*. My guess is, he's got a proposition for you."

Sam nodded as if considering it, not wanting to seem too eager to meet the man.

"I told you I'm thinking of going into business for myself," he said.

"All right, then," said Dolan. "That's what I'll tell him." He nodded the others back toward the door. "Obliged for the rye." He started to turn and leave. The other two followed suit.

"Hold on, fellows. I'm coming," Sam said. He pushed himself up from his chair.

Dolan chuffed and shook his head.

"No offense, Jones," he said with a slight grin, "but you are an aggravating man."

"I've heard that," Sam said.

Burke pulled the dusty blanket back and held it as Dolan and Ho filed through.

"After you," Sam said to Burke, standing firm until Burke left in front of him.

He followed Burke out onto the street, and the four of them walked abreast toward the town livery barn where Sam had left his dun stabled during his days in town. On the way down the street, Sam saw the young woman, Lilith, seated at a whetstone sharpening knives out in front of a mercantile store. Her peddler's wagon sat at a hitch rail. She looked up at Sam with a guarded smile as he and the three men walked past her. But before he could return her smile, she lowered her head quickly as Jon Ho glared at her.

The four turned down a narrow alley to the livery barn and when they reached the end, the three gunmen lagged back a step. Sam turned quickly and saw they had stopped in their tracks.

"Oh, I meant to tell you, Jones. You won't need your horse," said Dolan.

Sam knew instantly that something was wrong. He started to swing his Winchester up, but before he could, a lariat whistled in and looped around him, waist high. It tightened around both arms at his elbows and pinned the rifle down. He struggled. A hard yank on the rope jerked him off his feet. No sooner had he hit the ground on his back than another lariat swung in. The rope clenched tight around both his ankles. He felt the strong pull of horses draw both ropes tight.

"Good roping, vaqueros!" Dolan said to two Mexicans seated atop their horses, lariats in their hands.

Sam struggled again, but he felt the lariats draw tighter from either end.

"Whoa, now, look at Jones here!" shouted Dolan with a dark laugh. Stepping in, he clamped a boot down on Sam's wrist and jerked the Winchester from his hand. "Better give me that before you shoot your foot off."

"He went down hard," said Burke, as he and Jon Ho stood back watching.

Before he straightened, Dolan jerked Sam's Colt from its holster, and removed the two scalp hunters' guns and the bull scrotum from behind Sam's belt. He

pitched the scalp hunters' guns over in the dirt, but held
Sam's Colt and the pouch in his hand. He inspected the
initials and smiled to himself.

"You sure carry a lot of stuff, Jones," he said. Then
he stepped back and gave the two Mexicans a nod; they
loosened the tension on the two ropes a little. Dolan
rested a boot down on Sam's chest, holding him to the
dirt. He grinned down at Sam.

"You've been playing hard to get," he said. "But I can
tell you've been waiting for an offer from Segert or Madson, either one." As he spoke, one of the Mexicans looped
his lariat around his saddle horn, stepped down and
quickly, deftly looped a length of the rope around Sam's
wrists.

Sam resisted, but ended up lying helpless, his hands
tied together and clamped to his belly.

Dolan cocked Sam's Winchester and aimed it down
an inch from his face.

"Untie his feet," he told the Mexican. To Sam he said,
"Make a false move, I'll open your skull for the buzzards."

Sam just stared up at him. He heard footsteps coming up from behind him. They stopped only a few
inches from his head.

"Here he is, boss," said Dolan. "Trussed up like a
game bird."

Sam stared up as a tall, broad-shouldered man in a
silvery gray suit and polished Mexican boots moved
around and stared down at him from behind a cigar.

"Well, well, Joe," said Segert. "You don't look near
as tough as I'm told you are."

Sam didn't answer. He wondered why Segert called him Joe.

"I found this on him, boss," said Dolan. He handed Segert the pouch. Segert turned it in his hand with interest. "Curtis Rudabell's tobacco pouch," Segert said down to Sam. "Curtis would never give this up."

"I took it off a dead man," Sam said bluntly. "He wasn't going to be needing it."

"Sounds reasonable to me," said Segert. He studied the pouch, then sighed and said to Sam, "You come up here, shoot a couple of scalp hunters and bang a few heads at the cantina. You figured bouncing drunks at the Fair Deal was going to get you a job offer? All you did was cost me money, me and Madson both. Now, what did you figure that would get you?" He chuckled to himself.

Sam started to talk. "From what I've seen, you or Madson either one could use—" But Dolan's boot jammed down harder on Sam's chest, stopping him.

"We've got nothing to talk about, Jones," Segert said to Sam, gripping the pouch. He took a step back and said, "Dolan, show our pal around these Twisted Hills some, see if this Blood Mountain Range is a place where he truly wants to be."

"What about that bull's bag?" Dolan asked, nodding at the scrotum in Segert's hand.

Segert hefted the bag in his hand and said, "I know who to ask about this. Get our pal up and out of here," he said, realizing that calling him Joe had been a mistake.

Sam watched Segert step back out of sight. He felt a pair of strong hands behind him pull him to his feet.

The hands reached down and loosened the lariat from around his boots, and Sam stepped out of it.

Standing in front of him, the Winchester still aimed and cocked, Dolan said with a thin, crooked grin, "Here we go, Jones. Looks like you're going to ride with us after all." He called out, "You ready to show him the countryside, Mick?"

"Damn right, I am," said the deep, nasal voice of Mickey Galla.

Sam glanced around and saw the muscle-bound Galla step up onto one of the horses the Mexicans had been riding. Galla's nose was still crooked and purple, matching his dark-ringed eyes.

Dolan chuckled at Sam's surprise.

"You see, Jones, we're all just one big happy family when a stranger comes busting in uninvited." He gave a sharp nod. Sam almost flew from his feet as the lariat drew tight and yanked him, forcing him to turn around and stagger along, struggling to stay afoot, knowing what falling would mean.

"Enjoy your ride," Dolan called out to him as Sam ran awkwardly, his hands tied, his arms tied down his sides. "I'll tell Graft you won't be needing your table any longer."

Chapter 11

———

Sitting atop a trail that led down to the desert floor, the Hooke brothers and Preston Kelso looked down the trail behind them. Their attention had been drawn to the sound of horses' looping hooves, and as they sat cocked half around in their saddles, they saw the four riders come into sight.

"I'll be doubly damned," said Kelso in a gruff tone, seeing Sam on the end of a rope staggering along at a trot behind the approaching riders. "Looks like Dolan and Galla have joined up."

"Yeah," said Hazerat. "Looks like they've mistook Jones for a stray calf."

"We'd better move along before they recognize us—" said Charlie Ray, cutting himself short. "Damn it, too late," he added, ducking his head a little and starting to turn his horse away from the riders.

"Sit still," Kelso growled at him. "They've seen us. Don't slink away like a sheep-killing dog. We ain't done nothing."

"Hell, I know it," said Charlie Ray, trying to recover. "I'm just ready to get going."

"Well, settle down," said Kelso. "I want to hear what our pal Jones has done to curdle their milk so bad."

"Yeah, me too," Hazerat said. He chuckled. "It's awful damn hot to be traveling afoot."

As they watched the riders draw closer, they saw Sam go down and tumble and roll a few yards along the rocky trail until he managed to raise himself back to his feet.

"Now, you know that had to hurt," Charlie Ray said with a cruel grin.

The three sat staring until Dolan, Galla and the two Mexican vaqueros rode up and stopped a few feet in front of them. Kelso touched the brim of his oversized sombrero toward Dolan and Galla. Then he leaned sidelong in his saddle and looked at Sam.

"Howdy, Jones," he said, giving a mocking wave of his hand. "What brings you out running on such a day as this?"

Galla handed the rope over to one of the vaqueros. He raised his hat and wiped a bandanna across his sweaty forehead.

Dolan grinned and gave a nod back toward Sam.

"Segert asked us to air him out a little. Must've thought he was spending too much time indoors. Ain't that right, Jones?" He looked back at Sam, who stood bowed at the waist, trying to catch his breath. His hat was gone, his clothes ragged. His tied hands were bleeding from stone cuts. He didn't lift his head.

Dolan gave the Mexican a nod; the Mexican yanked on Sam's rope, forcing him to look up.

Sam's face was covered with welts, cuts, bruises and

dried blood. His blackened eyes had swollen almost shut.

"I said, *Ain't that right*, Jones?" Dolan repeated.

Sam still didn't reply. He stood swaying in place, but with his shoulders level in spite of his ordeal.

"Guess he didn't feel like stopping," Dolan said to Kelso. He gave a shrug. "What brings you three out this way?"

"Tired of sitting in town so long," said Kelso. "After two weeks of feeding worms, I thought I best get to moving around some. Any word from Segert on when he might need some gun hands?" he asked.

"No," said Dolan. "But it won't be long. So don't wander off too far."

"We won't," said Kelso. He looked at Mickey Galla and said, "Mick, what brings you over from Madson's bunch? Wasn't they feeding you well enough?"

Galla looked him up and down, and gave him a bored half smile. "Don't you suppose if I thought it was any of your business, I would have written you a letter about it?"

"No offense intended," said Kelso.

"Preston, the only time you *don't offend* is when you keep your yapping mouth shut," said Galla. He sat staring hard at Kelso.

Kelso ignored the muscle-bound gunman's insult and turned to Dolan to change the subject. He nodded toward Sam.

"Jones there had Rudabell's bull bag on him earlier today," he said.

"I know," said Dolan. He sat staring, offering no more on the matter.

Uncomfortable with Dolan's silence, Kelso felt he had to say more.

"Told me he found ol' Curtis dead, and took it off him," he said, hoping for more of a response.

"So I heard," said Dolan. He sat staring again.

Damn it to hell. . . . Kelso fidgeted and looked all around.

"All right, then, we'll be seeing you," he said. He jerked his horse's reins and veered over to the edge of the trail and started around the four. Passing Mickey Galla, he saw him give a smug grin as he observed Kelso's large sombrero.

"If you run across any Apaches, keep your britches up, Preston," he said. "You've got nothing left to lose on top."

"Smart son of a bitch," Kelso grumbled under his breath.

Galla chuckled, watching the three leave. Then he turned to Dolan and said, "How much farther to that water basin?"

"Two miles, maybe less. Why?" said Dolan. He started to turn his horse back up the steepening trail. But he stopped, seeing Galla bounce down from his saddle and walk back to where Sam stood bowed and panting.

"Hear him, Jones?" Galla said. "Two more miles to water." He patted Sam's sweat-drenched shoulder. "Hell, there's no need in you having to walk that far." He bent quickly, picked Sam up by his knee and his throat and raised him high over his head.

Dolan sat watching the feat of strength in awe.

Just as quickly as Galla had grabbed and lifted Sam, he slammed the Ranger down flat on his back in an upswirl of dust. What little breath Sam had left burst from his lungs.

"Jesus, Mick," Dolan said at the sound of Sam hitting the trail and lying limp. He gigged his horse forward to where Galla stood brushing dust from his shirtsleeves.

"All right, vaqueros, pull him these last miles," Galla said to the two Mexicans. "It's too damn hot for a white man to walk."

"Check yourself down, Mick," Dolan cautioned him. "We got to do this thing the way Segert wants it done."

"I know that," said Galla. He looked up at Dolan. "But have you ever had somebody slam a rifle butt into your nose?"

"No, I haven't, but—"

"It hurts like hell—I can tell you that much," Galla said, cutting him off. He adjusted his raised shirttails back into his britches and turned to his waiting horse. "So, there's that," he concluded.

For a mile and a half the Ranger tried to force himself back into consciousness, but he was too battered and exhausted to collect himself and struggle back up to his feet. Realizing that the horses dragging him were now at a walk, he struggled instead to keep his head up off the rocky trail and bore the impact of the ride on his left shoulder, which he kept tucked in a way to protect his chin.

The last few minutes of the ride, he began hearing

the sound of rushing water to his right, but he dared not shift his shoulder and head around to see where the sound came from for fear he would not manage to regain his protective position. Most of the pain he had felt earlier from the dragging had turned to a dark numbness that he was grateful for. Yet there was still enough pain from the dirt and grit in his eyes and his mouth to make up for it.

Outlast it. . . . Outlast it. . . . Outlast it . . . , he repeated over and over to himself. At length a soothing darkness fell over him and he turned loose of the trail and let it disappear from beneath him.

After what felt like no more than a few seconds, a hand was laid heavily on his shoulder and shook him roughly.

"Has the son of a bitch died on us?" Sam heard Dolan ask Mickey Galla.

Sam gave no response. Instead he kept his swollen eyes shut, listening, needing to gather enough strength to make one last attempt to save himself should the opportunity arise.

"Naw, he's alive," Galla replied. "Damn shame too," he said, drawing Sam's Colt from behind his gun belt, where he'd stuck it earlier. "Now I'll have to waste two bullets on him."

"Two?" said Galla.

"Yeah," said Dolan. "One to kill him, another to keep him that way." He cocked Sam's Colt.

"Killing him with his own gun," Galla remarked. "You must be cold as ice."

"I never claimed to be otherwise," said Dolan. But as he spoke, he uncocked Sam's Colt and let it hang in his hand. "First, let's get some water and let him simmer awhile. I hate killing a man, him not even knowing it."

"Yeah, me too," said Galla as the two turned and walked away. "It just ain't the same as seeing their eyes get real big and scared looking."

"I bet this one don't look that way when the time comes," said Dolan.

"Yeah, how much?" said Galla.

"How much what?" said Dolan.

"You said you bet," said Galla. "I say, how much?" He grinned.

"Five dollars," Dolan said. Then he chuckled. "And you said *I'm* cold as ice. . . ."

Sam lay listening to their footsteps move away from him, across the rocky trail. No sooner had he thought them out of sight than he began to test his ropes. First the one around his hands, then the one around his bloody wrists.

Tight . . . too tight . . .

Struggling against his returning pain, he cocked his boot around until he could see his spurs, the big rowel broken off one and only a stub sticking out. With all of his waning strength, he cocked his boot around at what he would otherwise consider to be an impossible angle and began picking at the rope around his waist with the sharp stub.

Even in his half-addled state, his mind flashed on the young Apache warrior who had done much this same thing to escape the scalp hunters. Same circumstances, same desperation. But the thought was gone as quickly as it came to him. Right now, his own survival was all that mattered. When the picking and cutting caused the rope to come apart, he looked through swollen, bleary eyes in the direction of the two gunmen and the two vaqueros—the sound of them through a sparse stand of young pine saplings, their voices mingling among the sounds of the rushing stream.

As soon as he had freed his bruised and cut hands, he untied the lariat knot at his waist, loosened it and wiggled out of it. As quickly as he could, he belly-crawled off the trail toward the sound of the stream just beyond a rocky edge. Reaching the edge, he looked down, seeing the water swirling and thrashing along twenty feet below.

"The son of a bitch is getting away!" he heard Galla's voice cry out behind him. A gunshot erupted from the trail, and a bullet struck a rock four feet from Sam.

"Shoot him!" Dolan's voice shouted. Another gunshot erupted. But now the Ranger had pushed himself over the rocky edge.

Luckily the water was deep enough. But just barely, he noted to himself, holding his breath, sinking, and at the same time feeling the current roll him along, sweeping him downstream. He heard more gunshots resounding in the distance, from that world moving away behind him. Bullets streaked down though the water in looping half circles and fell away to the rocky bottom.

To stop himself from tumbling along forever, he

spread his arms and grabbed at stones his size and larger, his battered hands pulling him ever upward through the cool swirling pool. When he had laddered himself up the rocks, his face came up above the surface so suddenly that it caught him by surprise. He let out his remaining breath, but with his boots filled with water, he dropped back under before he managed to recatch it.

The water had him. He dragged himself with his hands, back up the stones, strangling on water, swallowing it, coughing it out, his oxygen gone, only more water with which to replace it. Yet he felt himself moving upward again, only this time taking forever.

This is drowning. . . . This is drowning. . . .

Then, as suddenly as before, just as the world started growing dark and silent around him, he plunged upward into the world of air, his boots seeming to weigh more than he himself. He bounced along now in the swift water, his heavy boots serving to at least keep him upright, like a human buoy.

But it was water much more shallow now. *Thank God. . . .* He bounced and bobbed along, seeing a sandy, gravelly bank to his right, knowing that above it lay the trail—the same trail that would bring the gunmen down on him any minute. He knew he had to work his way to that gravelly bank and get up out of there.

Even as he told himself what he had to do, he had already begun scrambling against the current and the rocky bottom, pushing himself shoreward with hands and feet, scrambling through chest-high water that pushed with the force of a raging beast. But as he struggled, coughing, strangling, heaving up water, he began to feel that raging beast lessen its hold on him. The water was soon at his waist, then lower, and lower.

Finally he found himself splashing through water at his calves, then at his ankles. Stumbling forward in his heavy boots, staggering unsteadily, he reached the shoreline and dropped to his knees and swayed back and forth for a moment. *Huh-uh, can't stop now,* he warned himself. *Get up, get moving!*

He tried. He pushed himself halfway to his feet. But that was as far as he could go. He had forced himself as hard and as far as he could. He had lost all of his strength, his energy; he had become a spinal creature, operating strictly on the pulsing remnants of nerve signals between mind and body. And now even that left him.

He stopped there in the dirt like a run-down clock, his arms outstretched slightly to the side, and pitched face forward onto the cool wet gravel. A looming blackness moved in around him and swallowed up his senses. He couldn't even struggle against it. He moved along in the blackness much the same as he had moved along in the swirling current, except this was by far more peaceful. In this blackness, he lost all sense of time.

He only realized he'd lost consciousness when the voice of the gunmen standing above him forced him to regain it.

"I don't know how he made it this far," he heard Galla say, standing over him. "But this is as good a place as any, I expect."

Sam looked up at him and Dolan and saw them waver

in place, as if he was looking at them through a watery veil. He heard one of them lever a round into a rifle. Didn't he . . . ? He drifted, certain the sound came from his own Winchester. He drifted some more, for how long he did not know. But in what could have been a second, or an hour, he was stirred by the sound of another voice.

"Joe? Joe, wake up. We must hurry," he heard Lilith say in a hushed and harried tone. "They will be coming for you."

"Lilith . . . ," he whispered. He managed to open his swollen eyes enough to see a foggy image of a woman kneeled over him.

"Can you hear me, Joe? Can you stand up? Here, let me help you to my wagon."

"I—I can walk," Sam said, pushing himself with all his strength, yet still only managing to get onto his knees. He tried again, this time with Lilith looping his arm over her shoulder.

"Quickly, quickly," she said in a lowered tone. "I have seen what these men are capable of doing. They will kill you, and they will kill me for helping you."

"Then . . . why?" he asked, staggering to the rear door of the peddler's wagon only a few feet from the water's edge.

Lilith half shoved him inside the wagon and over onto the bunk bed.

"*Why?* you ask," she said. She quickly placed a pillow under his head and laid a canteen up under his arm. "I help you because you helped me. I saw what they did to you in town, and I followed you here." She looked off in the direction of the gunmen farther upstream. "Now I must leave you and pull this wagon out of here before they arrive."

Sam nodded, but her words were already growing farther and farther away.

Chapter 12

When Sam awakened again, it was in the long shadows of evening. He had felt leaves and vines brush along the wagon's side the last few yards. Then the wagon had jostled to a halt alongside an ancient and grown-over stone ruins that had pressed itself so long against the mountainside that the two had become one—the mountain having taken in man's orphaned hybrid creation and fostered it to its stony bosom. As the peddler's wagon had stopped, a panther stood up atop a vine-clad wall, spun silently and vanished in a wisp of fur and claw.

Sam stood shakily in the darkness of the wagon, braced against the side frame, when the rear door opened and Lilith stepped up inside.

"Where . . . are we?" Sam asked, feeling cracks in his swollen lips reopen when he spoke.

"Somewhere safe where we will not be found," Lilith said quietly, as if not to disturb the quietness of the ruins.

"We left tracks," Sam cautioned her.

Without reply she slung a loaded knapsack to her

shoulder, picked up a small lantern and stepped back to the open door.

"Come," she said, gesturing him down through the open door. "You must lean on me."

"I can walk . . . I think," Sam said, everything looking grainy and offset through his swollen eyes.

Yet, when he stepped down to the ground behind Lilith, pain in his ribs and shoulders caused him to falter and almost fall. She grabbed his arm and steadied him.

"We must take Andre and go deep into the mountainside," she said patiently, drawing him to her side. "Tomorrow or the next day, perhaps you can walk. Tonight you can help us both by doing as I say."

"Yes, ma'am," Sam said quietly, allowing his weight to shift a little onto her as they walked to the front of the wagon. When they stopped beside Andre, the wagon horse looked around at Sam and seemed to perk up. He twitched his ears.

"Look, Joe," Lilith said quietly. "Andre remembers you—he likes you."

"I like you too, Andre," Sam managed to say through his pained lips. He reached out a bruised hand and rubbed it down the horse's soft, warm muzzle. "Obliged for the wagon ride, Andre . . . ," he said.

"Don't thank him just yet, Joe," Lilith said. "You have a longer ride ahead of you." She helped him lean against Andre's side as she unhitched the horse from the wagon.

"Are we far from Agua Fría?" Sam asked.

"Yes, far enough anyway," she said. Then she gestured for him to climb atop the horse's bare back. With her pushing his rump upward, he managed to fall over atop the horse and straighten up some, in spite of the overall pain from being dragged. She hefted the knapsack from her shoulder up behind him and patted it down in place. Sam turned enough to place a hand on the sack to steady it.

She shook her head and smiled a little at his inability to not take part in things.

"Old habits," he offered in a lowered voice, trying not to disturb his cracked lips.

With a length of leather rein she looped around Andre's muzzle, Lilith led the horse forward through a courtyard of waist-high weeds, of wild grass and ironwood brush and ironwood trees grown up through the petrified limbs and carcasses of its generations past.

Across the courtyard, weaving through embankments of spilled stones and downfall branches, Lilith stopped the horse at a black open mouth in the rocky mountainside. She stopped long enough to strike a match and light the lantern in her hand. She adjusted the globe down on the lantern and blew out the match.

Sam watched through the narrow slits of his eyes as a circling glow rose around Lilith and the horse.

"Watch your head, Joe," she said. He did. Bowing forward on Andre's back, he cradled the pain in his ribs against the lesser pain in his forearm and rode forward, the clop of the horse's worn metal shoes resounding both before and behind them.

They moved on.

For half an hour the horse plodded farther and farther from the dim, rough-edged opening behind them until the entrance itself fell away behind a turn in the rocky path. The swaying circle of soft lantern light was all that accompanied them deeper into the stone belly of the mountain. Sam let his swollen eyes close for a few minutes until the horse stopped at the mouth of a cave.

"We are here," the woman said, her voice low yet still carrying the hardpan twang of an echo. Sam opened his eyes enough to see that they were standing beneath a wide, low ceiling supported by thick timbers that time had aged and dried to a consistency of granite.

Sam shoved the pack off into Lilith's arms and slid carefully and painfully down from the horse's back. He let her help him over to a low rock worn slick from where countless humankind had seated themselves for centuries past. He sat dawn and leaned back against a stone wall and looked all around. In the circle of lantern light, he looked at a burned and blackened ring of rocks on the stone floor. He looked at the black-smudged ceiling, where smoke had loomed and seeped upward into the hillside to dissipate as it found its way skyward.

Lilith set the sack on the stone floor, untied a blanket roll from atop it and rolled it out.

"Lie down here," she said. "Rest while I gather wood for the fire. I will heat some water and wash your cuts. I have some cloth for bandages." As she spoke, she took out a thick candle, stood it on the floor and lit the wick.

"Gracias," Sam said. He scooted down painfully onto the blanket, but looked all around. "Wood . . . ?" he said. Candlelight flickered around him.

Lilith nodded.

"It's not so far away as you think," she said. "There are other openings farther back that lead out." She gestured toward the blackness on the other side of the wide stone chamber. "That is what makes this a good place to hide. There is always a way out ahead of anyone who follows you here."

"What can I do, Lilith?" Sam asked.

"You can lie still and rest," Lilith said. "The wagon is hidden and we are safe here. Let me build a fire and take care of you," she said softly.

He lay watching her as she stood and walked to the horse. In a moment she was swallowed up by the darkness. Andre scraped a hoof and chuffed toward her. Then the horse settled and stood as silent as stone, the candlelight flickering shadowy on its flanks and in its dark eyes.

At the bottom of the hill trail, Hazerat and Charlie Ray Hooke reined up on either side of Preston Kelso. The three sat staring out along the meandering trail running out of sight across the desert floor. It had been yesterday afternoon when they met Dolan, Galla and the two Mexicans dragging Sam along the high hill line. After riding on, Kelso had been silent and brooding as they'd ridden throughout the night, stopping only long enough to eat and rest their horses.

"I don't like it," he said out of nowhere.

The Hooke brothers gave each other a blank look.

"What's that, Preston?" Charlie Ray asked cautiously.

"The short-lipped way he was treating us," Kelso

said, staring straight ahead, where a roadrunner sped out of sight behind a rise of dust.

"This would be Daryl Dolan we're talking about?" Hazerat ventured quietly. The two waited and watched as Kelso only sat in his tense silence.

Finally he spoke toward the wavering desert.

"Segert has got him out here poking his nose around, seeing if I was lying about anything."

"You mean . . . ?" Hazerat hesitated, glancing at Charlie Ray as if for permission. "You mean like telling him about the Apaches taking all the bank money?" he said.

"Something like that," Kelso said in little more than a growl. He reached his fingertips up under his oversized sombrero and head bandage and rubbed them around atop his raw head. His hand lowered and reached inside his shirt and grazed his healing arrow wounds.

The Hooke brothers looked at each other again.

"I don't mean to further aggravate an already testy situation, Preston," Charlie Ray said. "But that *was* a lie. Hell, Hazerat and me backed you up in it."

"I know that, you damn fool," Kelso barked harshly. He thought about what Jones had told him, about finding Rudabell scalped and dead alongside the trail. Was there a chance that Rudabell had stuck the saddlebags under a rock? It was something he would have been prone to do, to keep Apaches from getting it—if he'd had time, Kelso thought.

He considered it in silence for a moment longer. The only way to sort things out was to go find Rudabell's body. Then figure out everything from there. Meanwhile, these two believed he had the money buried, so let them keep thinking it for now. He nudged his horse forward onto the desert floor.

"This must mean we're leaving," Hazerat said to Charlie Ray under his breath, with a sarcastic snap, seeing Kelso moving forward.

Charlie Ray shook his head.

"We're too far in to back out now, Hazerat," he said quietly. "We lied to Crazy Ray Segert for him. If there's any money out there, I damn sure want a big taste of it." He nudged his horse forward behind Kelso, Hazerat doing the same right beside him.

"Yeah, damn it," said Hazerat, "in for a penny, in for a pound, I reckon."

They rode on.

Knowing the desert better than the Hooke brothers, Kelso led them three miles out, parallel to the trail. It was in the full bore of the blistering afternoon sun when he knew they had ridden long past the place where he'd hightailed it away from Rudabell. Now he could pick up the trail with the hoofprints he and Rudabell had left no matter how faded he found those prints to be.

Following those prints, Kelso knew, would take them past the place where he'd left Rudabell all alone to face the lawman who'd been dogging them since Nogales. Somewhere between there and where the Apache had skinned him like a rabbit, he thought bitterly, he'd find Rudabell's body, the way Jones said he would. He only hoped that Jones hadn't told Dolan the same thing before they'd killed him.

That damn bull's bag . . . , he cursed to himself. Who would ever have thought something like that could trip him up like this?

"Just where the hell are you taking us, Preston?" Hazerat finally blurted out. He'd been forcing himself to keep quiet all day. "Are you lost?"

Kelso stopped his horse suddenly, swung it around in the sand and stared harshly at Hazerat.

"I'm not lost, you damn fool!" he shouted. "There's the trail within spitting distance." He pointed off in the distance to their left. The three looked out through the wavering heat.

"Easy, Preston," Charlie Ray said, seeing how close Kelso was to going for the new Colt on his hip. "We know it's over there." He tried to humor the irate gunman staring at them both from under the brim of the oversized sombrero. "Don't we, Hazerat?" he said.

"Yes, *hell yes*, we know it's over there," said Hazerat. He pointed toward the distant trail. "What we don't know is why the hell the trail's over there and we're riding all the way out here. My horse is ready to quit on me soon, if I don't get him some solid footing!"

Kelso took a deep, calming breath and withdrew his hand from the butt of the Colt.

"All right," he said. "We've been riding out here off the trail because I figured neither of you wanted to end up like this." He reached up and patted his large sombrero. "Don't you suppose the damn *'paches* ain't still scouring that trail like hawks, just looking for the next ones passing by?"

That stopped Hazerat cold.

"Jesus . . . ," he said, looking toward the trail with a whole different expression.

"Yeah, that's what I thought," said Kelso.

Charlie Ray just stared, wondering how much safer it really was here, three miles to the left of the trail. But he kept the thought to himself.

"Just so happens," said Kelso, "I was turning somewhere along about here anyway—going back along the trail, seeing who's riding along there watching us from afar." He looked back and forth between the two. "If that's all the same with the Hooke brothers," he added sarcastically. "These know-everything sons a' bitches," he growled, jerking his horse toward the trail three miles away.

"Let's go, Haze," Charlie Ray said quietly as Kelso rode away through the sand.

Moments later, on the trail, the three looked all around, but found no fresh sign of Apaches—no recent prints made by unshod horses. They did pick up some older prints with edges that were worn down from the night winds and now appeared to be hoofprints left by some passing ghosts.

"Here we are," Kelso said, stopping, looking down at the jumbled wind-worn prints, nothing to tell even an experienced tracker which tracks might have been his and Rudabell's or which ones might have been those of the lawman following them.

Hazerat and Charlie Ray looked skeptically at each other, then nudged their horses over alongside him.

"What makes you so sure, Preston?" Charlie Ray asked.

Kelso just glared at him and swung his horse off along the trail. The two followed, looking down at the trail and off across the desert on either side. When Kelso stopped again, they circled and stopped too as he slipped down from his saddle and picked up a spent rifle shell. He pitched the shell up to Charlie Ray without saying a word, then stepped back up and rode forward.

A mile farther along, Kelso stopped again, this time pointing off to the right where all but a single set of prints veered off along a thinner, narrower path leading upward across a ride of sand. He pointed at the single set of prints and ran his finger along the trail following them.

"There I go," he said. Then he pointed off along the thin path up the sand ride. "And there goes Rudabell and the lawman."

"So," said Hazerat, looking along the set of tracks on the main trail, "we go this way, we'll find the money you hid, eh?"

"In a minute," said Kelso.

"*In a minute . . . ?*" said Charlie Ray. "What about the money? What about the damn 'paches watching this trail *like hawks*?"

"I said *in a minute*," Kelso repeated in a strong tone.

"First I want to know about my pard, Rudabell." He nudged his horse forward in the wavering heat. "You don't side with a man as long as me and Curtis rode together and not want to know what became of him."

They rode on.

When they'd followed the thin path over a mile, they stopped again where a flurry of faded hoofprints lay in the sand. From this point only one set of prints led off across the sand. The second set led to a dead horse resting in the sand, a saddle leaning sideways against it.

Kelso glanced at the animal, now merely bones and decomposing flesh. His eyes then wandered off the path where a strewn pile of rock lay as if thrown down from the distant hills by the hand of God.

The rocks where Jones said he'd dragged the body . . . ? he asked himself.

"What the hell . . . ?" said Charlie Ray, nodding toward Kelso. He nudged his horse along behind him as he spoke. Hazerat followed.

They stopped on either side of Kelso's horse as Kelso stepped down and walked forward to where strewn scraps of clothes lay all around the skeletal remains of Curtis Rudabell.

"Well, adios, ol' trail pal," said Kelso toward the bones, feigning a look of sadness as the Hookes walked up and stood on either side of him. "I'd take off this hat were it not for my condition," he said, giving the Hookes each a piercing look.

The brothers took off their hats grudgingly and held them to their chests.

Kelso stepped around the skeleton and began turning over any rock that one man might be capable of overturning.

"What are you doing?" Charlie Ray called out.

"What do you *think* I'm doing?" Kelso replied. "I'm gathering some stones to roll over him—keep the creatures from scattering his bones." He glared at them. "Don't think it will offend me if you give me a hand here."

"Preston, I'm just going to throw this out. You're acting plumb unnatural over a no-good bastard like Rudabell. Are you sure you and him was all that close? I heard once that you tried to kill him in his sleep."

"What are you saying, Charlie Ray?" Kelso asked, his gun hand going once again the butt of his new Colt.

Charlie Ray and Hazerat had both already managed to slip their guns from their holsters; they held them ready at their sides.

"I'm saying you're acting like a man who's feeling his way along, trying to figure things out as you go."

"Yeah," said Hazerat. "So stop Sally-gagging around. Where's the money?"

"All right," Kelso said. "I've gone as far as I can go. It's time we had an honest talk about this."

"I'll say it is," said Charlie Ray. Both his and Hazerat's guns cocked and leveled at the same time, before Kelso got a chance to draw. "Now lift that Colt with two fingers like it's red hot and drop it to the ground."

"It's a brand-new gun!" Kelso protested, glancing down at the rocky sandy ground.

"Drop it, or drop *with it*," Hazerat said firmly.

"Damn it to hell, all right," said Kelso. He raised the Colt with his finger and thumb and let it fall. "I hope neither one of you thinks I was out to deceive yas?"

The Hooke brothers didn't answer, slowly lowering the hammers on their guns.

Chapter 13

For two days and nights the Ranger rested, recuperating from the countless bruises, cuts, abrasions and pain that being run to exhaustion and dragged through the rocky hill country had brought upon him. On the third day, seeing that he was fully conscious and more able to get around on his own, Lilith placed a tin cup of coffee in front of him and seated herself on the blanket beside him.

"I must leave here and return to Agua Fría for a day," she'd told him.

Sam just looked at her.

"I will be missed by business owners who are expecting me," she explained. "Soon someone will come looking. It is always better to not be noticed."

Sam nodded and sipped his coffee.

"Also, it is how I support myself," she said. "Aside from peddling home goods, I sharpen anything that requires an edge. 'Axes, knifes, scissors or saws, Lilith Tettovia sharpens them all.'" She smiled as she quoted her business slogan. "It is the trade I learned from my father, and he from his father before him."

"I understand," Sam said. "It's what you were doing when I saw you outside the mercantile."

"Yes," she said, an air of resolve in her voice. "And it is what I will be doing until the day I die." As she spoke, she reached her fingertips to his bruised forehead and pushed aside a strand of his hair. "I have come to accept that we are all what we are. I was short with you when we left each other on the trail. For that, I apologize. I know you are one of those men, yet I feel there is something different about you." She paused, then added, "I hope I am right."

Sam studied her face in the glow of the small fire. A sadness had shown itself in her dark eyes, then vanished as quickly as it had appeared. Was there something else there, he asked himself, something between them?

Yes. He believed there was. He only returned her gaze in silence. There was nothing more he could tell her, about himself, about why he was here, about how far he actually was from being the kind of man she'd labeled him to be.

After a moment, she stepped away from him, back to the horse.

"Anyway," she said, "you will be all right here. I should be back in two days." She took a small four-shot pepperbox vest gun from under her shawl and handed it to him. "There is a panther who thinks this ruins belongs to her. If she gets unruly with you, just scare her away with this if you can."

"I generally get along with critters," Sam said, turning the small gun in his hand. "If you see a chance, please check on my dun at the livery." He hefted the little pepperbox. "And if you happen upon a *real* gun somewhere . . . ?"

"Of course, if I can," she said. She stood up and walked to where Andre stood chewing on a mouthful of dry wild grass she'd carried and piled in front of him.

"What about Segert and his men?" he asked as he'd watched her feed and ready the horse. "Won't they be asking you questions?"

"No," she said. "Even if they saw my wagon tracks, the tracks did not reveal who they belong to." She looked over at him and smiled. "Like all who live here in these Twisted Hills, I have learned how to avoid Segert and Madson and their men. It is how life is here. Anyway, I sharpen the knives for Segert's hacienda. I am a person who is seen, yet not seen."

Sam watched her pick up a rope hackamore she'd fashioned and slip it over Andre's head.

"Then you know Segert?" he asked.

"Yes," she said, "but only as one for whom I provide a service. I know his cook. But I have never spoken to Segert himself."

"Be careful," he said.

"Yes, I will, Joe," she said. She stepped away from Andre and over to where Sam sat. She picked up a thick candle from the floor and lit it from a flame in the small fire. "When I return, I will continue to take *good care* of you . . . if you will allow me to, Joe." She gazed down at him in the flicker of firelight.

There it was again. Something he'd seen in her dark eyes, some slightest suggestion in her words. . . .

"Obliged," he'd said, not about to say more right then, lest he find himself mistaken.

He watched as she led the horse away, and continued watching as the glow of candlelight moved away, out of sight along a stone corridor, and disappeared ahead of a soft echoing click of hooves.

The following day, some of his soreness gone and his body felt more rested and recuperated from his ordeal. Sam pulled on his shirt and boots and ventured along deeper into the mountainside. The woman had told him there were other paths to the outside world should they need them. He decided it would be a good idea to learn where they were ahead of time. He checked the small pepperbox pistol and stuck it down behind his belt. Using a long walking stick he found leaning against the chiseled stone wall, he set out walking stiffly, the glowing lantern swaying in hand.

He traveled down the stone corridor, seeing now and again the flickering light passing across ancient drawings on either side and looming on the soot-smudged ceiling overhead. Like a scholar walking the hall of some ancient museum exhibit, he witnessed layer over layer of time recorded and passed forward one generation to the next. When the exhibit fell away and the drawings spaced out less and less and finally ran out altogether, he stopped at another wide-floored cavern and looked at three black holes—pathways exiting on the other side of the mountain.

As he walked toward the three exits, he felt a rumble deep down in the earth's belly. And he felt his feet shift back and forth like a drunkard's on the stone floor. Yet, before he could even brace himself against it, the world beneath him seemed to drop an inch and the rumble stopped as suddenly as it had begun.

He stood still for a moment with his hand and walking stick pressed against the wall. He moved his hand when he felt a slight stream of dust sprinkle down from the ceiling. But when he looked up, he saw no place for the dust to have come from, no small crevice, no tiny crack in the stone artwork. Only crudely drawn moon-like faces with mouths and eyes agape stared down at him. Obscured in torch smudge from centuries past, stick figures danced around licking flames, wielding spear shafts above ornate and feathered heads.

Time to go, Sam told himself.

From the three corridors facing him, he chose to follow the one that had a footpath that appeared the most worn down in the center. Reasoning this exit to be the closest and for that purpose the most used, he walked into it with the lantern held before him. When he'd walked no more than a hundred feet and rounded a turn, he felt a difference in the freshness of the air around him. In the distant blackness he saw a jagged slash of light as slim as a needle. Yet, upon following the slash of light, he watched it grow into a doorway wide enough for man and horse.

Moments later he stood in a shaft of afternoon sunlight and looked across more ruins. He saw more piles of fallen weathered stone, and tangles of vines, some as old and thick as trees. A remaining tracing of stone outlined what he decided could have been a public marketplace complete with a tiled floor somewhere down there beneath the encroached moss, earth and fauna.

Across Sam's perceived and long-abandoned marketplace stood a wall ten feet high. The wall, interlocked in itself as if by wizardry, tipped forward at a deep angle from the pressing back of cast-off mountain stones that had tumbled down and gathered there behind it. Vines and thorns like a shredded flowered curtain draped from the wall's edge to the ground. In the moss and shadow behind the curtain lay a pool of water, a thin stream still trickling into it.

As he stood looking up, Sam saw the panther stand up atop the wall in a rustle of dried brush weed and stare down at him from thirty feet away. The panther Lilith had warned him about?

Probably, he told himself.

But it didn't matter. The cat was there, staring him down, growling, poised low in its front shoulders.

Easy. now.

Sam took a slow step backward, raising the small gun from behind his belt. He cocked it. He knew the pepper-box was useless at this distance. More than likely, it would be useless even if he were closer. But it might scare the animal away, distract it long enough for him to duck into the cavern and get out of sight. But even as he thought it, he saw the cat spring down from the wall in a flash of fur and the whip of its tail land facing him—less than twenty yards away now, he reminded himself.

He prepared to back up another step, out of the shaft

of sunlight back into the mountain, his finger on the trigger, ready to pull it, for all the good it would do him. But as he started his slow, cautious step, the cat only stepped forward with him.

"Now what?" Sam whispered to himself. He didn't want to shoot the animal and send it off wounded. Especially now, he thought, suddenly noting two rows of dark sagging milk teats lining the cat's underbelly.

Seeing the cat drop lower, he tensed his fist around the pepperbox, ready to fire.

Please don't . . . , he thought, staring into the cat's determined eyes.

He backed one more step, yet still the cat came forward, dipping farther, ready to launch itself into him.

"Here goes," he whispered aloud. He saw the cat ready to pounce. It was coming, gun or no gun. He tightened his fist around the gun, squeezing the trigger.

But before he got the shot off, he felt another rumble rise in the ground beneath his feet. The cat felt it too, he could tell.

The animal swung its head back and forth, not knowing what to make of the world trembling beneath it. The big mother cat looked back at Sam, but he could see any idea of lunging at him was gone, overshadowed by a much greater threat, that of the world coming apart around her.

She bared her fangs in a silent hiss. She spun in a flash and shot back across the ground and leaped atop the wall, all in what appeared to be one single seamless move. Sam swayed with the rumbling earth and steadied himself. In seconds the earth settled and he found himself standing alone, a small gun pointed aimlessly across the ruins. Weeds, brush and vines trembled in place and settled as if swept by some strange passing breeze.

Sam lowered the pepperbox but continued to stand for a moment, listening closely to the earth beneath his feet. He looked around at the stone pathway leading into the belly of the mountain, questioning the safety of going back inside.

As he wondered, he heard the tumbling, thrashing, tree-splitting sound of a mammoth boulder that had broken loose from its seating higher up atop a sloping bed of scree and rolled, bounced, lunged and finally plowed its way through a talus ledge and launched out off the mountainside. The earth rumbled again when the boulder landed farther down.

All right, he thought, nodding to himself, taking some sort of solace in the fragility of life. Yet instead of walking back inside, he walked out and across the open space and found a long, narrow, weathered stone ledge standing knee high to him. He sat down to rest on the narrow ledge, noting how his backside extended out inches beyond it. Curious, he turned and looked down into a deep overgrown trench running in a straight line behind the ledge.

"What the . . . ?"

He stood up and dusted his seat, realizing he had perched himself on some ancient public privy. Standing, he looked all around as if to make certain no one had been watching him.

"Enough for one day," he whispered. Satisfied that

he had not been seen by anyone in the present, he shook his head, smiled wryly to himself, embarrassed somehow, and limped across the ruins and back inside the mountain, as if leaving thousands of ghosts there in the marketplace to scratch their heads in wonder.

Chapter 14

On the morning of the third day, the woman returned, finding Sam seated on a stone slab out in front of the entrance to the deep cavern. The walking stick leaned against a low broken stone wall; a pot of coffee boiled on a bed of coals and low flames in front of him. He sat with a tin cup of coffee in hand, a blanket around his shoulders, another blanket piled on the wide stone slab beside him. The knapsack lay off to the side.

Leading Andre into the ruins from the place where she'd left the wagon hidden, she looked around, seeing the blankets, the knapsack, the campfire.

"You have moved out," she said. "Was it the darkness or the loneliness?"

"Neither," Sam said. "It was an earthquake."

"Yes, I know," she said. "I felt it in Agua Fría. There were windows broken. Some livery horses spooked and broke through the corral rails."

"No one hurt, I hope," he said.

"No one injured," she said. "There was only the surprise of it." She stopped Andre a few feet from the fire and looped his lead rope around a spur of rock.

"I met the she-panther you told me about," Sam said.

"Ah, and what did you think of her?" Lilith asked.

"She's pushy," Sam said. "I wouldn't be surprised if she has cubs nearby."

"She is pushy . . . and she *always* has cubs nearby," Lilith said. She smiled at Sam and said, "Speaking of surprises, I have one for you."

"Oh?" said Sam.

"Wait here. I'll only be a moment," she said.

Sam watched as she walked away in the direction from which she'd come. In a moment she reappeared out of the surrounding vines and foliage leading his dun by its reins.

Sam set the cup down and stood up.

"How in the world . . . ?" he said, at a loss for words.

"It was easy," she said. "I told the hostler you sent me for your horse. I paid him, had this fellow saddled up and I led him away."

"No one tried to stop you?" Sam said.

"No one even saw me," she replied, "and believe me, I checked all the time on my way here, to make sure I wasn't followed."

Sam took the dun's reins and rubbed its muzzle. The dun chuffed and sawed its head a little as if glad to see him.

"But wait," said Lilith. "I have more."

Sam watched her step back, open a saddlebag flap and pull out his Colt and the two guns he'd taken from the scalp hunters, Ollie McCool and Bo Roden.

"Well, well," Sam said, taking his Colt in one hand, the two extra guns in his other, "I wasn't even going to ask if you managed to get a rifle. These three sidearms are going to do just fine."

"Oh, but I did get a rifle. A French rifle. It's in the wagon," she said, smiling proudly. "And a bandoleer of cartridges for it. I also found a second horse for the wagon. Andre is delighted."

Sam looked impressed.

"You've had a really good trip," he said.

He checked the guns over good and found his Colt loaded. He shoved it down into the waist of his pants.

"Yes, I have," she said, watching him intently. "Now that you have guns, and your horse, what will you do when you leave here?" she asked almost warily.

"I'm not going to lie, Lilith," Sam said. "I'm going after the men who did this to me."

That much was true, he reminded himself. He'd tried working his way into the gang and he'd failed. His next move would be to fight his way through the gunmen, get to Segert and Madson and take them both down. He realized a large part of it was now personal—vengeance for what had been done to him. But it was still his job. Now that he was getting over his last round with the gunmen, the next round was waiting to be fought.

She looked concerned for him.

"But, Joe, this time they will kill you," she said. "You are lucky to be alive right now, after what they did to you."

"I know," Sam said. "But I can't let it go, Lilith," he said, realizing he couldn't tell her why.

"But it seems so senseless—" she said, not getting her words all the way out before he cut her off.

"It's something I don't want to talk about," he said. "I'm going and that's all there is to it."

She stepped in and stood closer to him, only inches away. "Have you thought about me while I was gone?" she asked with a cool level gaze.

Sam caught the look and the meaning right away.

"Yes, I have," he said. He hesitated for a moment, then said quietly, "I have to be honest with you, Lilith. . . ." He stopped, finding himself stuck for words. He was not going to be honest with her and he knew it. For just a second he felt tempted to reveal his true identity. But then he caught himself. No, he couldn't do that. Deceit was a part of the job he was on. He knew that coming in. There was no changing it now.

"What is it, Joe?" she asked, seeing the look of regret on his face. "You can tell me."

Huh-uh, don't do it, he told himself.

"You were right about me. I am a gunman. I'm not better than the rest. You don't want to pin any hopes on me."

"Yet you're honest enough to tell me," she said, defending him from his own accusations.

"Stop it, Lilith," he said softly. "You deserve better. Don't mislead yourself."

She seemed to consider it for a moment and take a breath.

"All right, Joe," she said. "If we stop here, we are only two people who have helped each other, and now it is time we go our own way."

"Yes," Sam said, gently, yet firmly. "I think that's best." He watched her walk to the stone slab, sit atop it and look into the low fire.

"You are much better now, I see," she said, without looking at him. "Tonight I am tired from the trail. But in the morning I will leave."

"You don't have to leave," Sam said.

"No," she said. "I have a long, hot ride ahead of me to San Carlo. It is best—"

"San Carlo?" Sam said, cutting her off. "That's straight up the middle of the Blood Mountain Range—right through the Apache stronghold. You can't go there alone."

"Yes, I can," she said. "I can, and I must." Her eyes turned up from the fire to his as he walked over and sat down beside her.

"What's so important about you going to San Carlo?" he asked.

She looked back into the fire for a silent moment.

"Every year my father and I go there to pay tribute my father owes to a great Mexican don who holds title to the land we live on, who even owns the wagon I drive." Sam saw her eyes well up; he saw a tear spill down her cheek. "My father is gone, but his debts are not forgiven. It is my duty to go."

"But you can't go alone, Lilith," Sam insisted.

She turned her gaze to his.

"How else can I go, Joe?" she said. "I am now a woman on her own. I must do what it takes to live here."

"But it's too dangerous. They'll kill you. It makes no sense to do something that's going to get you killed."

"Oh . . . ?" She gave him a knowing look.

"It's different," Sam said, realizing her point. "I have to go after these men."

"And I have to pay the tribute owed to Don Marco

for the land on which I live, and the wagon which I use to make my living." She paused, then said, "Whose journey makes more *sense*? Which is more important?"

Sam considered it for a moment. He knew where Madson and Segert were. He knew they would be there. It would be a week's ride to San Carlo, another week back. Settling with these gunmen would have to wait. The woman had risked her life taking him in.

"I want to ride to San Carlo with you," he said.

"It is a long ride," she said. "Are you sure you are up to it? You can stay here and rest and mend awhile longer."

Sam gave a wry smile.

"I'm one of those people who heal better when I keep moving," he said.

"What about going after the men who did this to you?" she asked him quietly.

"Forget them," Sam said. "I've had a change of heart. This is more important to me."

She reached over and took his hand.

"See?" she said. "You tell me you are a bad man, yet I see so much good in you."

Sam held her hand in return.

"Don't go seeing too much good in me, Lilith," he cautioned her quietly. "One thing I've learned about life is there's a surprise around every turn."

"Yes, I know," she replied quietly. "Living here in the Twisted Hills, I have learned that very thing myself."

It had been two days since Kelso and the Hooke brothers had their *honest* discussion about the stolen bank money they were searching for. Kelso had finally told them the truth about the money, how he'd gone off and left it with Curtis Rudabell—*for safekeeping*, he'd explained. Since their honest talk, they had scoured the desert floor along the bottom of the Twisted Hill line, turning over every rock that lay near the trail where Kelso and Rudabell had split up when the lawman had gotten too close on their trail.

"Split up, *ha!*" said Hazerat, recounting what Kelso had told them. He and Charlie Ray sat slumped in their saddles, watching Preston Kelso from horseback in the blazing afternoon sun. Kelso had walked ten yards down a rise of loose sand and turned over a large stone. "First gunshot, I bet Preston lit out like a streak. Left ol' Curtis out here to die alone."

"Yeah, I can see it that way myself," Charlie Ray said, without taking his eyes off Kelso. "We best be careful he doesn't leave us the same way."

"He tries, he'd better know we'll kill him," said Hazerat. He turned his head to the side and tried to spit in contempt. But in that arid furnace, all his spitting amounted to was a gesture and a dry puff of air. Dust stirred from his mustache. He didn't even bother swiping a hand across his dry lips. "I'm on a tempted urge to kill him anyway," he added.

The two quieted down when Kelso walked back to his horse standing beside Charlie Ray and stepped up into his saddle.

"Next ones you get, Charlie Ray," Kelso said, lifting his canteen by its strap and uncapping it.

Charlie Ray looked off along the trail in front of them, leading upward onto a rocky hillside.

"Brother Hazerat and I got the last six or seven, Preston," he said sidelong to Kelso. "It seems to me you've got some catching up to do."

Kelso took a short sip of warm water, lowered the canteen and capped it.

"Don't make me remind you, Charlie Ray, you and your brother wouldn't even be out here if it weren't for me," he said.

Charlie gave a dry chuff.

"That's my point exactly, Preston," he said.

The three turned their horses back along the trail and nudged them along at a walk without another word on the matter.

They rode forward for the next hour, sharing the burden of overturning stones along their way until they'd ridden up off the sandy desert floor onto a rocky sloping hillside. When they stopped again and the three stepped down from their saddles, Kelso looked all around at the countless stones lying strewn all over the rocky terrain. Hazerat and Charlie Ray stood slumped, looking all around.

"Jesus . . . ," Hazerat murmured under his breath, seeing the endless enormity of the task lying before them.

"The quicker we get started, the quicker we'll get done," Kelso said. He took a deep breath and a step forward.

Hazerat and Charlie Ray looked at each other.

"For God sakes, Preston!" said Charlie Ray. "We can't overturn every rock in the Mexican desert!"

"What's worth doing is worth doing right," Kelso

said in a dry, hoarse voice, as if reciting the words mindlessly from some imaginary text.

"Uh-oh, the heat's making him loco," Hazerat said to Charlie Ray, looking Kelso up and down. "We need to get out of here into some shade. My horse is starting to falter at a walk."

"We're not going anywhere except to turn the next stone," Kelso said with the ring of rusty iron in his dry voice. "This damn money has gotten me arrow struck and cost me my hair. I'm not leaving this hellhole without it." He started to throw his hand to his new Colt, but seeing Charlie Ray crane his neck and look out around him, Kelso followed suit.

A drift of trail dust had risen beyond a sand rise.

"We've got company," said Hazerat, a worried look already coming to his face. "I knew if we stayed out here too long, we'd get ourselves seen."

The three gigged their tired horses forward and rode at a stiff run the last two hundred yards up the rock-strewn hillside. When they stopped behind a large land-stuck boulder, they jumped down from their saddles and took position, rifles in hand.

"Don't let the heathens get too close before we blast them out of their saddles," Kelso warned in a whisper, even though the riders were still a good way off. "They're dead shots with them arrows, up close."

With a battered telescope raised to his eye, Charlie Ray watched intently for a few moments until three horses topped up into sight as if rising out of the earth. Charlie Ray let out a sigh of relief.

"Fellows, we're in luck," he said. "It's not 'paches—it's the scalp hunters, Fain and the Mexican, Montoya."

"Who's the third?" Kelso asked, squinting out suspiciously at the riders with his naked eyes.

"The third is a packhorse, Preston," said Charlie Ray. "If we play our cards right, we can eat something besides hardtack tonight."

"What are those fools doing out here?" Kelso asked aloud, staring out, still wary.

An hour passed before Fain, Montoya and their supply horse drew up along the trail below. They looked down at the tracks of the three horses and all around at boot prints leading to and from stones that had clearly been overturned. Then they turned their horses and followed the hoofprints winding up the hillside among broken rock and large boulders.

As they neared a mammoth land-stuck boulder towering above smaller boulders surrounding it, Preston Kelso yelled out to them.

"Stop right there, misters," he said, lying atop the boulder, the heat of its hard hot surface burning his belly even through his clothes.

The scalp hunters stopped and looked up, their hands chest high away from their weapons. Fain's large gun barrel welt had healed, but Montoya sat stiffly from the bullet wounds in his side and his shoulder.

"Preston Kelso, is that you?" Fain called out toward the boulder, recognizing Kelso's rough, raspy voice.

"Yeah. What of it?" Kelso returned in an unfriendly tone.

"Well, it's us," said Fain, "me and Montoya." He didn't know what to make of Kelso's less than warm reception.

"I'm not blind," Kelso replied. "What the hell are you doing out here?"

"Looking for you three," said Fain. "Segert sent us to round you up."

Kelso murmured to himself, "That's what I was afraid of." He started to take aim on Fain's chest.

"We've got a big job coming up," Fain called out, not realizing he was a split second away from a bullet through his heart. "Dolan says Segert needs all the men he can gather."

Kelso's finger eased off the rifle trigger.

"You two are riding for Segert now?" he called out.

"Yep," said Fain. "He redeemed our guns from Graft and fed us dinner before we left."

"And he's not mad at me for nothing?" Kelso asked, listening closely to how Fain answered him.

"Mad? No . . . ," said Fain, in an even tone. "Dolan told him he saw you riding this way the other day. Said, get you back to Agua Fría and all of us get ready to make some money."

"I can use that," Kelso said, grinning. He stood up and slid down the backside of the boulder to where the Hooke brothers met him, their rifles at port arms. "Come on, fellows, Lady Luck is not only knocking—she's about to beat our doors down."

"What about this money out here?" Hazerat asked.

"It'll have to keep," said Kelso. He looked at each brother closely and said, "And it has to be our little secret."

The two nodded in agreement.

"Meanwhile," said Kelso, "let's get cracking and see what Segert has in store."

They grabbed the reins to their horses and led them down from the boulder to where the scalp hunters sat atop their horses waiting for them. As they arrived, Fain gestured toward overturned stones lying here and there on either side of the trail.

"You fellows looking for something out here?" he asked.

"No," Kelso said gruffly. "And if we was, whose business would that be but ours?"

"I understand," said Fain. Changing the subject, he jerked his head toward the packhorse. "If you're hungry, we've got beans, dried elk, hoecake and coffee."

"Damn right, we're hungry," said Kelso. He stepped over to the packhorse as if to start eating right then and there. The horse shied back from him.

Montoya had sat quietly beside Fain, but now he pushed up his sombrero and said, "Ask him about Jones."

"No, forget it for now," said Fain.

"What's that?" said Kelso, overhearing them. "What about Jones?"

"He is out here," said Montoya. "We saw him with the peddler's wagon earlier today. He and the woman are traveling together."

"You saw them, where?" Kelso snapped his head around and looked back and forth as if the wagon might be sitting nearby.

"West of here, earlier today," said Montoya. "Headed up through Apache land."

Kelso looked off in that direction and scratched his beard, realizing how easily Jones might give up what rock the money was buried under if he saw a gun pressed to the woman's head. But before he could say anything, Fain cut in, saying, "We was wanting to go kill Jones for what he done to us and Petty. We didn't know how you fellows might feel about it."

Kelso and the Hooke brothers looked at one another. Kelso took on a wry smile.

"Anything I can do to help a trail pard, I'm always in for it," he said to the scalp hunters. "After what Jones did to yas, I say we help run him down and kill him on our way to town."

"It'll be morning before we catch up to them," Fain said.

"Morning or night doesn't matter to us," said Kelso. He took the packhorse's reins from Montoya. "We can head that way now, and eat later, far as we're concerned." He looked at the Hookes. "Ain't that right, Hazerat, Charlie Ray?"

"It's the gospel," said Charlie Ray. He and Hazerat both nodded.

Chapter 15

It was near midnight when the scalp hunters led Kelso and the Hookes up into the hills and found the tracks where the peddler's wagon had rolled along earlier that day. Once upon the wagon tracks, the men stopped long enough to water, grain and rest their horses while they themselves ate and drank hot coffee. They rested for a few minutes around the small campfire burning in the cover of a huge boulder standing on a rocky hillside. When they stood up to gather their horses and ride on throughout the night, Kelso stepped over ahead of Montoya and untied the lead rope to the packhorse.

"We can't have you leading this horse with your shoulder still mending," he said. "I'll take it for a while, and then we'll have these two pull their turn."

"Obliged," Montoya said, looking a little surprised at Kelso's generosity.

Vincent Fain crushed out the fire with his boot. They finished gathering and saddling their rested mounts and stepped up into their saddles.

"Lead us on, Fain," Kelso said. "You're the one found them."

Holding the packhorse's lead rope, the animal drawn close to his side, Kelso and the Hooke brothers let their mounts fall in behind the two scalp hunters as all of them put their animals forward in the chilled desert air. The five of them rode single file throughout the night, speaking little as they wound downward turn after turn along the steep hill trail. Overhead, a three-quarter moon stood amid a purple-blue velvet sky, lighting the trail with the help of a million glittering stars.

They rode steadily in the tracks of the peddler's wagon, as quickly as the darkened trail would allow. At the first streak of dawn on the eastern edge of the universe, they had reined to a halt atop a bulging stone cliff on the downslope a hundred yards above the desert floor. Their horses' nostrils puffed steamily in the chilled and grainy morning air. As Kelso raised his canteen to his lips for a drink of cool water before the day's heat got to it, Fain sidled up to him on the stone ledge.

"I've never heard of you being so obliging, Preston," he said, having given the matter much consideration throughout the night.

Kelso just looked at him as he lowered his canteen from his lips, capped it and hung its strap around his saddle horn.

"No offense intended," said Fain, "but is there bad blood between you and Jones? Because there's bad blood between us and Jones."

"Yep," Kelso said flatly. He turned his head from Fain and gazed out across the sandy desert below them.

"Might I ask just what it is?" Fain ventured.

"No, you might not," Kelso said in a short tone. He leaned enough to look past Fain at Hazerat and said, "Haze, come take this packhorse for a spell."

Hazerat huffed and jerked his horse back a step before turning it on the cliff facing. He spoke under his breath to his brother.

"Why the hell am I the one to—?"

"Don't start," Charlie Ray warned him in a guarded tone, cutting his complaining short.

Hazerat stepped his horse over to Kelso and took the packhorse's rope from his hand.

Before releasing the rope, Kelso looked him up and down in the purple light of dawn.

"Everything all right with you?" he asked.

Hazerat snatched the rope from him.

"Couldn't be better," he said sharply.

"Is he always that way?" Fain asked as Hazerat reined his horse and the packhorse away.

"What way?" said Kelso, and before Fain could say another word, Kelso yanked his horse's reins, spun the animal in a puff of steam from its warm muzzle and rode off the cliff ledge. The Hookes followed, Hazerat leading the packhorse.

"I never knew Segert's gunmen acted so odd," Fain said under his breath to the Mexican.

"I saw something change for them as soon as we found the wagon tracks," Montoya said. "I don't like how he offered to take the packhorse."

"I know," Fain whispered. "We best watch these sons a' bitches close, Montoya."

"I watch all sons a' bitches *close*," the tall Mexican

replied. They reined their horses around and put them forward onto the trail. Kelso and the Hookes lagged behind until the two scalp hunters were back in the lead.

Sam sat in the driver's seat of the peddler's wagon, Lilith sitting beside him, holding a ragged parasol above their heads. Sam's dun walked along behind the slow-moving wagon at an easy pace, his reins hitched to a rail near the rear door. At midmorning the heat of the day had gathered and pressed down on the desert floor with no breeze, and no letup. Beneath the blazing sun, heat wavered its way back upward to a blue and perfect sky. Lilith had been talking to him when he shoved the parasol aside and rose in his seat enough to look back over the top of the wagon.

"What is it, Joe?" she asked, seeing the look on his face when he sat back down and slapped the reins to the two horses' backs.

"We've got riders coming," Sam said. He slapped the reins to the horses' backs again, forcing them to quicken their pace.

Lilith leaned sidelong in her seat and looked back along the trail, seeing only dust. She lowered the parasol, folded it and stuck it back under the seat.

"It's probably nothing, Lilith," Sam said. But he slapped the reins again. "But it's best we get off this open floor, just in case."

Lilith watched him reach under the seat and pull out the Gruen rifle she'd brought him. He stuck it up on the floor and leaned it against himself.

"What can I do, Joe?" Lilith asked.

"You can take over the reins and keep these horses moving," Sam said. "I don't know if their intentions are good or bad, but they are trying to catch up to us. I want some cover around us before I stop for them."

Lilith took the reins and scooted over to Sam's side as he looked over his shoulder again. He could see the riders had already gained on them. As he questioned their intentions in his mind, a bullet zipped past his head.

A second following the bullet, the sound of the shot rolled forward, out across the hill line.

"Not good," he said to Lilith. "Keep them moving. We need some cover."

"What kind of men attack a peddler's wagon?" she asked.

"These kind," Sam said, having recognized the two scalp hunters riding out in front of the others. "The two out front are Vincent Fain and Carlos Montoya. I shot a friend of theirs and put them in the infirmary for a few days. The other three are Segert's men."

"Segert's men?" She sounded surprised. "They are after you for shooting a scalp hunter?" she asked.

"That would be my guess," Sam said. He leveled the untried Gruen rifle back along the top of the wagon and took aim. As he did so, two more bullets zipped through the air, near him. A third nailed the back of the wagon. He thought about the dun back there, in the line of fire. He fired a shot; the bullet went wide of the target. He allowed for the gun sights being off and fired again. His shot missed, but he could see by how the riders separated that the bullet had been close.

"Can you run this rig right up the slope and get us off these sand flats?" he asked, shouting above the roar of the horses' hooves, the jingle of gear and tack.

"Yes," Lilith shouted in reply. "I can hold them. What are you going to do?"

"I've got to get the dun out of there before he gets his head shot off," Sam said. "Can these horses pull any faster?"

"No," Lilith shouted. "This is all they can do. The wagon is too heavy to go very fast." She adjusted the reins in her hands and slapped them to the horses' back. But there was nothing to be gained by her actions. The horses' heads were down, their legs plowing at the rocky dirt trail.

Wild shots continued to zip through the air as Sam climbed atop the wooden wagon and moved at a low crouch on the swaying, rocking rig until he reached the rear corner where below him the dun ran along in a gathering cloud of trail dust.

A shot thumped into the rear of the wagon. Sam climbed down over the edge, Gruen rifle in hand, onto the top iron rung that laddered down the side. More shots zipped, spun and thumped into the rig. But Sam would not stop. He climbed down until he could reach the dun's reins and untie them from the rig. Before untying the dun, he reached the rifle out and shoved it down into the saddle boot. The dun seemed to know what was coming next.

With a free hand Sam loosened the reins, swung a leg out over his saddle and dropped into place. He immediately veered the horse away from the rig and touched up its pace as he turned it in a wide circle out of the roiling trail dust. He jerked the Gruen rifle back up from the boot and back into play. As the wagon rolled on along the trail, he slowed the dun, raised the Gruen to his shoulder and took aim on the front rider, recognizing him to be the tall Mexican he'd shot in the Fair Deal Cantina.

His first shot didn't make contact, but as the big .50-caliber bullet spun through the midst of the riders, it caused them to scatter out. He levered another round into the seven-shot Gruen's chamber. Luckily, Lilith had brought a pouch full of cartridges along with the big French rifle.

As the five riders drew closer, Sam took another aim on the Mexican front rider. This time when he squeezed the trigger, he saw the rider pounding along a few feet behind the Mexican sway in his saddle and begin to flop back and forth as his horse cut away from the others.

"I'll take it," Sam said, realizing he'd fired at the tall Mexican but had hit the nearest man instead. He levered another round into the Gruen's chamber. Built almost identical to the 1860 Spencer rifle, the Gruen was a good hard-hitting rifle that just needed getting used to, Sam knew. He was sure he'd work that out before the day was over, he told himself, raising the rifle back to his shoulder, feeling the dun slow and circle beneath him.

A good rifle, a good steady horse beneath him, he thought. What else did a man need? He aimed in again on the Mexican. But this time as he squeezed the trigger, he saw the rider fly from his saddle before the shot caused the rifle butt to kick against his shoulder.

What's this? He stared out, puzzled, knowing that one of the other riders had just shot the Mexican from behind.

Lowering the rifle, he circled back, putting the horse into a fast run toward the wagon as he saw Lilith drive it at an angle upward onto the long slope reaching up the hillside. She had good control of the rig, he could tell. But when he'd met her, she was having trouble on the hillsides. He wasn't going to take a chance, not with gunfire filling the air around them.

He raced on toward the wagon, gunshots still resounding behind him. Yet, in front of him, he saw the woman slow the wagon on the upward slope and duck in among large stones seated deep on the rocky hillside. *Good move,* he told himself, knowing that once in those rocks, with good rifles and enough cartridges, he and the woman could hold off an army—for a while anyway. A while was all he needed. Once he began inflicting wounds, knocking riders from their saddles shot after shot, it wouldn't take the riders long before they decided he wasn't worth what it was costing to kill him.

On the desert floor, Kelso and the Hooke brothers had brought their horses to a halt, but kept them moving back and forth, keeping themselves from being an easy target. A hundred yards behind them the Mexican, Montoya, had circled back to check on Fain, who lay alongside the road, flat on his back, one foot still tangled and jammed into his stirrup. Clutching a gloved hand to a new and bloody shoulder wound, Montoya rode up behind the others, who turned their horses to meet him.

"What the blazes is this?" Montoya asked, gesturing toward his bloody shoulder.

The three men looked at one another, then back at the Mexican.

They all three shrugged. They didn't know. Kelso sat with his new Colt hanging from his hand.

"Do not think you can shrug me off!" Montoya shouted. "One of you shot me! Which of you did this?" He paced his horse back and forth as he spoke, a rifle in his hand.

"Don't get your drawers in a knot, Mexican," said Kelso. "You act like this is your first gun battle or something."

"No, it is not my first gun battle," Montoya raged. "I have been in many! But in none of them have I had to worry about my own *compañeros* shooting me from behind!"

Kelso gave a chuff and a halfhearted grin.

"Well, get used to it," he said. "It happens all the time. A man can't always make a bullet go where he wants it to. One of us shot you and that's that. End of the story. Hell, it might have been Fain, for all we know."

"Fain was already dead!" said Montoya. "I saw him fall before this shot was fired." Blood ran down between his fingers as he gripped the wound tight. As he spoke, he let his horse come to a halt.

"You'll see yourself fall too," Kelso said. "Unless you keep that horse moving."

"I know how to look out for myself," Montoya said, stepping his horse back and forth in the sand. "But it is hard to protect myself with my own men shooting me from behind."

"You're not going to let this go, are you?" Kelso said quietly. The Hooke brothers sat staring blankly.

"Let it go?" said Montoya, still fuming in anger. "Hell no, I am not going to let it—"

The sound of the big new Colt cut the Mexican short as it bucked in Kelso's hand. Montoya rocked back and forth with a stunned, enraged look on his face. Then he toppled backward from his saddle as his horse stepped out from under him. He hit the ground in a puff of dust.

"I didn't think the son of a bitch was ever going to shut up about it," Kelso said. He turned the tip of the Colt's barrel to his lips and blew away a string of curling smoke. "He acted like everybody's supposed to live forever."

Charlie Ray looked off in the distance at the place where the wagon had rolled up out of sight into the hills.

"We'd better get a move on if we're going to pin Jones down and find out where the money is," he said.

"First things first," said Kelso. "Let's get off this blasted desert and into the rocks ourselves. We make too good a target out here with our backsides exposed." He looked all around as he spoke, recalling the last time on the desert floor and what the sound of gunfire had brought down on him.

"Why don't we hit Jones head-on from right here?" Hazerat asked. "Get it over with."

"You need to talk to your brother, Charlie Ray," Kelso said. "He's starting to sound like a damn fool."

Charlie Ray turned to face Hazerat.

"As far as we are from Jones, he can pick us off one at a time in a head-on rush. Besides, we need to pin him down and catch him alive if he's going to tell us anything. Wouldn't you agree?" he asked sarcastically.

"Yeah, I agree," Hazerat replied with equal sarcasm, "since you put it that way. I was just asking, is all."

The three turned their horses to the hills and gigged the tired animals out across the desert floor.

Chapter 16

When Sam arrived up on the hillside where Lilith had taken the wagon behind the shelter of a large boulder, he slipped down from his saddle and hurried to her. She sat against a rock, holding a cloth against a bullet graze across her forearm. She looked up at him with a slight smile and tried to play off her wound.

"Look at me," she said. "If my father was here, he would chastise me for being such a clumsy duck." She held her forearm up for him to see.

Sam kneeled. He leaned the French rifle against a rock and took her arm in his hand.

"Are you all right?" he asked, ignoring her critical remark. "Are you hit anywhere else?"

"No, I am fine, Joe," she said, taking her arm back from him. "How about you? Are you all right?"

"I'm good," Sam said. He took the cloth from her forearm. She watched as he tore a long shred down one edge the length of the bloody cloth. He folded the rest of the cloth, held it on the shallow bullet graze and tied it down in place with the shredded length.

"You appear to be good at this," she said, watching

him work deftly, tying the bandage, making sure it wasn't too tight on her arm.

"We learn as we go," he said, revealing nothing of his past that might lead her to his true identity. He let her lower her arm to her lap.

"If these are Segert's men," she said, "it will not be long before Dolan and the others will arrive."

"Yes, I figure as much," Sam said. "Only this has nothing to do with Dolan and his pals dragging me out of town. This is over a whole other thing that happened out on the desert. Preston Kelso thinks I have some bank money buried out here."

"Bank money?" said Lilith. She pulled her arm back from him. "You robbed a bank?" she asked quietly as she worked her hand a little to test for any stiffness from the bullet graze.

"No, nothing like that," Sam said, not liking the disappointed look she gave him. "Kelso thinks I did, though. In his mind, that's enough to make him want to come after me and force me to show him where the money is."

"Oh. I see," she said. But Sam saw that she only half believed him. That was all the explanation he could give her, regardless of what it caused her think of him.

"This is not the time to talk about it, Lilith," he said. "The whole thing isn't true. But Kelso thinks I know where the money is hidden. He wants to take me alive and try to get it out of me. If you're with me, it's likely he'll think that I'll talk instead of allowing you to be hurt."

She looked puzzled. "But you say you don't know—"

"That's right. I don't," Sam said, cutting her off. "But

that only makes it worse. I can't tell him anything, no matter what he would do to me, or to you either."

She looked frightened by his words.

"Then—then what will we do?" she asked.

"You'll stay down, Lilith," Sam said, clearly, calmly. He reached around and took the French rifle in hand. "If this Gruen is as good as it's supposed to be"—he lifted the long-distance sights atop the rifle chamber and stood it up in place—"I'll get them in my sights and kill them."

Lilith gave a little gasp.

Sam stopped adjusting the rifle sights and shot her a grave, serious look.

"I'll kill them before they kill us," he said. "Because in the end, that's what Preston Kelso intends to do."

"No matter what you tell him?" Lilith asked in a shaky tone.

"Yes, we will die, no matter what I tell him," Sam said with finality. "Now, stay under cover while I get us out of this," he added as he stood and cradled the French rifle in the crook of his arm.

Behind the boulder where the wagon sat, and where he'd tied the dun's reins, he took the pouch of rifle ammunition from his saddlebags. Slipping the pouch strap over his shoulder, cradling the Gruen in his arm, he climbed the iron rungs up the rear of the wagon. Atop the wagon, he stepped over onto the rough sloping surface of the large boulder and walked upward in a crouch to where a thin broken stone shelf offered natural footing for a man wielding a long-range rifle, and deadly intent.

He located the largest boulder out there and decided

that would be where they had left their horses. They were on foot now, no doubt about it, he told himself. He laid the cartridge pouch on the rock and adjusted the French rifle down onto it, making himself a good solid shooting foundation.

These men knew he and the woman were ducked down in the rocks; they had seen no long rise of dust on the pathway leading up the hillside. They knew roughly where to find him, he thought, having been in this same situation many times before. What they would do now was skirt along on the hillside, behind cover, rock to rock, until they could pin him down and decide when to rush him. Once they did that, they would try their best to take him and the woman alive. And then the games would begin, Sam told himself grimly.

He flipped the yardage sight up on the rifle barrel and aimed it at a stone standing in the settling trail dust they'd left behind. They were in the rocks now, headed this way, he decided. He sighted the French rifle in and waited, scanning back and forth among the larger rocks in the afternoon sunlight.

Nothing moved or stirred on the hillside in front of him. But he knew they were there. On the desert floor to his left, now that the wavering heat had subsided enough for him to see a little more clearly, he eyed two bodies lying sprawled in the sand. Even with his naked eyes, he could make them out as the scalp hunters, Montoya and Fain. Not far from Montoya stood his lone horse, an afternoon breeze lifting at its mane. Fifty yards away stood Fain's horse. By dark the two horses would be standing together against the coming night and what it brought down from these rocky slopes.

Another few moments passed without event. Then, as he continued scanning down the rifle barrel, he saw a scrawny jackrabbit streak from behind an upstanding stone and race away skittering over rock and barrel cactus until it vanished somewhere down near the desert floor.

Here we go, Sam alerted himself, locking in on the rock cover the rabbit had given up. No rabbit headed to the open desert this time of evening. In the afternoon heat, even a rattlesnake would only send the creature moving a few grudging yards out of striking range. Huh-uh, Sam decided. Only man caused this much disturbance. He waited, ready and aimed.

A moment later, the French rifle snug to the pocket of his shoulder, his eyes focused down the long-range sight, he spotted his target. The gunman, this one Charlie Ray Hooke, rose in a crouch and moved forward quickly from the cover he'd taken over from the rabbit to a newer, closer spot ten feet in front of him. But, moving in a line facing the Ranger, he didn't make it. Before he could swerve in behind his next rock, he stopped, bolted upright onto his toes and flipped sidelong and backward onto the rocky ground.

Sam's long-distance shot resounded as Charlie Ray hit the ground. A string of blood followed him backward, splattering wide on his chest, his face. On the ground beneath him, a spray of blood pointed out along the dirt behind him.

From his position, Sam heard Hazerat crying out to his brother.

"Charlie Ray! Charlie Ray!" Hazerat shouted, suddenly grief-stricken. His voice echoed, following Sam's rifle shot off across the hills and desert floor.

One down, two to go, Sam told himself, ignoring the cries of Hazerat.

He levered out the smoking cartridge and levered a new round into the rifle chamber. He raised the rifle to his shoulder again and began scanning the hillside near the spot where Charlie Ray lay dead in his own blood. What Kelso and his pals didn't know, he told himself, was that he had an advantage. These men thought they were fighting one of their own. They were wrong. They were fighting a lawman—and it made a difference; he was certain of it. As he scanned the rocks, he caught sight of Hazerat Hooke standing up in a crouch behind a waist-high rock and looking over toward his brother's body. Sam took quick aim and fired again.

Behind the boulder, Preston Kelso reached up and pulled Hazerat straight down beside him. As Hazerat hit the ground, a shot from a long ways off along the hillside ricocheted off the rock and zinged away wildly in the air.

"Stay down, you stupid son of a bitch!" shouted Kelso. He swung his rifle around and poked it into Hazerat's chest. "Make another move like that and I'll kill you myself!"

"That's Charlie Ray lying out there!" Hazerat shouted.

"I aim to go get him, pull him back here! He might still be alive!"

"Yeah," said Kelso. "And he might be lying there scratching a galled ass, but I find it hard to believe." He looked around quickly, then back to Hazerat. "This Jones fellow is a good long shooter. But he can't see any better than we can in the dark. Soon as the sun's gone down, we're going to slip in and rain hell on him. He'll do what we tell him to once he sees some cold steel along the peddler woman's neck."

"As soon as the sun's down," Hazerat said, "I'm going to get Charlie Ray and drag him behind a rock. Dead or alive, I can't leave him lying out there like that."

"All right, all right, *damn it*!" said Kelso. "Soon as it's dark, you drag him behind a rock, for all the good it'll do you. But you'd better be ready to back my play when the time comes."

"I'm ready," said Hazerat. "After what he's done to my poor brother, I won't rest until I see him dead."

Atop the boulder, Sam shouldered the ammunition pouch and cradled the French Gruen. Feeling the chamber warm against his forearm, he stepped down the side of the boulder onto the wagon top, then climbed down the iron rungs to the ground. He hurried over to where Lilith huddled against the rock where he'd left her.

"See?" she said nervously. "I stayed right here, just like you told me to."

"Good," Sam said, seeing the worried look in her eyes.

"Are you—? Are you all right?" she asked, sounding dry-mouthed and frightened.

"I'm good," Sam said, looking back across the hill-sides as he spoke. "I got one, but the other two will keep moving in closer on us every minute." While he spoke, he picked up the canteen, uncapped it and held it to her. "Here, drink some water. Try to settle yourself down. We've got a long night coming."

She accepted the canteen and took a short sip. When she finished, she handed it back to Sam.

"What are we going to do?" she asked.

"While we've got this big boulder hiding us," Sam said, "we're going to ease up the hill and find ourselves another trail before it gets too dark. We're going to stop the wagon and drop back along their trail and ambush them when they come looking for us."

"We are . . . ?" She seemed uncertain about his plan.

"Yes, we are," Sam replied with confidence. He reached down and pulled her to her feet. "Don't worry. We got one, we'll get another. We'll get both if they keep coming."

They both hurried. When they left the cover of the large boulder, Sam rode his dun at the rear of the wagon. With Lilith at the wagon reins, they moved up the winding trail as the sun dropped out of sight over the jagged twisted hilltops. By dark, they had turned left onto a trail that reached around the rocky hill and led down into a narrow canyon. At the point where the trail began to angle down, Sam circled the wagon and rode beside her a few yards, looking all around.

"Stop here," he said finally. Around them the shadows of night had begun to creep down the hillsides and cast them purple-black against the darkening sky. The trail behind them became obscured by the grainy evening light.

Lilith brought the team of horses to a jolting halt.

"Set the brake and tie the reins good," Sam said. "We're going to leave the rig here."

"But what about Andre and the new horse?" she asked.

"They'll be all right," Sam said. "They'll be here. We'll be back there." He gestured toward the trail behind them. "I'll find a place where they'll have to moonlight themselves to us. With any luck, we'll end everything right there."

"All right," Lilith said. She hurriedly set the wagon brake and tied the reins around the tall brake handle. Standing, she searched herself quickly, almost frantically. "Do you still have my pepperbox? Will I need it?"

Sidling close to the wagon, Sam reached a hand over to her.

"*Yes*, I still have it," he said, "and, *no*, you won't need it. Let's hope not, anyway."

Taking his hand, she stepped over from the wagon seat and lowered herself behind him on the dun.

As he put the dun forward at a walk, they heard a hard eruption of gunfire from the trail, somewhere near the boulder where they'd been taking cover.

"Sounds like we left at the right time," Sam said to her over his shoulder.

Two more shots exploded on the trail below them.

"Yes, yes, you were right. They were coming right then to kill us, these evil men," she said. Sam felt her shake her head back and forth against his back. "I'm glad it's you with me," she said softly. He felt her tighten her arms around him. "Do you mind if I hold you this way?"

"Be my guest," Sam said. He touched his boots to the dun's sides. They rode forward along the winding trail.

When they neared the run in the trail that led back down toward the large boulder, Sam stepped the dun over onto the hillside and they both slid down off the horse's back. There were tracks they'd left riding back from the wagon, but there was nothing he could do about them now. He had kept the horse as close to the rough edge of the trail as he dared without risking that the animal would twist a hoof or slip and fall in the loose gravel. This would have to do, he told himself.

They walked up the steep rocky hillside among boulder and stone ledges, and through sparse growth of pine and ironwood until they reached a shallow overhang with a thick short wall of stone lining its front edge. Inside the overhang, Sam led the dun downward over a sunken boulder and stood it in the darkness. Then he hurried back up to where Lilith sat against the front stone wall.

"I haven't seen anything," Lilith whispered.

"Good," Sam said, swinging the ammunition pouch from his shoulder, laying it atop the stone. As she kneeled beside her, he inspected the front of the hillside facing the trail up the hillside. A glow of moonlight had already seeped into the night sky. The trail was dark but visible from where they lay. Sam leaned the French rifle against the stone wall and sat in silence, waiting, watching the trail below.

In moments when the chill of night began to make itself felt with a promise of the cold to come, without a word, Lilith moved over against Sam and put her arms around his shoulders, drawing herself even closer. Sam breathed in the fragrance of her, and reminded himself that he was there to keep them both alive throughout this long and deadly night.

PART 3

Chapter 17

Preston Kelso had no idea how he and Hazerat had gotten separated on the rocky hillside. One minute Hazerat was there, moving forward with him, only a few feet away. The next minute, he was gone. *Damn it! How hard can it be to stay low and keep moving forward,* Kelso thought. But Hazerat was an idiot, and in an idiot's mind, Kelso supposed, the least little thing could get him lost and confused. That had been a few minutes ago. They'd heard shots from Jones' direction; they'd ducked down and fired back blindly. But now the shooting had long stopped.

So what was this?

Kelso ventured a peep out from behind the rock where he had hunkered down through the gunfire, his rifle across his lap. Now the gunfire was silent. Still, no sign of Hazerat—the idiot son of a bitch.

Kelso stood up warily into a crouch and walked out from behind the rock cover. Evening curtains of darkness had pulled across the hill land. Every rock stood bathed in shadow.

"Hazerat . . . ," he whispered as loud as he dared.

When he heard no reply, he whispered again, "Hazerat, damn your eyes! Answer me." *You idiot bastard*, he growled to himself. But again no reply. After two more tries, he cursed under his breath and crept forward toward the mammoth boulder. If he had to pull Jones down and hold a boot on his throat to find out about the money, he would. And he'd be damned if he was sharing one thin dollar of it with Hazerat—that idiot turd. . . .

He crept forward slowly.

In the grainy darkness ahead of him, he thought he saw the outline of a man on the moonlit side of the boulder. But when he drew closer and called out again, he still got no reply. And yet there Hazerat was, just standing there beside a tall cactus outside the boulder's dark shadow, bare-headed, looking stupid, Kelso thought to himself.

Jones was gone or else Hazerat wouldn't be standing there like a goose looking for thunder, Kelso decided. He straightened as he walked closer and circled the spiky cactus.

"There you are, fool," he grumbled in a whisper. "Why didn't you answer me?" He looked closer at Hazerat as he stopped and stood ten feet away. "What's that on your face?"

But as soon as he asked, he saw what it was, and he recoiled and felt a scream well up in his tightened chest.

Mercifully, Hazerat was dead. Blood ran down from his empty eye sockets. In the dark blood, his eyes dangled by their thin tendon cords on either cheek. His mouth lay agape and empty, a black cave carved free of its lips, soft tissue, teeth and bone matter. His scalp was missing. His abdominal cavity had also been cut open sternum to crotch, its contents jerked out, much of it flung aside like that of a field-dressed deer. His own belt around his neck held him pinned to the cactus.

Kelso managed to keep his scream down to a short, painful whine. He turned back and forth quickly, wildly, searching the dark in every direction, his rifle raised at port arms. Yet, in a sudden grip of terror and panic, he fumbled with the rifle as he took his right hand off it and drew his new Colt. With a gun in each hand, he ventured forward. But he stopped and spun back and forth again, this time when he heard the sharp single yelp of a coyote in the darkness in front of him—then an answering yelp from the stones and darkness behind him.

These weren't coyotes, they were Apaches. He sidestepped warily away, with no direction in mind except to get out of the grainy light into the greater darkness of the rocky hillside.

"Stay back, you heathen sons a' bitches!" he shouted, as if shouting would do him any good. He sidestepped quicker, hearing the coyote yelps grow bolder, more intense—coyotes having fun, teasing a scared human. "You ain't fooling me. I know. I know!"

But the yelps continued, growing closer.

Kelso felt them pressing him in. He turned and ran up the hillside to keep ahead of them. He stopped and turned and raised both guns at his sides. He didn't know how many of them were circling him, only that he was outnumbered. They had killed Hazerat, maimed his body and left it there to scare him, and it had worked. He saw figures dart back and forth in the darkness, too fast to even identify, let alone take aim on. He backed around a tall rock, deciding this might be a place to huddle down, make a stand. Yet, before he could do so, he heard a yelp only inches from his ear, and felt a hand come out of the darkness and yank his rifle away from him.

He yelled as he ran blindly up the hillside, hearing shrill taunting laughter behind him. He raced from rock to rock, his Colt pressed to his side, lest it go the same way as his rifle. When he noted that the yelps and the laughter had fallen silent behind him, he stopped and hung against the side of a rock and wheezed and gasped for breath. They weren't gone, he knew. They wouldn't leave now, not while they had their prey outnumbered—not while they had him on the run like this. He sank down into the dark slice of shadow beside the rock.

'Pache . . . sons a' bitches. . . . He spat drily, and opened and closed his hand around the butt of the new Colt. Now they were being real quiet, slipping in on him unseen like ghosts? Yes, this was just like the heathen savages, he told himself. But he could play that ghostly slip-around game himself. He just needed to catch his breath for a minute.

His eyes searched the darkness back and forth, from rock to rock, seeing nothing. After a while, when his breath was restored and he knew he could make a good sprint up the hillside, he raised himself into a stooped position beside the rock and prepared to streak forward at full speed.

Let's see you catch this, you sneaking sons a' bitches. . . .

He launched himself forward on his toes, holding nothing back, gun in hand. Yet before he made three fast steps, a knee-length leather-laced moccasin jabbed out of the darkness into his running feet. He tripped, his boots tangling beneath him, and went down face-first, sliding forward a few feet even on the uphill ground. His new Colt flew from his hand and clattered on the hard dirt ahead of him.

He knew what had happened. He scrambled forward on his belly and reached for his gun. Yet as he saw it in the pale grainy light, the moccasin again came out of the dark. This time it clamped down on the Colt and pinned it to the ground. His hand fell atop the moccasin.

Above him, two hands pulled him up roughly, enough to flip him onto his back. Kelso stared up at a shadowed-out face, a wispy black looming silhouette—and a half dozen other wispy silhouettes looming around him. Kelso jerked out a bowie knife from his boot well. A moccasin kicked it away. One of the silhouettes picked it up and gave it to the one standing on his Colt.

Kelso lay helpless, surrounded, off his feet.

The young warrior, Luka, kneeled down beside him, holding the bowie knife and inspecting it as though it were a gift to him.

"It's you, you heathen son of a bitch!" Kelso said, his voice dry, trembling with terror and rage.

He caught a glimpse of one of the other silhouettes picking up the new Colt and turning it in his hands.

Luka yanked Kelso's sombrero and bandage from his head in one swipe and threw them both aside. Seeing Kelso's raw, grisly head, he said something in Apache that brought dark laughter from the others.

"That's it, laugh, you savage heathen," Kelso said to Luka. "I can't get nothing done on account of you—" His words ended in a nasal twang. Luka squeezed his nose shut between his thumb and forefinger.

Kelso's eyes widened as Luka shoved his head back at a sharp angle. Luka made one long, deep pull of his knife blade across Kelso's throat. He held a firm hand on Kelso's heaving chest, pinning him in place until the hapless gunman stopped thrashing.

Before dawn, the Ranger and Lilith rode down as quietly as they could from the sloping hillsides. Lilith drove the peddler's wagon; Sam rode the dun beside her, the butt of the French rifle resting on his thigh, standing ready in his hand. The night had passed quietly after the gunfire stopped. But Sam wasn't kidding himself. In these Twisted Hills, last night's silence could mean anything. He gave no thought to Kelso and the Hooke brother he hadn't shot giving up and going back to Agua Fría. But he did consider the Apaches. Not seeing them, not hearing them, didn't mean they weren't out there. The Blood Mountain Range had been their land for centuries. Avoiding them out here might require more luck than skill, he told himself.

They traveled along the desert floor, yet they stayed

close to the bottom of the sloping hillside, should they need to make a run for cover, or for shade when they needed whatever shelter was available for resting themselves and their animals.

They did not stop at first light, but rather ate some dried biscuits and drank canteen water while on the move. They kept pushing forward until midmorning. When they did stop, they stayed out on the sand flats, but kept close watch on the wavering heat that had set in, curtaining the wide desert floor.

"Are you sorry you came with me, Joe?" Lilith asked, the two of them standing with the dun on the thin shaded side of the wagon.

"Only if you are," Sam replied, gazing out, searching the endless wavering land.

Lilith smiled at him.

"That is no kind of answer," she said. She gave him a nudge in his side.

"That was no kind of question," he replied. He glanced at her, then back out across the burning sand. "As it is, I've got nothing but time," he said, although he knew better. He had plenty to do, most of it bloody and violent, in order to topple Segert's and Madson's gangs and stop the plundering across the U.S. border.

"I have to admit," he added, "it might be safer to mail your tribute to Don Marco every year, instead of traveling all the way to San Carlo."

"Mail in Mexico? Ha," Lilith said. "Mail that does not get robbed by bandits in Mexico gets sorted through, stolen and thrown away by the very ones paid to transport it."

Sam continued gazing out across the desert sands. Was she trying to keep him talking? If so, why? *Nervous,* he decided. Easy to understand after all they'd gone through the night before.

"I always say, you can't beat the American postal service," he said quietly.

"Mail is not the only thing wrong here," Lilith said. "I can tell you so many stories—"

"Hold it," Sam said, cutting her off. "What's this?" He continued to stare out across the desert floor, but now he raised the French rifle and started to put it to his shoulder.

Lilith stood tense beside him, looking worried.

Sam saw a large half circle of riders begin to close in around them, coming into view through the wavering heat.

Seeing there was not time to get the wagon up onto the hillside, Sam jerked the dun around to Lilith.

"Climb on," Sam said to her with urgency. "Take my horse and get out of here. I'll hold them off. Get into the hills."

Lilith grabbed the dun's reins and saddle horn and climbed up quickly. Out fifty yards, the riders drew in closer, still too far away to identify through the swirl of heat, the stabbing desert sunlight. She started to turn the dun to the hills. But then she stopped, seeing Sam with the French rifle, raised, aimed, ready to fire.

"Wait!" she said to him. "I know these men!"

Sam hesitated. He looked up at her.

"What?" he said. "Who are they?" He couldn't see how she recognized them from here. He could not yet make out anything about them, except that they were circling and moving in—never a good sign, he reminded himself.

"They—they are customers of mine. Please do not shoot," she said. Slipping down from the saddle, she put herself in front of Sam and let the dun's reins fall to the dirt.

Sam gave her a puzzled look, but he lowered the rifle a few inches.

"Customers?" He stared at the riders, then back at her. "What does that mean?"

"Please let me explain," she said.

"Feel free to," Sam said wryly, "before they nail us to the side of this wagon."

"They won't shoot unless you shoot first," she said. "I will tell you everything. But don't shoot. If you fire at them, I know they will kill you."

Sam lowered the rifle a little more. He stared at her, then out at the riders as they moved into clearer sight. Finally he relented and lowered the rifle down to his side. The riders were much closer now. He could see their dirty white peasant clothes, their rifles, the bando-leers of ammunition crisscrossing their chests.

"I hope you know what you're doing, Lilith," he said sidelong to her.

"Yes, I do," she said quietly in reply, stepping in, plac-ing a hand on his arm, as if helping him put the French rifle down. "Their people are rebels. They fight to free Mexico from its ruler, Jueto Umberto and his cruel *gen-eralissimo*."

"I can't help thinking I've heard all this before,"

Sam said under his breath as the armed riders, men and women alike, stepped down from their saddles, guns ready in hand. They walked up to Sam and Lilith, stopped and stood facing them.

The leader, a stout, scar-faced Mexican wearing a dusty strip poncho over his shoulders, looked Sam up and down, then turned to Lilith.

"I see you have a new father," he said to her with a short, knowing grin.

Sam gave him a curious stare.

"A new father?" he said. His voice demanded an explanation.

But Lilith cut in, her hand still on Sam's arm.

"Not a new father," she said. "This is Joe. He is a friend who I trust, or he would not be here with me."

The stout Mexican stood with a big German revolver cocked and aimed loosely in Sam's direction. He reached down for the French rifle in Sam's hand. But Sam didn't want to let go.

"Please, Joe," Lilith said. "Let him have it. He only wants to inspect it."

Now it was Lilith's turn to get Sam's curious look. Yet he let go of the rifle and watched the stout Mexican hold it, unload cartridge after cartridge into the dirt, checking the sleek action each time he levered it. Then he left the lever down, turned the rifle and gazed one-eyed down through the long barrel. He looked satisfied with the rifle.

"They are all like this one?" the Mexican leader asked Lilith, turning the empty rifle in his hands.

All right, now I see, Sam told himself. He breathed

a little easier, just starting to understand what was going on.

"Yes, they are all in the same condition," Lilith replied. "Used very little, some still with packing grease in their chambers."

"Good," the Mexican said. He handed the unloaded rifle back to Sam. With the wave of a thick hand, he gestured the riders forward. They hurried on foot and filed past Sam and the woman, through the wagon's rear door. Sam turned, Lilith and the Mexican flanking him, and watched three men throw aside a striped Mexican rug and lift a trapdoor with eager hands. Rifle after rifle appeared up out of the floor as if by magic. They moved from one pair of hands to the next, coming down out of the wagon to the rest of the waiting rebels.

"A gun runner," Sam said flatly to Lilith as even the Mexican leader himself stepped up into the wagon.

"Please, Joe, do not judge me harshly," Lilith said. "It was either do this or lose my wagon and everything else—"

"They know your wagon pretty well," Sam said. "This isn't your first dealing with them."

"No, no, it is not," Lilith said. "I am so ashamed for deceiving you." She stood with her head hung, but it was only for a second. Then she raised her face to his and tilted her chin up. "No, I am not ashamed," she said defiantly. "These are people who are struggling against a cruel, oppressive leader. They need help. I bring them that help. As an American, you should understand such a thing."

Sam had to digest it with one hard swallow.

"I do understand, Lilith," he said, letting out a breath. "I only wish you hadn't misled me."

"For that, I apologize, Joe," she said. "But I could not take a chance. You told me yourself the kind of man you are. I had to keep my intentions a secret from you."

Sam only nodded; he stepped back and watched as the Mexican rebels unloaded the hidden compartment beneath the wagon's floor. The rifles continued in their chain from wagon out to horses, where they were tied down behind saddles, five, six, seven at a time. Ammunition cartons were tied atop them. When the arms were unloaded, secured and readied for travel, a thin young man stepped forward with three canvas pouches in his hands. He held them toward Lilith, who only gestured him inside the wagon.

"All for the cause of Mexican freedom?" Sam said, seeing the man stoop inside the wagon and lay the gold pouches in the open floor compartment.

"It is gold that I must have in order to purchase more rifles and ammunition for them," she said in her own defense. "Again, I beg you, *please* do not judge me, Joe."

The stout Mexican stepped forward. He looked down at the cartridges still lying in the dirt. He gave Sam a wide smile.

"Leave the bullets there until we are gone, eh, *señor*?" he said.

Sam only nodded.

The leader turned to Lilith.

"We are grateful to you for your support. Now, I bid you and your *father* a safe journey," he said.

Sam held his peace until the leader and his riders had

turned and rode away. When their horses had climbed the sloping hillside and disappeared into the shelter of rock ledges and boulders, Sam stooped and picked up the cartridges and reloaded the rifle.

"What did he mean, you and *your father*?" he asked Lilith, standing up, rifle in hand.

Lilith shrugged.

"Who knows?" she said. "I am just glad that is over with." She gazed at him. "If you hate me now and wish to ride away, I will understand."

Sam looked all around. "I said I'd ride with you to San Carlo. I still will if that's where you're headed."

"No," she said. "Now that I am finished with the rebels, I can go home to Agua Fría."

"Then that's where I'll accompany you," Sam said.

"And when we arrive there?" she asked, pensively. "Will you forgive me for deceiving you?"

"I've been dealt worse," he said. He realized that he had been deceiving her and everybody he'd encountered since he left Nogales. "I think I can handle this."

Chapter 18

———————

In the afternoon, on the desert trail back to Agua Fría, the Ranger rode the dun alongside the peddler's wagon. He kept close watch on the rocky hillsides rising on the left of the desert floor. As the sun began to draw downward beyond the Blood Mountain Range and the land began to shed its heat, they moved up into the rocky hills to take shelter for the night.

Beside a thin runoff stream, they set up camp and built a small cook fire that, owing to the Apaches still prowling the hill country, they would extinguish as night closed in. The two had eaten hardtack and jerked goat meat in silence. With the dun and the team of wagon horses grained, watered, rubbed down from the day's dust and hidden from sight in the shelter of stone, Sam had walked to the stream and sat down on a thick long slab of limestone at the water's edge. He sat in the evening silence, sipping hot coffee, the French rifle lying across his lap.

The two hadn't talked any more about the rifles Lilith had sold to the rebel band. As far as Sam was concerned, the incident was not something he was supposed to get involved in. Under the Matamoros Agreement,

American lawmen had no business being involved in Mexican political situations. It was something he would never mention when reporting back to his captain. As soon as he accompanied Lilith back to Agua Fría, his only concern was to take down Segert's and Madson's gangs. In Segert's case, it would be a pleasure, owing to what he and his men had done to him.

"Joe, may I sit with you?" Lilith asked quietly, standing beside him at the water's edge, her hands around a tin cup of coffee.

Sam scooted over a few inches and gestured a nod at the space he'd made for her.

"Thank you," Lilith said. She sat down and gazed at stream in silence for a moment. Finally she said, "Who are you, Joe. What were you really doing in Agua Fría?"

Sam looked at her.

"Are we starting that all over now?" he asked. "Or are these just questions you're going to ask until you get answers that suit you?" He feigned his disagreeable attitude and started to stand up. But Lilith stopped him with a hand on his arm.

"You first tell me you are not one of these men who come here looking for gun work. Then you tell me that you are. I am only trying to find out what to believe."

Looking for a way out, Sam said coolly, "I didn't come here to run guns. That's something you can believe."

"All right, I deserve that," Lilith said. She paused, then said quietly, "But there are things about you that I still do not understand."

"Maybe you shouldn't trouble yourself," Sam replied, wanting the conversation to be over.

She ignored his effort to end it.

"I know that you are not a gunman like the ones who ride with Raymond Segert or Bell Madson."

"What makes you so sure?" Sam said.

"Because there are sacks of gold in the bottom of the wagon, and yet you have demanded none of it, in spite of how I deceived you into delivering the rifles."

Sam sipped his coffee and looked at her.

"How do you know I wasn't going to demand a cut of it before we get to Agua Fría?" he asked.

"Perhaps you were, but I don't think so," she said. "Perhaps you were going to kill me in my sleep and take it all for yourself," she added. "But I doubt that too."

"You've got a lot of doubts," Sam said. Again he started to stand.

She took his arm, but this time he stood anyway. She let her hand fall from him. He slung the coffee grounds from his empty cup.

"I'd best put out the fire," he said, "before we draw in every Apache in the range." He turned toward the fire.

"Joe, please," she said. "Tell me who you are and what you're doing here. It is important that I know."

Sam only shook his head. He walked to the small fire and rubbed it out with his boot.

"Don't sleep in the wagon," he said. "Get yourself a blanket." He nodded at the towering stones and boulders surrounding them. "We'll climb up there a ways and spend the night."

"But what about the gold?" she asked.

"We'll carry it with us," he said. He picked up a blanket from his saddle on the ground and walked to the wagon. She joined him on the way.

They took the three canvas pouches of gold from the wagon. Sam strung the pouches together with a strong strip of rawhide and draped them over his shoulder.

"We can keep these with us, or hide them overnight in the rocks," he said. "If Apaches come across us, we'll be protecting more than this gold."

"Yes," she agreed. "We'll hide it in the rocks."

Sam saw the troubled look on her face.

"As large as this desert is, it could be crawling with Apaches and they'd never come across us," he said, hoping to lighten her worry. "It's hearing gunfire, or seeing a bright campfire that draws them in."

"Let us hope we have neither," she replied.

With a blanket she picked up for herself from the bed, the two left the wagon and horses behind and walked to a narrow crevice leading up into the stonework above them. They climbed an uneven stairway of broken stone and partially exposed pine and ironwood root. On their way up, near the top of a flat cliff overhang, they found an opening in the stones beside them and shoved the pouches into it for the night. Sam covered the opening with a flat stone he loosened from the wall of the crevice.

They continued climbing fifteen feet up and over onto the cliff overhang that sank back into the hillside enough to hide them from sight, yet provided a good view of the hillside below them and the sprawling desert floor. Careful not to make a sound, they rolled out their blankets and adjusted themselves in the hard stone bed they'd chosen for the night.

Except for the harshness of their surroundings, the night passed uneventfully for the two of them, sleeping there among the rocks some thirty-five feet above the spot where their wagon sat out of sight behind a boulder. Twice in the early darkness, Sam was awakened from a light, watchful sleep by a chorus of coyotes out on the desert floor. He was familiar with how coyotes started their nightly yelping and baying in a large circle, a natural, ages-old cadence that stopped only when they had gradually drawn closer and gathered into a pack. He noted the distance between where that cadence began and where it stopped.

Good hunting, Sam thought, allowing himself to drift back between a thin sleep and waking vigilance. He spent the night blanket-wrapped, the French rifle resting in the crook of his arm. Five feet away, Lilith lay sleeping in much the same position, with the dead scalp hunter Ollie McCool's shiny Smith & Wesson snuggled to her bosom.

In the middle of the night, with a three-quarter moon overhead, Sam eased over and checked to make sure she was sleeping. Then he eased down the crevice and stopped where the two of them had hidden the pouches of gold among the rocks.

Before the first ray of sunlight blinked on the horizon, Sam shook the woman gently by her shoulder. As she awakened, she fumbled with the Smith & Wesson, as if trying to cock the big pistol. Sam reached out and took it from her hands. She looked up at him, bleary-eyed.

"Lilith, wake up," he said almost in a whisper.

"What is it?" she whispered in reply, growing more awake quickly, thinking she detected an urgency in his voice.

"Nothing," Sam said. "We just need to get an early start out of here." He was on one knee beside her, rifle in hand, and brushed a strand of dark hair from her face.

She relaxed and stretched and wiped a hand over her face, feeling better. She saw he had already rolled his blanket and was ready to leave.

"When I return to Agua Fría, I think I want to stay there for a while," she said.

"What about your business?" Sam asked. He stood, stepped back and rose on his toes and looked out past the edge of the cliff. The desert floor still lay cloaked in purple darkness.

"My sharpening can wait," she said. She pushed up to her feet and adjusted her dress. "Anyway, I get paid a small amount from the rifle deal," she said. As soon as she said it, Sam realized she wished she hadn't.

"Oh, a small amount?" he asked casually. "Who gets the largest amount?"

She didn't answer right away. Instead she attended to rolling up her blanket and tucking it under her arm.

"There is *always* someone higher up, who *always* gets the largest part," she said.

"I understand," Sam said, not wanting to push too hard for an answer. She turned toward the crevice they'd climbed the night before. But Sam guided her in another direction.

"This way," he said. "I found us a better crevice. This one is a game path—less steep."

She hesitated.

"But the gold," she said.

"It's only fifteen feet up the crevice," he said. "We'll reach it easier from down there, once we're ready to leave."

Lilith only nodded. She followed him to the far edge of the cliff and down another thin, narrow crevice. At the bottom of their downward climb, Lilith walked to the wagon while Sam gathered the horses and led them back to the campsite. When he'd returned with the horses, he saw Lilith bowed over a new fire she'd built. He walked over quickly and put out the fire with his boot.

Lilith looked up in surprise.

"I thought you'd want some coffee before we leave," she said.

"Not this early, not while it's still dark," Sam said. He gestured toward the desert floor. "A fire in this darkness can be seen for miles."

"I'm—I'm sorry, Joe," she stammered. "I don't know what I was thinking." She chastised herself as she stood up quickly and rubbed her boot back and forth with him. "I know better than to do something like this."

"Take it easy," Sam said, seeing her reaction. "Everybody makes mistakes now and then. Like as not, there's no one out there anyway. A few more minutes, we can make all the coffee we want. Just keep the fire low."

"Yes, of course," she said. She breathed easier and looked out across the grainy black desert floor. "I will not make such a mistake again, you have my word."

Sam watched her walk away toward the wagon. In the east, the first red-gold light mantled the edge of the earth.

By the time Sam had inspected and tacked the team of horses and saddled and readied his dun, the light had grown silver-blue across the endless ocean of sand. As he cinched the dun, he looked out across its back and saw something move at the bottom edge of the hillside. He settled his eyes in the direction of the movement and waited until he saw it again. There it was! A horse? Yes, a horse, he decided. But not just one horse. Now he counted three horses, spread out abreast, moving onto the trail slowly, soundlessly.

He sidestepped away from the dun and picked up the French rifle from against a rock.

Lilith saw him checking the rifle quickly as he kept an eye down on the lower hillside.

"What did you see?" she said, barely above a whisper.

"I see we've got more riders coming," Sam said, his voice not as guarded as hers. From their stealthy approach, he could tell the riders knew there were people up here. "This has got to be the busiest place I've seen in a while," he added.

"Oh no!" Lilith said. "What do you want me to do?"

"Take cover," Sam said. "I'll try to slip around the rocks and see how many guns are down there—"

His words were almost cut short by a booming voice in the rocks above them. "There's more guns than you can count on your fingers and toes," the voice called out.

"Segert," Sam said under his breath, recognizing the

voice he'd last heard before the Mexican vaqueros dragged him away in the dirt. He looked up at the big man standing in view twenty feet above him. The Ranger's first instinct was to raise the French rifle, take aim and fire. But as he cocked the rifle he saw a line of gunmen spring up from the cover of rock. He heard the clicking of rifles cocking as one.

"Don't do it, Jones," Segert said. "It'll only get you killed first thing before breakfast."

"I had nothing planned for today," Sam called out, not giving an inch, the French rifle ready to fire.

"Then think of that pretty little peddler gal," Segert called down to him. "It'd be a shame to splatter her head all over these hills."

Sam judged Lilith to be standing no more than six feet from him. Like it or not, Segert was right. If rifles started blasting here among these rocks, if a straight shot didn't kill her, a ricochet surely would.

Sam hesitated. He looked along the line of riflemen aiming down at him, some in tan Mexican army uniforms, some in trail clothes. *Federales* siding with Segert's gunmen, he told himself. What a dangerous mix.

"Joe, Joe, I'm scared!" he heard Lilith say beside him in a shaky voice. "Tell me what I should do, please," she added, her voice almost sobbing.

"What do you want, Segert?" Sam called out, hoping for a way out. "I figure whatever business you had with me ended when your gunmen used me to sweep the trail." Even as he spoke, Sam lowered the rifle an inch.

"You are a hard man to kill, Jones," Segert said with

a dark chuckle. "I've got to hand it to you." He made his way down the hillside, the riflemen following suit.

Sam watched, lowering the rifle more as the men closed down and lined up again ten feet from him and Lilith. Behind him, he heard more men move up from the side of the campsite.

Surrounded.

"You're right, Jones," Segert said. "You and I are finished with business. But the captain here has other business with you."

A thickly built Mexican soldier with a sharp black mustache stepped forward from the left, two soldiers with rifles flanking him.

"Yankee pistolero," he said. "I am *Capitan* Silvero. You are under arrest for the selling of firearms to the enemies of the sovereign government of Mexico and its peoples," he said. "Hand over your weapon," he demanded.

Sam allowed one of the two soldiers to take the French rifle from his hands.

"Is it the same as the others?" the captain asked.

The soldier inspected the French rifle in the grainy dawn light.

"*Sí, Capitan*, it is the same as the others," he said.

Sam took a deep breath and glared at Segert, who stood with a thin smirk on his face.

"It's a firing squad offense, I hear," Segert said.

Sam just stared. He got the picture. The other soldier leveled his rifle at his stomach. The one holding the French rifle reached out and lifted Sam's Colt from his side.

Daryl Dolan stepped into sight and stood beside Segert.

"I always admire a good firing squad," he said. "It's louder than a hanging, but still lots of fun to watch."

Two soldiers from the other side of the campsite dragged one of the rebels in front of Sam and threw the bloody man to the ground.

"Is this the man you received the rifles from?" the captain asked in a demanding tone.

"*Sí, sí*, it is him," the bloody man groaned over split and swollen lips. His eyes were too swollen shut to recognize anyone, Sam decided. But it made no difference. This had all been set up and played out before they'd even arrived. This was Raymond Segert's way of showing he owned the law in Agua Fría and the Twisted Hills, maybe in the whole Blood Mountain Range. Sam stared at the captain, then at Segert, then turned his gaze toward Lilith, who stood deliberately looking away from him, tears glistening in her dark eyes.

Chapter 19

Seeing that Lilith wouldn't face him, Sam started piecing everything together in his mind. He had actually started running some things through his mind the night before while Lilith slept. He had grown suspicious, and what was happening now only proved his suspicions right. The gunrunning was just one more of Segert's operations. The woman and her father must have been managing it for him for quite a while. Now that the father was dead, it fell to her to do Segert's bidding. Sam stared at her for a moment longer, then turned to Segert and Dolan.

"Firing squad?" he said. He shook his head slowly and added confidently, "I don't think so, not today."

Dolan grinned.

"I've seen men break down this way in the end," he said.

But Segert stepped forward and gave Sam a curious look.

"Not today, why?" he asked.

"Because if you shoot me today, you won't get the gold from the rifles *you* sold."

"I didn't sell rifles to the rebels," said Segert. "I'd be a fool to do that. The *federales* and I take care of one another in this range."

"Oh," Sam said, "then I suppose not getting the pouches of gold won't bother you at all."

"To hell with a firing squad," said Dolan. "Let me pop a couple in his noggin." He stepped forward beside Segert, his Colt coming up cocked from his holster.

"Stand down, Dolan," Segert barked. He turned and stared at Sam as he spoke to Lilith. "Where's that gold, little darling?" he asked.

"We hid it in the crevice," Lilith said, pointing up along the rugged hillside. "It's up there."

Segert gave Sam a look of satisfaction.

"Want to bet?" Sam said.

Segert's look of satisfaction turned disturbed.

"I moved it during the night," Sam said. "Go see for yourself."

"Now, why would you do that?" Segert asked. "Did dear Lilith do something to make you suspicious—make you think she and I might be in cahoots?" He gave Lilith a dark glare. She looked frightened.

"No," Sam said. "You did."

"Oh, I did?" said Segert.

"Yes," said Sam. "The first time I ever met you."

Segert looked puzzled.

"You called me *Joe*," Sam said. "The only person I told my name is Joe is her." He nodded at Lilith; she looked away. "Everybody else knows my name is *Jones*."

"Jones, Joe, who gives a damn?" said Dolan. "This

is nuts. Let me kill him." He tried to raise his gun. Segert shoved the barrel down.

"Stand down, Dolan," Segert growled, "or I'll have your gun stuck where you would never want it to be." He glared at him, then said, "Take Lilith up to the gold. Let me know if it's still where they hid it."

Sam, Segert and the Mexican all watched as Lilith and Dolan hurried to the crevice and began climbing up.

The Mexican captain looked concerned with the way this was going. He stepped closer to Segert.

"What is the holdup here, Señor Segert?" he said between the two of them. "You said this would be quick and easy, and no one would be any the wiser."

"It will be, Captain," Segert said, his fists clenched, straining to keep from shouting at him in anger. "You wanted to bust up a gunrunning operation. I'm giving you one. Stay back and shut up. Let me get it worked out."

The captain stepped back, red-faced, demeaned.

Segert turned back to Sam as he jerked out a handkerchief and wiped spit from his lips and settled himself down.

"What good is owning the Mexican government if you can't tell them what to do, eh, Joe?" he said with a sly grin.

"I've always said that," Sam replied.

"You've *always said that* . . . ," Segert laughed. Then he stopped and said, "See? Joe—Jones, whatever. That's the problem, you're just a little too quick for life in Agua Fría. Too quick with a gun, too quick thinking." He gestured toward the hillside where Lilith and Dolan had climbed out of sight. "The first time I heard of you, I knew you weren't going to last. You should have come in quieter—not cracking heads at a cantina, shooting up the local scalp hunters, all that. What the hell were you thinking?"

"Just trying to get myself inside where the money's being made," Sam said.

Segert reached out a thick hand and patted Sam on the shoulder.

"Well, it's a damn shame, is all I can say," he said quietly. He turned and looked up the hillside. "Hey, up there. What's the story?" he called out.

After a silent pause, Dolan called down to him from within the jaws of the crevice.

"It's gone," he said, his voice echoing slightly.

"Raymond," Lilith cried out, "it was here last night, I swear to you it was. You must believe me."

Raymond . . . Sam took note of her sudden familiarity with Segert.

"She's something, that gal," Segert said to Sam.

"Yes, she's something," Sam said flatly.

Segert gave him a curious look. Then his expression turned bemused.

"Don't tell me you've fallen for her," he said with an air of disbelief.

"No, I haven't," said Sam.

Segert considered it.

"So, if I were to say, Jones, tell me where the gold is or I'll kill her, you wouldn't bat an eye?"

"Segert," said Sam, hoping to strike down any such

idea, "right now, if you gave me a gun, I'd likely shoot her myself."

"Shoot her yourself," Segert chuckled. "See, you've got a way of making me laugh. I like that."

"Then here's something else you'll get a chuckle out of," Sam said. "I'm not telling you where the gold is, no matter what you do, no matter who you kill."

Segert's smile vanished. An ugly scowl swept over his broad face.

"That's just mean-spirited, Jones," he said, poking his finger against Sam's chest with each word. "If you're dead, and the woman's dead, what do you care if I've got the gold?"

Sam shrugged.

"Like you said, *mean-spirited*," he replied. Then he said, "But Bell Madson won't like it, you coming home without his cut of the rifle deal."

"Bell Madson?" said Segert. "The hell do I care what Madson likes or doesn't like? We're what you call *competidors*, him and me."

"Huh-uh." Sam shook his head. "There's not two gangs here, only one. And Madson's the boss," he said flatly. "I figured it out. I've never laid eyes on him, but I've already run into you twice. You're the one out here in the hot sun. Where's Madson? Or does he even let you know?"

Segert backhanded him; Sam's face snapped to the side. The two Mexicans grabbed him, held him in place.

"Now, look what you made me do," Segert said. "You're wrong thinking I won't have them kill you." He gazed off up the hillside, seeing Dolan and Lilith walking toward him, empty-handed.

"Son of a bitch . . . ," Segert cursed under his breath.

As Sam shook off the sting and the ringing of the broad backhand across his jaw, he almost smiled to himself. He'd just learned that what he'd thought was correct. Madson called all the important shots here. All he had to do was kill Segert and get him out of the way. He looked around and realized it was a tall order at the moment.

Dolan stopped beside Segert. Lilith stood to the side, giving Sam a look of disappointment, as if it were *him* who had let *her* down. He shook his head and looked back at Dolan and Segert. Dolan sucked at a spot of blood on his palm.

"I cut my damn hand on a rock because of this bummer," he said, giving Sam a scathing stare.

"Well, ain't that just a damn shame?" Segert said with sarcasm.

Captain Silvero stood over beside Lilith, watching, growing impatient.

"Señor Segert," he said, "may I now shoot this one for you? I wish to get my men to San Carlo before the heat of the day sets."

Segert gritted his teeth at the captain.

"Not until he tells me where the rifle gold is hidden!" he said. "Do you understand that?"

The captain stepped back and fell silent.

But Dolan cut in, stepping forward, only inches from Sam's face. "That's a damn shame," he said. "I really had hopes of seeing somebody die first thing this morning." He turned to Raymond Segert, not realizing how tightly wound Segert was from talking with Sam. He grinned and said, "Seems like we ought to shoot somebody—"

"Damn it to hell!" Segert shouted. He snatched Dolan's Colt from his holster before the gunman could stop him, spun and fired four bullets into the bloody Mexican rebel he'd questioned a moment ago and left lying in the dirt. The rebel jerked each time a bullet hit him, but with the fourth, he fell limp.

Gun smoke rose and drifted. The sound of the four shots echoed out across the desert floor. Sam wanted to turn his head and look through the grainy morning light. But instead he just stared straight ahead.

Uh-oh . . . , he said to himself.

At dawn, the Mexican soldiers had pushed the wagon backward until it sat near a small campfire they'd built. As dawn widened on the hillside, Sam stood with his hands tied behind him, the rope running around the wagon's rear wheel. Lilith walked up to him, leading Andre, who now had a saddle on his back. The other wagon horse still stood with the dun in the shelter of rocks.

"I—I want you to know, Joe," she said in a soft tone, "that this is not how I—"

"Let me ask you something, Lilith," Sam said, cutting her off sharply. "Was the man I buried for you really your father, or just some gunman Segert and Madson sent along to help you cross the desert?"

She looked stunned that he even considered such a thing. She shook her head and started to answer. But behind her, Dolan laughed and shook his head.

"Jones is not as stupid as he looks, is he, peddler gal?" he said to Lilith.

She ignored Dolan and gave Sam a look through glistening, tear-welled eyes.

"What you must think of me, Joe," she said, shaking her head slowly. "I suppose I deserve it."

"Not to break up her performance," Dolan said, still with a dark chuckle, "but to answer your question, Jones, no, he was not her father. He was an old gunman named Rowdy Bart Taggs. Knew the desert like the back of his hand—died in his sleep, the story goes." He gave Lilith an accusing glare.

"That's enough," Segert called out, riding up with four of his mounted gunmen bunched up behind him. He gave Lilith a nod and she stepped away from Sam and up into her saddle. Mexican soldiers milled around the campsite, their rifles leaning against upstanding rock. Captain Silvero stood watching Segert as if awaiting further orders.

Atop his horse, Segert looked back and forth between Silvero and Dolan.

"Here's the deal," he said. "As soon as the sun is cooking good and hot, tie *Joe Jones* down out on the desert floor a ways and let the sun boil his brain until he gives up the gold." He turned his gaze to Sam and added, "Joe, the sooner you tell them, the sooner they'll put a bullet or two through your head. Don't wait too long. It wouldn't make sense." He gestured toward the rising sun in the distant sky.

Segert looked down at Dolan and said, "Once he gives up that gold, get it to me quick, you hear?"

"You've got it," Dolan said. He stood staring at Sam.

"*Capitan*," Segert said, "as soon as this one's dead, you take your men on back to San Carlo—but not before, *su comprende*?"

"Yes, *I understand*," Captain Silvero said in a voice stiff with resentment.

Segert chuckled under his breath, turned his horse with Lilith and his gunmen and rode away.

No sooner had the riders gotten out of sight down the hillside than Dolan walked over to Sam and poked him in his stomach with his rifle barrel.

"I should beat the living hell out of you before we stake you out, making me have to stay back and do all this, as hot as it's going to get."

"It's a tough day for you, I admit," Sam said.

Dolan just stared at him.

"Why'd you come to Agua Fría acting like the cock of the walk anyway?" he asked. "All you did was give all the wrong people a mad-on." He grinned. "Now look at you."

Sam took a breath and let it out slowly. A lot of what Dolan said was right. Maybe he should have played things a little different. But it didn't matter now. This was the hand he held. He'd have to play it on out.

He saw the captain walk up and stop beside Dolan. He had his tunic open at the throat against the already encroaching heat.

"If it is all the same with you, *señor*," Silvero said to Dolan, "I start my men searching the hillside for the gold. When they find it, we can kill this one and go our ways."

"Suits me," Dolan said. "All Segert wants is the gold. After that, he don't care what we do with Jones here." He reached his gun barrel up and tweaked Sam's nose back and forth.

"It is settled, then," said Silvero. "I will send men up the hillside."

"Do it, *Capitan*," Dolan said. "I'll just go have coffee while we wait." He looked back at Sam and ginned again. "Don't go rushing off nowhere, Jones," he said. "There's going to be a whole lot going on here in an hour or two—wouldn't want you missing out on any of it."

"Wouldn't miss it for the world," Sam said, almost to himself.

He stood watching as the two walked away. No sooner had their backs turned to him than he felt around behind him and found the metal edge of the wagon wheel.

Sharp enough, he told himself. He twisted his wrists and began sawing his rope back forth on the wheel edge.

Chapter 20

It was daylight by the time the rope gave way against the sharp iron band circling the wooden wagon wheel. When the ranger felt the rope break, he made no changes in his stance. He watched the soldiers and the gunmen move about the campsite. By the time Dolan sent one of the soldiers to stand watch over him, it was too late.

Sam stared intently at the young soldier, and judged the distance from where he stood at the wagon wheel to the place where he knew the dun stood in the rocks. He saw the French rifle that the soldiers had taken from him. It was leaning against a rock near the young guard's side. He needed that rifle, first thing, he told himself. Yet he waited and watched until he felt the time was right to make his strike. When he saw the soldier's attention move away from him and out across the desert floor below, he knew he could wait no longer.

But just as he prepared to launch himself forward at the soldier, he felt the entire hillside tremble and sway beneath his feet. The tremor caused the young soldier to snap to attention and steady himself. Soldiers and gunmen around the campfire made remarks aloud as they staggered like drunkards. Knowing he might not get another chance, Sam didn't let the deep land tremors stop him; he leaped forward.

In one quick move, he knocked the soldier backward, grabbed the French rifle from against the rock and turned to make his run for the horses. Racing straight for the rocks where the dun stood, Sam heard someone by the campfire shout, "He's getting away!" But he didn't miss a step, not even as rifle and pistol fire erupted behind him.

As he streaked across the campsite, rifle in hand, guns firing behind him, in front of him, suddenly he heard the loud yelping and shouting of Apache warriors. They had sprung up on the hillside and come spilling down over rock and boulder like a swarm of hornets. Luckily, Sam veered around a large boulder toward the horses in time to hear three arrows whistle past him. He didn't slow down.

The soldiers and gunmen around the campfire wasted no time retaliating. They concentrated their gunfire on the rocky hillside above Sam, where warriors let out their war cries and fired at them on their way down, using rifle and bow. It was the chance he needed. He raced around a large boulder to where the dun and several of the soldiers' and gunmen's horses stood in a row, reined to a lariat line the soldiers had earlier strung from a tall rock to a thin single pine standing behind the large boulder.

Without slowing, Sam saw a young Apache warrior standing between him and the horses, drawing back the string on a bow. He only had time to veer a step to the side and hear the warrior's arrow whistle past him. Then, before the warrior could restring an arrow or even get out of his way, Sam charged through him. Knocking him aside with his rifle barrel, Sam slid to a halt at the rope line and hastily untied the dun and threw himself up into the saddle, rifle ready in hand. Along the line, horses whinnied and neighed and reared in place, having first been frightened by the earth rumbling and swaying beneath them, and now by the raging gun battle.

Around the boulder, the battle intensified. But it was their fight, not his, he told himself. In the dirt, the young Apache had collected himself and sprung to his feet. He raced toward Sam atop the dun with a knife poised and ready. But the dun bolted forward and climbed headlong onto the steep hillside, pitching a face full of loose rock and swirling dirt into the warrior's eyes. As the dun climbed and Sam hung on, the sound of a fierce gunfight exploded from the campsite behind him.

Just in time, Sam told himself.

Yet, even as the dun dug its way up the hillside, bellying down and pawing with all four hooves, Sam heard Apaches yelling at the bottom of the hill. Then he heard their rifle shots explode and felt the bullets kick up dirt all around him and the struggling dun.

The dun went down under him, sliding backward on its belly, losing ground, and Sam rolled off its back onto the hillside and tried dragging it forward by its reins. Bullets sliced through the air close to his head. With Sam's weight off it, the dun managed to kick and paw its way back up onto its hooves in a spray of gravel and dust. The determined horse dug upward; Sam dug and tugged and pulled upward right along with it. With one hand holding the reins, Sam swung the French rifle around with his other hand and fired at two warriors below him.

The warriors heard the bullet slice past them. Seeing the dun digging up the hillside, and both man and animal growing farther up and away from them, the warriors turned away and ran the few feet to the row of spooked horses. The terrified horses stood rearing and kicking, trying to free themselves from the rope line.

"Earthquakes and Indians . . . ," Sam murmured to himself. He shook his head. "What next?"

Twenty feet farther up, the hillside flattened a little, giving way to a gravelly bed of scree that stretched upward over a hundred feet and ran in an endless wide swath to either side. Sam looked back and saw the two warriors below, mounted now and forcing their horses up the hillside behind him. Knowing a straight climb would send him and the dun sliding and tumbling backward, he led the dun sidelong, cautiously, diagonally up through the loose shifting scree, each of his and the dun's steps sending loose streams of rock skittering down the hillside.

The dun grumbled as it fought for footing against the slippery gravelly talus. But the two continued upward, slowly, sidelong until at length both Sam and the dun stepped onto a solid narrow game path. Looking back down the hillside, Sam saw the two warriors negotiating the same trouble on the steep terrain. The fact that they were still there told him they wouldn't stop their pursuit unless he stopped them. But that had to wait for now, he told himself, hearing the battle rage down at the campsite. Any second other warriors could join these two.

He turned to climb atop the dun. As he did so, the earth beneath his feet trembled again, violently. He heard the bed of scree rattle; he saw it slide inches down the hillside on its own. The dun shied sidelong and stopped, its stance wide, trying to right itself on the face of an unsteady planet.

"We can't wait for this," Sam said to the wary dun. He settled the horse as the world around them jarred to a halt. Then he swung up into the saddle, rifle in hand, batted his heels to the horse's dusty sides and rode away.

At midmorning Sam and the dun had topped the highest paths over the hill and descended the winding switchback trail down to the desert floor. As the path led him across a rocky stretch of broken stone and sand, Sam stopped the dun and stepped down from his saddle. He looked back at the trail dust rising and looming up the hills behind him. From the far sides of the hills, the sound of battle still resounded, but it had become less fierce, he noted to himself.

As he flipped open the saddlebags and grabbed the other gun he'd taken from the other dead scalp hunter, Bo Roden, he studied the hills in either direction. He hoped the Apaches might ride on and leave him. But he doubted they would. He checked Roden's big black-handled Colt, made sure it was loaded and shoved it down in his waist. From the dun's saddlebags, he took out a tin of bullets and filled his front trouser pockets. Somewhere in the heat of things, he vowed to himself that he was taking a holster belt off Segert's body—or the body of one of his gunmen—to make up for the one he'd lost somewhere as he'd been dragged around Agua Fría.

With the French rifle in one hand, he led the dun back and forth along the sandy ground until he found fresh tracks leading out onto the desert floor. He wasn't about to let Segert slip away from him now—not after all he'd gone through.

A half hour later, he had found the fresh tracks of many shod horses. Deciding the tracks could only belong to Lilith, Segert and his gunmen, he had followed them out and along the desert path to the trail back toward Agua Fría. From here to Agua Fría, if that was where they were going, as it appeared to be, he could trace their trip in his mind almost mile for mile. On this trail, it was a certain bet they would stop to water their horses and rest for a night or two at the old ruins where he himself had stayed.

"And that's where we're headed," he said to the horse beneath him, as if the animal had inquired. The dun perked its ears at the sound of his voice.

Sam only rubbed the horse's warm withers and rode on.

Two miles farther Sam felt a bullet thump, ricochet and whine away, followed by a rifle blast on the trail behind him. In reflex, he batted his boots to the dun's sides and looked back as the horse bolted into a hard, fast pace. Behind him he saw the number had grown from two to three Apache warriors riding toward him. There could be others joining them anytime.

"Get us out of here," he said down to the dun. He wasn't going to be shot at from behind if he could keep from it.

Another bullet fell to the ground behind him as Sam and the dun sped away. He had a move in mind, but he'd have to put more distance between himself and the three warriors in order to make it work. He flipped the rifle around and jammed it down into the saddle boot. He needed to get out of rifle range, he told himself. Lying low and forward on the dun's back, he batted his boots harder to the horse's sides, asking even more than the tiring animal had already given.

"Go, go, go!" he shouted.

The dun found more somehow. The horse chuffed in protest as it sped along, its hooves digging deeper, stretching longer, dangerously longer; but Sam felt them moving away from the pursuers. He looked back, and the three warriors appeared smaller behind him. They were coming fast, but their ponies were no match for the dun.

When he felt he had all the ground he needed, slowing only a little, he veered the dun out away from the trail just below the crest of a low rise and swung wide into a world of sand and squatting cactus. As the horse made the swing, Sam sat back on the reins and brought it to a hard and treacherous halt, sand flying and swirling up around them both. The dun whinnied long and loud but backpedaled quickly against the bit in its mouth.

Before the horse had even completely stopped, Sam doubled the rein on one side and twisted the dun's head so sharply the animal starting toppling to the ground on its side. As it went down, Sam jerked the rifle from its boot and leaped from the saddle at just the right second. As the dun flopped onto its side, he pressed its neck down with his left hand, letting it know what he wanted.

With the horse stretched out in the sand, Sam laid the cocked rifle out across its back, across the saddle. He took aim on the warrior to his right as the three warriors topped the rise and came speeding down the trail, abreast in a rise of dust.

Whether or not the warriors saw that he and the dun had circled out and dropped to the dirt in a shooting position, he had no idea. He squeezed the trigger and let the hammer fall.

The warrior on his right flew twisted and limp from his horse's back and rolled to a halt in the dirt, his arms and legs spinning askew like broken pinwheels.

Sam heard the other two warriors shout as they separated and spread out. Sam levered a fresh round and took quick aim again. He'd caught them by surprise. He knew his advantage would run out fast. This was their land. There was no contesting it.

He squeezed the trigger again. Another warrior fell. But his horse sped on, the third warrior running along its far side, keeping the horse between him and Sam's rifle sights.

But Sam had seen this trick before. He turned on his belly, keeping the rifle to his shoulder as the two horses and the warrior sped along the trail. He waited, sighting in on the riderless horse, knowing the warrior was lying low on the other horse, just beyond it. At any second the warrior would either break forward past the lone horse or rein his horse down suddenly and drop back behind it. Either move he made, Sam's rifle would be ready. He would take aim and fire.

But Sam didn't have to take aim. He already had it. Watching the riderless horse, he saw the warrior's horse falling back quickly—saw its rump coming into view. He targeted it and let it slide farther back until the warrior came up into sight, his rifle raised and ready.

But in the split second it took for the warrior to draw a bead on him, Sam squeezed the trigger and felt the slam of the rifle's recoil against his shoulder. The shot resounded and echoed along the hill line. The third warrior flew away from his saddle, rolled along the trail and fell limp in a large puff of dust. The two horses sped along the trail and began to wind down as Sam stood bowed at the waist and looked all around.

As he searched back along the trail, he picked up the dun's reins and jerked them tight while he booted the horse's rump—not hard, just firm enough to let the dun know what he wanted. The dun rolled up onto its hooves in a spray of dust. The Ranger swung his right leg over the saddle and rose with the animal beneath him, his rifle in hand, ready to ride.

He looked around again as the horse shook itself and slung its head. Patting the dun's withers, Sam gave the animal a touch of his boots and put it forward at a walk along the empty trail.

"That was good," he said to the horse. "Real good." He relaxed in the saddle, let out a breath of relief and rode along slowly until they came to the fork in the trail that would lead them to the ruins. In the sky, the sun began to stand lower toward the western horizon. "I don't know about you," he said to the dun. "It feels like it's been a long day to me."

Chapter 21

———

In the ruins, Mickey Galla sat on a cap rock atop a long mound of dirt and stone that had once been a lookout wall. He gazed almost blankly off into the shadows of evening. Holding a stone in either hand, he raised and lowered each in turn. His rifle was leaning against the stone he sat on, its barrel pointed at the sky. When Clyde Burke walked up quietly behind him, Galla didn't even turn toward him.

Burke shook his head, watching Galla raise and lower the heavy stones in his hands. An hour earlier Burke had looked up and seen the muscle-bound gunman lying on his back, pushing a much larger stone down from his chest with both hands. Now this.

Jesus.

"Hello the lookout," Burke said, stepping up onto the mound.

Galla didn't answer.

"Hello the lookout, damn it," Burke repeated in a stronger tone.

"I heard you. You don't have to yell," Galla said, still

raising and lowering the rocks without looking around at him.

"I didn't want to surprise you, cause you to drop something on your foot," Burke said.

"I'm all right," Galla said, still staring out as he continued lifting the stones, one on either side, sitting rigid except for his bending elbows. "What do you want?"

"What do I *want*?" Burke stopped and stood staring at him from five feet away. "I don't want nothing," he said. "I was just talking to Segert. He said tell you to keep a close watch back along the trail him and the peddler gal rode in on."

"I've got it covered," Galla said. He stopped lifting the stones, stood up and stepped around the rock and sat back down, facing out in another direction.

Again with the stones, Burke told himself, watching the broad-shouldered gunman begin his routine again. After watching for a moment, he had to say something.

"What do you get out of all this?" he asked, trying not to sound too critical.

"You have to ask?" Galla replied, his shoulders and upper arms bulging inside his shirt.

Burke shrugged; he didn't get it.

"Anyway," he replied, "Segert said him and the woman is riding on, taking four riders with them. He wants us wait here for Dolan and the ones he left back there." He jerked his head in the direction of the distant hill line. "They're bringing the gold from the rifle deal."

"Yeah? Why'd he not bring it?" Galla asked, still lifting the stones one after another in steady repetition.

"He ain't got it," said Burke. He stepped in closer and lowered his voice. "Said Jones got his hands on it and hid it, bigger than hell." He gave a short chuckle. "I *know* you remember Jones," he added, referring to Galla's broken nose still healing from Sam's punch with a rifle butt.

Galla stopped and looked around at Burke with a flat stare.

"You being funny?" he asked.

Burke lifted his hands chest high in a show of peace.

"Segert said they heard gunfighting behind them coming across the desert last evening," Burke said. "So, he says stay on our toes."

Galla stared hard at him again.

"He didn't mean it how it sounds," Burke put in. "He means expect anything."

"I know that," said Galla, going back to lifting stones. "What was the peddler gal so broken up about?" he asked.

Burke shook his head.

"Damned if I know," he said. "She's done nothing but cry and sniffle ever since they rode in. Might be she's crying over Jones. Anytime I talk about him, she starts in again. What time she ain't crying, she's stropping a knife she carries. I decided it best that I shut up. So I did."

Galla grinned a little to himself, gazing out along the desert trail.

"Do you remember how you did it?" he asked.

Burke stood staring at him for a moment, and finally said, "Go to hell, Mickey," and turned to walk away. But then he stopped and looked back at Galla from the edge of the high lookout mound. "One more thing," he said. "The woman warned us both to look out for a she-panther laid up here."

"Do I look like I need *warning* to you?" Galla asked over his shoulder without looking around. He raised the stones high, flexing his shoulders and massive arms. He hurled the stones one at a time out off the top of the mound. The stones fell and hit the side of the dirt slope with solid thuds.

"Not to me, you don't," Burke said; he shrugged. "What the hell do I know?"

On Sam's ride back to the trail, he'd swung past the bodies of the two warriors lying sprawled in the dirt. Dust had already settled in a dry hazy layer on their open eyes. On the ground near one of the warriors lay a battered telescope similar to the one Sam carried most times. Amazing how gear had a way of changing hands out here, he told himself.

Walking along toward the third body, he picked up a battered hat that had flown from the warrior's head as he fell from his horse's back. Sam turned the hat in his hands, realizing that he'd seen it before—early this morning when it had been sitting atop Daryl Dolan's head. He let out a breath and sailed the hat away and walked on to the third dead warrior.

Looking down in surprise, he saw his own Colt stuck down in a wide leather bullet belt circling the warrior's waist. The last he'd seen his Colt, it had been in the hand of Captain Silvero, he reminded himself. Stooping down, he picked up the Colt and unbuckled the bullet belt. There was little question how the gun battle had turned out. This one had plundered a hat and a pistol and hurried out to join his two fellow warriors as soon as the battle had swayed in their favor.

Buckling the bullet belt around his waist, Sam gazed back in the direction of the hills where the battle had been fought and wondered which way the rest of the Apaches had gone afterward. He checked the Colt and shoved it down behind the belt. He wasn't going to stay in one spot long enough to find out, he decided. Then he remounted the dun and rode on.

Yep, amazing . . . , he thought, feeling the bone-handled Colt lying hard against his belly, glad to have it back.

He rode on until deep in the afternoon, keeping the dun paced at an easy clip, letting the horse rest in the cooling breezes off the Blood Mountain Range. At a water hole in a stone tank just off the desert floor, he watered the dun and himself, and let the horse pick at clumps of dry, thin wild grass while he sat watching the fall of night on the long trail behind him.

The dun walked up and stuck its wet muzzle against his shoulder and chuffed.

"Sure," he said as if in reply, "ready when you are."

He dusted his trousers, capped a canteen and swung up into the saddle, rifle and canteen in hand. He turned the dun back onto the trail toward the ruins at a walk. An hour later, he chucked the horse up into an easy but steady gallop and did not stop again until he saw the hoofprints he followed lead off the desert floor and up in the direction of the ruins high on a rugged hillside.

When another hour had passed, Sam stopped and

stepped down from the saddle and looked up at the black outline of the old earth-covered ruins standing against a purple starlit sky. He continued to follow the hoofprints until at a fork in the trail he swung right and took a thinner path around the ruins to a rear entrance he'd found the other day.

In the dark, he led the dun through the ancient empty marketplace he'd found, staying wide of the grown-over wall where he knew the she-panther nested above her domain. As they entered the long black tunnel through the hillside, the dun looked back across the wide marketplace and grumbled and muttered under its breath. Sam gave a short, easy jerk on its reins and walked on, leading the dun into the darkness.

But before he and the horse had gone fifty feet into the black tunnel, Sam froze when a lantern flared bright and sudden fifteen feet in front of them. He raised the rifle one-handed, but didn't get it cocked. He saw the broad shoulders of Mickey Galla as Galla leaped from a hollow in the side of the cavern tunnel and stabbed the butt of a rifle straight into his face.

"Damn, Mick, don't kill him!" said Burke as Sam slammed down against the stone floor.

Galla grabbed the dun's reins from Sam's hand.

"I didn't kill him," Galla said, "not yet anyway. I want to break a few bones, snap a few fingers first."

"No," said Burke, "first thing is, we find out what happened back there—find out where's Dolan and the others." He paused, then said, "Maybe find out who's carrying the gold for the rifles, if you get what I'm saying."

"Yeah," said Galla, "I get what you're—" His words stopped as the earth rumbled and swayed beneath them.

"What the hell?" said Burke, trying to steady himself on his feet. He looked up in the lantern light and saw a stream of dirt spill down from the ceiling. "Whoa! Is this place falling in on us?"

"I don't know," Galla said. He swayed sidelong; so did the dun, getting spooked. Yet, in an instant, the earth made a hard thump. Galla tightened his hold on the dun's reins and settled it. With his free hand, he reached down and grabbed Sam by his collar. "But let's get the hell on out of here, just in case it is." He reached down, picked up the French rifle Sam had dropped and stuck it into the dun's saddle boot. He snatched Sam's newly recovered Colt from his gun belt and held it out for Burke.

Burke hurried over, took the Colt and shoved it down into the waist of his trousers. With the glowing lantern held up before him, Burke took the lead. They left the chiseled-out tunnel the same way Sam and the dun had come in, Galla dragging Sam along the ground like a bundle of rags. When he heard Sam groan, he looked down and shook him vigorously by his collar.

"I hope that rifle butt hurt as bad as I meant for it to," he said.

They stopped outside the tunnel and Galla dropped Sam flat on the ground at his feet.

"The hell are you fixing to do?" Burke asked, holding the lantern over closer.

"I'm fixing to wear a pair of boots out on this no-good ambushing son of a bitch," Galla said. He drew a boot back to give Sam a kick.

But Burke stopped him.

"Hold it, Mick!" he said. "Ain't you the least bit curious how come Jones shows up instead of Dolan and the others?"

"No, not particularly," Galla said.

"I am," said Burke, stepping in front of Galla. "Dolan's supposed to be bringing the gold."

"He's . . . not coming," Sam groaned from the ground, a hand covering his bleeding nose.

Galla stepped around Burke and stood looming over the Ranger with his big fists clenched at his sides.

"How about anytime I want to hear from you, I'll crack another rib?" Galla said. He drew his boot back again.

"Jesus, Mick!" said Burke. "Leave him be, at least until we know what's going on out there. He could be pulling a whole band of 'paches on his trail."

Galla settled and stepped out of Burke's way.

Burke set the lantern on a flat rock, reached down, pulled Sam up and propped him against a rock.

"You know the question," Burke said, looming over him. "How come you're showing up instead of Dolan?"

"Like as not, Dolan's dead," Sam replied, tilting his head back, holding his throbbing nose. "An Apache war party hit the camp. I took Dolan's hat from a dead warrior on my way here."

The two stared at him.

"Too bad for Dolan," said Burke. "What about the gold

for the rifles? Are we supposed to believe the 'paches took it?"

"I don't know," Sam said. "The last I saw it, I got up in the night and moved it."

"What do you think?" Galla asked Burke as they stared down at Sam.

"So far, it's all sounding the same as what Segert said before he left," Burke replied.

"It's the truth," Sam said.

"What do you think?" Burke asked Galla.

"I think if we're not hearing the truth, we will be when I commence kicking him all around the clearing." Galla stepped forward again and drew back a boot.

"Damn it, Mick!" said Burke. "Why do I keep having to say this? Let the man talk. You can kill him anytime."

"I hid the gold up in a crevice," Sam said, stalling for time, looking for a way off the spot. "The next morning Segert and some soldiers surrounded me. The Apaches hit before I told anybody where I'd hidden it."

"Yeah?" said Galla. "How'd you get away? They just let you walk off over the hillside?"

Both gunmen chuckled.

"I'd already worked my hands loose," Sam said. "When the Apaches struck, I made a run for the horses, got one and got away. This is the truth, so help me."

"You believe him, Mick?" Burke asked. As he spoke, he cocked his rifle.

"Mostly," Galla said, staring down at Sam. "Except I never knew an outlaw in my life who'd run off and leave gold behind, 'pache raid or not."

"I'm having trouble with that part myself," Burke said. He seemed to consider the matter, then said, "Go on, now, kick something loose. See if his story changes any."

"It's about time," Galla said. He stepped forward and drew back a boot.

"Hold it," Sam said. "All right, you got me. I didn't leave the gold behind. I'm no fool. I brought it with me."

The two gunmen looked at each other with slim grins of satisfaction.

"Give it up," Galla said.

Sam sighed, blood running down from his nose, through his beard stubble, dripping off his chin. He shook his head.

"There's plenty for the three of us," he said, bargaining now.

"But even more for *two*," Galla put in.

"All right," Sam said. "I hid it up there, right on the other side of the wall." He gestured a nod toward the heavily vine-covered wall. "Just in case I ran into trouble here," he added.

"Which you did, as fate would have it." Galla grinned and said to Burke, "Stay here. I'll go make sure he's not lying. Soon as I lay my hands on the gold, stick a bullet in his head." He pulled a thick candle from his shirt pocket and walked across the grown-over stone-tiled floor.

"My pleasure," Burke said to Galla, staring down at Sam from behind a cocked rifle.

Chapter 22

Both Sam and Clyde Burke waited and watched as Galla leaned his rifle against a stone and climbed the vine-covered wall. Atop the wall, he stood up in the purple moonlight, lit the thick candle and held it out on the wall's far side. He looked back and forth along a deep tangle of brush, dirt slope, stone, scrub pine and ironwood.

"Damn, what a mess," Galla called out. Looking down, he walked along the bed of vines capping the wall.

Sam almost held his breath, getting ready for his chance to make a grab for Burke. He knew there was no more than a fifty-fifty chance at best that the panther would be lurking on the other side of the wall. But it was the only plan he could come up with at the time, his nose pouring blood, his mind still cloudy from the rifle butt he'd taken to the forehead.

"See anything over there?" Burke called out, watching Galla take a step down the brush-covered slope on the other side.

"There's nothing *to see* down there," Galla replied. "Jones is lying. Put a bullet in his head."

Burke looked down at Sam with a thin, cruel grin.

"You heard the man, Jones," he said. He leveled the cocked rifle an inch from Sam's face. "Tell the devil in hell to save us a place," he said with a dark chuckle.

Sam had nothing to lose. He tensed, ready to make a grab for the rifle barrel and shove it away. But before he could, Galla called out, "Wait! I do see something— saddlebags, I believe. They're stuck down deep under some brush."

Saddlebags?

Sam stared up toward the wall in disbelief.

"Are you sure?" Burke called out.

"Pretty damn sure," Galla said, sounding excited, picking his way down the steep slope. "They're tan, sand-colored, you could say."

Tan, sand-colored? Sam had no idea. . . .

"Lucky for you, Jones," Burke said to Sam. "You can stand up if you want. But this won't change nothing. You're still going to die."

Sam pushed himself to his feet and stood beside Burke.

"I'm going to have to reach through some brush and pull them up," Galla called out over the wall to them.

"Get it done," Burke shouted in reply.

Sand-colored? It suddenly struck Sam what Galla was about to grab from down in the brush.

At the same time the realization struck Sam, he and Burke heard the snarl of the big panther on the other side of the wall. With the snarl came the chilling scream of Galla as the cat locked itself around his arm when the muscle-bound gunman had reached down and tried to grab its hunkered-down back.

"Holy Joseph!" Burke cried out toward the sound of

man and panther fighting it out beyond the wall. "I'm coming, Mick!" he shouted.

But before he knew what had hit him, Sam was at his back. He threw an arm around Burke's neck and yanked him backward off his feet. A shot from Burke's rifle exploded wildly in the air. Then the rifle left Burke's hands and turned around quickly in Sam's.

"Don't shoot!" Burke pleaded, having to raise his voice above the raging loud melody between man and cat.

"Then don't move," Sam replied. He reached down, jerked his Colt from Burke's waist and cocked it in his face. He clamped a boot down on Burke's chest. Over the wall, the cat battle raged. Galla screamed; the panther snarled and growled. The sound of brush breaking filled the ancient marketplace. Tree limbs and brittle dry vines thrashed and snapped. A black cloud of bats rose from the brush and screeched off into the night.

"For God's sake, Jones!" Burke pleaded. "You've got to help him. You can't just let that thing kill him!"

"Oh, I don't know," Sam said calmly, speaking above the terrible snarling, thrashing and screaming. "They're both holding their own."

"Burke! Help!" Galla shouted. They saw him throw a naked bloody arm up over the top of the wall and start to push himself up. Then his eyes opened wide, as did his mouth. He screamed as the two watched a big tan paw swing up over his shoulder and pull him back down. A deep, vicious growl resounded behind him.

"Please, Jones, do something!" Burke said.

Sam considered it for a second. He couldn't just let the man get eaten alive.

"All right," he said. He watched as Galla struggled all the way atop the wall, naked, save for a torn boot and what remained of a shredded shirtsleeve hanging down his bloody back. Sam watched as Galla jumped to the ground. He took aim on the panther as the she-cat sprang atop the wall behind Galla and perched there for a moment.

"Shoot it! Shoot it!" Burke shouted.

Sam had the cat in his sights, though he pulled his shot up, hoping to scare the cat away. But the cat would have none of it. The bullet hit the top of the wall, the shot resounding loudly in the night, and the sound only appeared to enrage the big cat more. Instead of vanishing with her tail down, she leaped from the wall and landed ten feet from Galla, who was having a hard time getting to his rifle.

"Jesus!" Burke mused. "That is one bad, angry cat."

Sam didn't reply. He stood watching as Galla got his rifle and faced the crouched, growling cat.

Sam felt a little sorry for the cat, seeing the naked, bloody gunman aim down the rifle barrel, ready to pull the trigger. But amazingly the panther, unimpressed with the pointed rifle, leaped forward onto Galla's chest as the bullet zinged past her head.

Galla went down, the cat on his chest, mauling, biting, scratching. She held his head in her forepaws for a moment and ran in place on his stomach as fast as she could with her rear paws. Blood flew. Galla bellowed in pain. Burke couldn't watch. He turned his face away. Sam took aim on the moss- and dirt-covered stone floor, only inches from the cat.

His shot sent dirt and rock chips from the floor, stinging the cat's sides. This time the cat turned to run. But Galla, dazed and seeming to forget that his main objective was staying alive, instinctively grabbed the cat's tail with both hands and pulled her back into the fray.

"The son of a bitch has lost his mind!" Burke remarked. "He's wanting more!"

Hoping Galla realized what a mistake he'd made grabbing the cat, Sam fired again. This time the cat stopped, ducked and looked squarely at him and Burke.

"Don't draw her over here!" Burke bellowed.

Sam held his aim, the rifle hammer cocked and ready, now level on the cat herself. As much as he hated to do it, the cat had to be stopped.

The cat snarled at him and Burke as Galla lay inching himself away, across the ancient marketplace. Then, as quickly as the cat had struck, she turned instantly, raced away twenty feet and stopped and sat in the outer edge of the lantern light. She sat for a moment licking her bloody front paw. A second later she was gone—vanished with the flick of her long tail.

Sam and Burke looked at each other.

"All right, Jones, I'm just going to say this—see what you think," Burke said with a hand spread. "I'm betting that there's not a man in ten thousand ever seen something like we just saw right here."

Sam shook his head slowly.

"I can't argue it," he said.

From the ancient marketplace floor came a pained whimpering sound.

"Help . . . me," Galla said.

Burke looked at Galla, then at Sam.

"All right," Sam said. "I'll help you get him cleaned up and comfortable before I leave. How far ahead of me are Segert and the woman?"

"Four hours, more or less," Burke said.

"Okay." Sam nodded and said, "Here's the deal. I'm not going to kill you."

"Obliged," Burke said.

"But I'm taking your guns and horses when I leave," Sam added.

Burked shrugged and said, "Hell, that goes without saying, I suppose." He paused and said, "What if the 'pache is headed this way, us without guns and horses?"

"Hope for the best," Sam said. "I'm taking them anyway."

In a glowing circle of the lantern light inside the cavern, Sam stood watching Burke sew up open claw gashes and deep teeth marks on Galla while the big gunman lay trembling in pain. Sam watched, as did the dun and the two gunmen's horses, their heads lowered, seeming interested in watching needle go through bloody flesh and pull it back together.

"I—I won . . . didn't I?" Galla said in a weak and shaky voice.

"Yeah, you sure did," Burke agreed. He gave Sam a skeptical look.

"A fair fight . . . and I won," Galla mumbled. "How's . . . the cat doing?" he asked, as if to sound gracious in his victory.

"Oh, I'd say she'll get over it well enough," said Burke, sticking the needle through more gaping bloody flesh. "Funny thing, she didn't even ask about you," he added.

"I won . . . I won, I won . . . ," Galla repeated, growing weaker with each word. He slumped back against a rock and gazed off to the darkness of the cavern.

Sam watched Burke continue with his sewing for a few minutes longer. Then he leaned around and studied Mickey Galla's dull blank eyes.

"You can stop sewing anytime," he said to Burke. "The man's dead."

Burke stared at Sam, his fingertips and the front of his shirt covered red with Galla's blood.

"But I'm almost done," he said.

"I know," said Sam. "But he's dead. Stop sewing on him."

"Oh . . . ," Burke said. He let out a breath and blotted his sweaty forehead with the cuff of his shirt. "I hate getting so close and having to stop." He looked all around. "But I guess I ought to anyway."

Sam nodded and stood back by the horses.

"I would," he said.

Burke stood up and sighed, the threaded needle hanging in his hand.

"I have to stay here by myself until somebody comes along with a horse for me?" he asked.

Sam considered it.

"How long have you been outlawing, Burke?" he asked.

"Long as most anybody you'll ever meet," said Burke. "I've rode with all of them, both sides of the border." He grinned. "Man oh man, the tales I could tell and the hangings they would cause."

"Is that a fact?" Sam said, thinking about what he'd just said.

"Not that I would, though," Burke said quickly. "Least-wise not to anybody outside our own circle."

"I hear you," Sam said. "Want to ride along with me toward Agua Fría, break off before I get to Segert's place?"

"Yeah, I can do that," said Burke. "To tell the truth, I never liked this place." He gave Sam a curious look. "You're going to go kill Raymond Segert first thing, aren't you?" He looked Sam up and down appraisingly.

"That is my plan," Sam said. "Can you blame me, after everything he's done to me?"

"Naw, I can't blame you," said Burke. He gestured his bloody hand toward Galla's body. "Any reason we can't leave him lying here?"

"None that I can think of," Sam said.

They turned to the horses. Before getting into their saddles, Burke uncapped a canteen, washed blood from his hands and dried his hands on the front of his shirt.

"Not that it matters, Jones," Burke said, "but what about that gold?"

"What about it?" Sam asked him.

"If it's not here anywhere, where is it?" Burke asked.

"It's where I told you and Galla the first time," Sam said. "I left it in the crevice. When the Apaches hit the camp, I lit out."

"You wasn't just making that up?" Burke said.

"Not a word," Sam said.

"Damn, we should have listened," said Burke, chastising himself and Galla. "Now that things are more or less settled between you and me," he said, "how would you feel about going back there and finding that gold? Split it right down the middle?"

"I don't think so," Sam said. "The Apaches will be crawling all over the hills for a while. Anyway, like we said, I've got a score to settle with Segert."

Burke stopped short and said, "I hope you're not harboring a mad-on at me, for being in on that dragging." He gave a slight shrug. "I was only doing my job."

"Naw," Sam said dismissingly. "What's a dragging more or less?"

"It's big of you to feel that way," Burke said, taking Sam's words seriously. "Fact is, we was told not to kill you, just scare you some, make you think we was going to."

Sam just looked at him.

"It's true," said Burke. "Segert said teach you a lesson about stirring things up at the Fair Deal, costing him the money Graft paid every week for us for keeping down trouble."

"All about business, huh?" Sam said.

"Yep," said Burke. "Most likely had things gone on the way they were meant, you'd be riding for Segert right now."

"But it was Lilith—" Sam stopped and corrected himself. "I mean the peddler woman who saved me," Sam said.

"Only because Segert told her to," said Burke.

"Then she set me up?" Sam said.

"I figure Segert got jealous of you and her, saw she

was falling for you, decided to get rid of you in the end," Burke said. He shrugged and grinned. "Just my opinion, for what it's worth."

"Falling for me . . . ?" Sam murmured. "She was going to let them kill me."

"I have learned in life that none of us are perfect," Burke said in a sage tone.

."I'm with you there," Sam said.

Chapter 23

On their way to Agua Fría, Clyde Burke told Sam about all the banks, railroads and payrolls he and the other men riding for Segert and Madson had robbed over the past two years. Sam listened to names, banks, towns, gunmen involved, men murdered. He tried to absorb as much of it in his memory as he could as they rode on through the night. Burke also told him about how the two gangs were set up. In truth, there were not two gangs at all, he'd admitted. As Sam had suspected, Madson was the real leader. Sam had already decided as much. It was going to take some time getting to Madson.

Segert was just Madson's *segundo*—his second-in-command, Burke had gone on to tell him.

"Anyway, none of it matters much now," Burke said finally. "Madson's taken his best men and pulled out of here. Built himself a fine hacienda somewhere thirty miles west above Twisted Hills. I've never been there, but they say it's built like a fortress, stone walls and all. It would take an army to get inside it."

They rode on through the night. Near dawn they had stopped at a water hole to water their horses and fill their canteens. While the horses drew water, Burke stood beside Sam, the two of them gazing off across the desert. In the east a silver-gold mantel crested the horizon.

"It's too bad how things turned out here between Segert and me," Sam said. "I really wanted to ride for him. Still would, if he hadn't treated me the way he did."

"If you don't mind me saying so, Jones, you came on a might too strong to suit Segert. He's used to people bowing and scraping. You come in kicking ass and thumping heads."

"Yeah," Sam conceded to him. "I think you're right, looking back on it," he said. "I'll remember that the next time I go looking for gun work."

"I can't help thinking that you wouldn't be looking for gun work for a good long time, if you played your cards right," Burke said. He gave Sam a wry grin as they rode along.

"You're still talking about the gold for the rifles, huh?" Sam said.

"I can't turn it loose," Burke said. "It's too much gold just lying there, nobody getting any good out of it. He took a sidelong step away from Sam. A small gun cocked in his hand.

Sam turned, facing him.

"Don't try nothing, Jones," Burke said. "I'll kill you graveyard dead."

"Um-umm," Sam said. "After me not killing you, giving you a horse . . ." His disappointment expressed itself in his voice.

"It was *my* horse to begin with," Burke reminded him. "You just gave it back to me."

"Still," Sam said.

"Still, nothing," said Burke. "I ain't leaving gold to waste. You ought to understand that, being an outlaw yourself."

"I'm not taking you to it," Sam said. "So put it out of your mind." He tried to dismiss the matter and turn away.

"You say that now," Burke replied, reaching out, poking his arm with the gun barrel, causing Sam to turn back to him. "But you'll think about it along the way, all the whores you can diddle in Vera Cruz, all the dope, the whiskey. We'd be living in what they call *ex-tasy*." His eyes grew excited just talking about it. He smiled to himself and let his gaze drift upward toward the sky.

Sam's rifle butt came around and smacked his gun hand soundly. His hideout revolver flew into the water. He yelped like a kicked dog. He started to charge at Sam, but he saw Sam's rifle cock and level at his chest.

"Hold on, Jones! Let's talk this thing out," he pleaded.

"I thought we just did," Sam replied. "I've gone as far as I can with you."

"Please, no, don't kill me!" said Burke. He fell to his knees, clenching his throbbing hand. He sobbed and bowed his head. "Please don't . . . ," he said, weak and pitiful.

Sam glanced all around the black jagged silhouettes on distant hill lines.

"This whole country sits around waiting to hear a gunshot," he said. "Get on your feet. I'm not going to kill you."

"You're not?" Burke sniffled and stood up, dusting

his knees, looking embarrassed. "You could have said so to begin with," he said stiffly.

"I'm saying so *now*," Sam countered. "I'm taking your horse. You're on your own."

"My *horse*?" said Burke. "Jesus, Jones! I'd've been better off if you took it at the ruins. What am I going to do now?" He swung his arms around, gesturing at the vast endless desert hills.

"You can sit here and figure it out," Sam said. "Fish your gun out and dry it. If I catch you near me again, I'll kill you before we say howdy."

"Even if I can find the gun, it's a Navy cap and ball," said Burke.

"If you live long enough, you'll find another gun," Sam said reassuringly. "They seem to drift around everywhere." He turned to the dun and swung into the saddle as Burke cursed and bent and pulled off his boots.

"I ain't forgetting this, Jones," Burke warned, rolling up his trouser legs. "You'd better *hope* you never see me again."

"I'm already there," Sam said. He turned the dun, rifle in hand, and batted his boots lightly to its sides. He heard splashing and cursing behind him as he rode away.

At midmorning, Reuben Grafton stood out in front of the Fair Deal Cantina, looking at the single rider coming into town from the hill trail leading down to the desert floor. Grafton's eyes were still puffy and purple from a beating he'd taken at the hands of Jon Ho and some other Segert men after Burke, Dolan and the two

Mexican vaqueros had dragged Sam away on the end of the lariats.

As Grafton stared, he watched the lone rider pull his horse over to the hitch rail out in front of the mercantile and step down and spin its reins. Only as the rider stepped out onto the street did Grafton recognize him.

"Oh, hell, Jones—" Grafton said under his breath, seeing Sam tip his hat up on his forehead. The cantina owner rubbed his hands nervously on his bar apron and looked around at his cantina with a grim worried expression. Seeing no one watching from the cantina's brand-new wooden double doors, he ran along the middle of the street, keeping silent, but waving his arms at Sam.

Sam walked on, rifle hanging in one hand, his right hand close to the butt of his bone-handled Colt standing behind the leather bullet belt around his middle.

When Grafton got close enough to not be heard in the cantina, he called out to Sam in a guarded tone.

"Jones, go back, go back! Four of Segert's men are in the Fair Deal. They'll kill you!"

Sam kept walking.

"*Buenos días*, Grafton," he said without slowing a step.

"Good morning, yourself," said Grafton, tagging alongside backward beside him. "Do you hear me, Jones? Four of them, four of his best—half drunk and killing mean."

Sam kept walking.

"Who are they?" he asked.

"Tom Mullins," said Grafton. "Dirty Tommy . . . ?" He continued tagging along backward, facing Sam.

"Don't know him," said Sam.

"Sudio Arpai, the Argentine?" said Grafton.

"Never had the pleasure," Sam said, still walking.

"Jon Ho, the Chinese half-breed?"

"I've got him," Sam replied.

"Some new man," said Grafton. "I've never seen him before."

"That's four all right," Sam said, staring straight ahead.

"Wait, Jones, damn it!" said Grafton. "You can't go in there. They'll kill *me too*!" He grabbed Sam's arm.

Sam stopped and looked at Grafton's hand. Grafton dropped it quickly. Sam looked at his bruised, mending face.

"Kill you for what?" Sam said.

"Jon Ho told me if I ever see you coming and don't warn them, I'm a dead man," he said firmly.

"So what are you doing here?" Sam asked.

"What do you mean?" Grafton asked.

"I mean, get on in there and warn them," Sam said. "Do us all a favor."

Grafton gave him a stunned look.

"You mean . . . ?" His words trailed.

"Yep, that's what I mean," Sam said. He started walking again.

Grafton stood in the street, watching him walk on.

"Don't you go fighting and shooting inside the Fair Deal, though," he called out. "I've got myself new oak doors, a brand-new mirror—this one has a fancy Spanish frame. Wait till you see it."

"I'm happy for you, Grafton," Sam said flatly over his shoulder. "I'll be real careful."

But before he'd gone three more steps, a shotgun blast from inside the Fair Deal sent the middle of the big double doors flying in chunks and splinters out onto the street. What was left of the doors swung back until one fell off its hinges. A hand shoved the other broken door open and three men walked out and spread out along the street facing the Ranger.

"Looks like they know I'm here," Sam said.

"There was no call for doing that," Grafton said angrily. "All's they had to do was walk out."

"Better clear out, Grafton," Sam said, still walking, "unless you want some of this."

"For two cents, I would take them on with you," Grafton said, seething in anger. But when the tall Argentinean with the smoking shotgun broke the gun open to reload one of its double barrels, Grafton slunk away to the side and called out to the three. The Argentinean stared at Grafton, then at Sam from beneath a lowered black sombrero brim trimmed in silver and red embroidery.

"Believe it or not," Grafton called out to him, "I was on my way to find Jon Ho just when you fellows stepped out," he said quickly as he moved away toward an alley. He offered a wide, frightened grin. "How's that for coincidence?"

Jon Ho . . . Sam looked at the gunmen as Grafton disappeared around the corner of an alley. There were only three, he reminded himself. Where was Ho? He looked all around. Jon Ho was not in sight. But on a balcony on the second floor of the adobe and stone hotel, Sam saw the woman and Raymond Segert, the two having come out to investigate the shotgun blast.

"Well, well, look, darling, it's Jones," Segert called out aloud for both Sam and Lilith's benefit. "I bet he come to save you from me." His voice had a slurred whiskey edge to it. An Army Colt conversion hung in a shoulder holster under his left arm.

Sam kept the three gunmen in the corner of his eye and looked up at Segert.

"Where's my gold, where's my men?" Segert asked bluntly, his hands spread out on either side supporting him on the balcony rail.

"The gold is where I left it," Sam said. "Your men got attacked by Apaches. My guess is they're all dead."

"Damn the luck," Segert said. He pounded a fist on the railing.

"Joe, I am so pleased that you're alive," Lilith said, near tears, her voice trembling.

Sam just stared up at her. He wanted to hear what she said, but he wasn't going to let the three gunmen catch him off guard.

"Me and this she-bitch has fought all night and all morning over you, Jones," he said. "All she's done is cry and take on over you—me, the one who's given her everything!"

"You gave me *nothing*!" Lilith screamed. "Nobody has ever given me anything!" She swung her arm wildly. "Except for this man." She pointed down at Sam. "He is the only man who has done anything for me without demanding something in return. I'm only a peddler girl! Who cares what happens to me?" She swung her arm again, as if to wipe the world away. "All of you, go to hell."

Sam could see that she too had consumed her share of whiskey.

"Nothing, *ha*!" Segert screamed in reply. "Look what she done to me, Jones!" He half turned, his arms spread wide. Sam saw the handle of a dagger sticking out of his shoulder, a wide stream of blood down the back of his wrinkled white shirt.

"Please tell me you came here to kill this pig," Lilith called down to him.

Sam didn't answer her. But he did say to Segert, "You need to put something on it, Segert, and get on down here."

"Put something *on it*," Segert said as if in disbelief. "You mean some salve, some ointment?" He laughed aloud. "A poultice maybe?"

Sam just stared at him.

"You still make me laugh, Jones—whatever the hell your name is," Segert said.

"Come down, Segert. It's time," Sam said with finality.

"Please! Please kill him, Joe," Lilith sobbed. "Please kill him for me. . . ."

Sam only stared, keeping watch on the three gunmen who had also started watching the spectacle play itself out on the balcony above them.

"Listen to her, Jones!" Segert raged. "But I warn you now, she is no angel. Not this one! Angels can fly!" He grabbed her and lifted her over his head in spite of the knife stuck deep in his shoulder. "She can't fly!"

Lilith screamed long and shrill as he hurled her off the balcony. Sam winced as she hit the hard stone-tile street out in front of the hotel. Her scream halted. She lay as still as the stones beneath her.

Sam turned his rifle up and aimed at Segert. His shot sliced through Segert's throat and took out the intricate nerves and tendons that served to hold his head erect. His head fell onto his shoulder like some broken child's toy. Blood, tendon and bone matter splattered on the adobe behind him.

Sam wasted no time. He spun toward the three gunmen, his big Colt coming up fast from behind the bullet belt, cocked and ready.

The gunmen looked stunned, stunned at what Segert had done to the woman, stunned at what Sam had done to Segert—all of it happening so fast it wouldn't be easy to recall except as one instinctive reflex, relentless and mindless in its violent conclusion, even to men such as these.

Yet, as Sam's Colt leveled at them, the three gunmen snapped out of it. Sudio Arpai, the Argentinean, fired first. The shotgun bucked in his hand, even as Sam fired and put Dirty Tommy Mullins flat on his back beneath a looming mist of blood.

The Argentinean saw his buckshot dig up the street ten feet short of his target. He charged forward with a loud yell, shortening the distance to make his next shot count. But as he yelled and charged, Sam's big Colt bucked again. The blast sent a bullet straight at Arpai.

It hit the tip of his gun barrel, dinged off it, tore through his eye and out the back of his head. Arpai staggered sidelong, reaching up, knocking the big embroidered sombrero from atop his head. He stared dumbly at Sam for a second through one eye and one bloody black socket. Then he swayed and melted to the ground.

The third gunman, a new man, stood frozen in place, his hands chest high.

"Don't shoot," he said. "We ain't reached no agreement yet."

"What?" Sam asked. He held the smoking Colt ready to fire again.

"We never talked about how much I get paid or nothing," he said. "It's all still open to discussion . . . far as I'm concerned I ain't took this job yet."

"Get out of here," Sam said. "Don't stop, don't look back." He waved the Colt toward the edge of town. The new man ran as if Sam might change his mind. He glanced sidelong at his horse standing at a hitch rail as he passed it by and kept running.

Sam looked all around, then walked to where Lilith lay in the dirt. He quickened his pace when he thought he saw her move a little. Watching, he saw it again, the slightest movement of her head there on the dirt.

"Lilith?" he said, running to her now.

He turned her over onto her back and cradled her on his lap.

"Joe . . . Joe," she whispered. "You came for me. . . ."

It wasn't true, but what did it matter at that moment? Sam decided.

"Keep still, we're going to get you a doctor," he said.

But she didn't listen to him. She raised a hand to his cheek. Her voice sounded normal enough, but listening closer, Sam could hear something broken deep inside her chest.

"Somebody get a doctor," Sam shouted to the empty street. *Un medico . . . consiga a un medico!"* he repeated in Spanish. "Please! *Por favor!"*

"Shhh," Lilith said, touching his mouth, feeling his lips tremble a little. She managed a thin smile. "I'm going to be all right. You came for me . . . and I will be all right."

"That's right," Sam said. "I came here for you. I'm here for you and you're going to be all right."

"Hold me, Joe. All this time, you never held me," she whispered. "Why is that . . . ?"

"But I'm holding you now, Lilith," Sam said. He bowed, drew her up to him and held her as a man should hold a woman. "I'm here, and you're going to be all right." He believed that she would be, could be, if someone would hurry, get a doctor. *"Please* get a doctor!" he shouted.

No one replied, but he saw people hurrying away. Were they getting a doctor? He was certain of it.

But as he held her up, her cheek pressed to his, he felt her stiffen in his arms. Then he heard the rifle resound from somewhere a long ways off.

No! No!

He held her away from him and looked at her. He saw the bullet hole in the center of her forehead; he saw what the exit wound had left lying spread along the street. He laid her down gently as if not to disturb her, and he stood up, looking at the blood all over his hands.

He wished he *had* come for her, the way she'd made it up in her mind—had taken her up and ridden away, her and him, the dun beneath them.

Stop it. . . .

"What are you doing here?" he whispered to himself. He shook his head and turned and looked off into the distance. He saw a single rider making a hard run toward the hill line, dust roiling up behind him. *Jon Ho?* He'd bet on it.

But Jon Ho would keep for now. Segert was dead. But Sam knew he'd be coming back for Jon Ho and the others—for Madson and all his men, he told himself. He felt a tremor deep in the earth as he walked back to the dun. Yet after a powerful swaying second, the ground settled and jarred underfoot. He walked on almost aimlessly, everything around him feeling foreign and unreal.

It was moments later when he swung up onto the saddle, noting that he had washed his hands somewhere between here and where he had held the woman, the woman who had died in his arms.

"Lilith," he whispered. Lilith with a last name he couldn't even pronounce. He touched back on the reins and directed the dun onto the street.

"Let's go," he said to the horse. "It's time you started earning your keep." Yet he patted its dusty withers, knowing the dun to be among the best he'd even ridden.

Talking to your horse . . .

The dun chuffed and blew and haughtily shook out its dusty mane, as if agreeing with him. He put the horse forward at a gallop, needing to leave some miles between himself and Agua Fría. As he rode, he looked down at the Colt standing at his waist. He placed his hand on the gun's bone handle.

"You've made your rounds," he said. "Good to have you back."

First to your horse, now to your gun?

So what? he told himself. *Sometimes that's all you get. Sometimes it's all that makes sense.* And he rode on, seeing the woman's face, knowing he'd be seeing it all the way to Nogales, knowing he'd be seeing it for a long time to come.

Arizona Ranger Sam Burrack is back!
Don't miss a page of action from
America's most exciting Western author,
Ralph Cotton.

SHADOW RIVER

Available from Signet in March 2014.

Blood Mountain Range, Old Mexico

Above a stone-lined water hole seated in the foot of the Twisted Hills, Arizona Territory Ranger Sam Burrack lay on his belly in the arid dirt hidden between two brittle stands of mesquite. On the sand flats a hundred yards below him, he saw four men on horseback riding toward the water hole at a gallop. Their duster trails flapped in the hot Mexican wind like tongues waggling from the mouths of lunatics.

With a dusty telescope to his eye, he moved from face to face, studying the men in the circular lens. The only face he recognized was that of Clyde Burke, a gunman he had left at this same watering hole a month earlier. The other men were just three hard-set faces darkened out beneath wide hat brims. Sam lay in wait like some predator of the desert floor, his duster and trail clothes long faded to the color of desert and stone.

At midmorning the scalding sun had already cast and drawn a wavering curtain of heat between a clear blue sky and a rolling desert floor. Behind him at the edge of the water hole, Sam had left his dun and a spare horse, a mottled white barb, to draw their fill, having tied their reins around a rock spur standing up from the gravelly sand.

And now to wait, he told himself.

He lowered the telescope and let his mind pore over the events leading up to now.

It had been a month—over a month, he decided—since he'd left Crazy Raymond Segert lying dead on a hotel balcony in Agua Fría. He had no regrets about killing Raymond Segert. It had been his job to bring down the outlaw leader. Yet, recalling that day, he still saw the body of a peddler girl named Lilith Tettovia lying dead in the street below the hotel balcony. Segert had thrown her over the balcony rail, but it wasn't the fall from the balcony that had killed Lilith Tettovia. Her death had come from a bullet through her head as Sam had held her weakened body in an embrace.

Four inches to the right, the bullet would have struck him in the back of his head. But as it turned out, the bullet came in just over his shoulder and hit her squarely in her forehead. He still hadn't decided if the long-range rifle shot had been meant for the woman or for him. But he had a strong feeling it was for him. Whomever it was meant for, the shot was made by one of Segert's men, a Chinese-Mexican named Jon Ho. Sam had every intention of killing Jon Ho, he reminded himself.

He was still working undercover; he was still careful to keep his identity a secret.

His objective a month ago had been to infiltrate the gangs operating back and forth across the border out of

Agua Fría and the Blood Mountain Range. He hadn't been successful in joining either group of outlaws, but he had found out that the two gangs were, in reality, only one gang run by one man—Bell Madson. It was useful knowing the head of which snake he needed to cut off. Now that Segert was dead, Madson was, without question, the head of the snake.

Sam had also established himself as a hardcase, a gunman who was out to do anything that had a dollar attached to it. While Madson might not trust him yet, there was no one on Madson's payroll who suspected him of being an Arizona Ranger working on the sly. Even better, he reminded himself, after killing Madson's right-hand man, Crazy Raymond Segert, in a straight-up gun battle, there would be few in the gang who would be quick to lock horns with him mano a mano. Strange as it sounded to him, he had established himself as an outlaw a lot faster than it had taken him to establish himself as a lawman. And he had managed to do it well enough that most hardcases prowling the desert knew him—or thought they did.

Good enough . . .

Now he was back on the job.

Sam remained in the mesquite cover the next twenty minutes, watching the four riders draw closer to a path leading up to the water hole, riding abreast, ahead of a wide, roiling stream of trail dust their horses raised. Sam shook his head. *Nobody rides abreast this time of day,* at least nobody who wanted to keep the hair atop his head. When he raised the lens back to his eye, Sam looked out past the four riders all the way across the sand flats to a stretch of sloping hills standing beneath the Twisted Hills. At this time of morning, he could still see the hills well enough to distinguish any signs of life and what those life-forms might be. Another hour or so and the wavering heat would obscure these foothills from view for the rest of the day.

Good Apache weather, Sam told himself.

The Apache knew this; they used the time of day or night to their advantage. Their knowledge of earth and weather was as instinctive to them as the scent of blood to a wolf, the sense of sight to a hawk. Sam knew that not seeing the Apache in the foothills this time of day did not mean they weren't there. It meant they knew the desert wouldn't yet hide them from watchful eyes. When the wavering heat overtook the flatlands, the Apache would venture down. They would cross toward the place where they had first spotted the wide trail dust.

So, here we go . . . , Sam told himself. It appeared his first job of the day would be to save the hides of some of the men he was sent here to kill. That struck him as darkly ironic. Rising onto his knees, his rifle pressed to his shoulder, he levered and cocked at Clyde Burke from ten feet away.

"*Whoa* now!" Burke shouted, all four riders and horses started at the sight of something rising up from the sand that way, sand pouring down from Sam's shoulders. The riders struggled to keep their spooked horses from bolting away beneath them.

"Everybody, freeze up!" Sam shouted, hoping that he wouldn't have to fire his rifle. On the slimmest out-side chance that the Apache in the foothills hadn't seen the trail dust, he didn't want to send a rifle shot resounding in a five-mile radius.

The three other men tightened on their reins, but kept their hands chest high. So did Burke.

"Jesus, Jones!" he said. "What the blazing hell are you doing here?"

"I felt bad leaving you, so I came back," Sam said, thinking quick. He stood up, the rifle still pointed and cocked.

"After a *month*?" Burke said. The other three men watched and listened.

"I got sidetracked," Sam said. "But I'm here now. I even brought you a horse."

"As you can see, I already acquired a horse. A gun, too," said Burke. He gave a mirthless grin. "Like you said, there seemed to be plenty of guns and horses drifting around out here."

"Glad it worked out for you," Sam said, not sounding like he cared one way or the other.

"And I heard how you were *sidetracked*, too," said Burke. "I heard how you killed Segert and a couple of his men in Agua Fría. Stuff like that always gets around."

"I was ambushed by them," Sam said. "I did what any clear-thinking man would do. I killed the ones I should. I chased away the one that had no stake in the game."

Burke nodded. He stared at Sam as he spoke to the other three gunmen.

"Pards," he said sidelong, "this is Jones, the man I told you about. Be advised that every damn thing he just said is most likely a blackguarding lie."

"So, this is Jones," said a tough-looking gunman wearing a high Montana-crowned Stetson. As he spoke, his hands lowered a little. He and the other two men began to inch their horses away from Burke and form a half circle around Sam.

"Clyde," Sam said calmly, his rifle still leveled at Burke's chest, "you might explain to your pals how the closer they try to get around me, the tighter my finger gets on this trigger."

Burke knew enough to realize that this man Jones had no hesitancy about killing. Yet he only sat staring at Sam.

"I meant to tell you fellows," he said to the other three. "Jones here is one of them suspicious kind of folks, always thinks everybody is out to get him."

"Adios, Clyde," Sam said with finality. He braced the rifle in his hands, ready to fire.

"Hold it, Jones!" said Burke. He quickly recommitted to raising his hand chest high. He gave the other three men a jerk of his head, calling them back in. "There's no need in you breaking ugly the first smallest thing we might disagree on."

As the three inched their horses back beside Burke, Sam kept his rifle tensed, ready.

"We disagree on a lot, Clyde," Sam said. "The last thing you told me was that I'd better hope I never see you again."

"It was?" said Burke, looking surprised. Sam saw that he wanted to ease the tension, get the rifle bead off of his chest.

"It was," said Sam.

"All right," said Burke. "I admit I was piqued at you, leaving me out here with no horse, no gun, Apache crawling all around—"

"The question is," Sam said, cutting him off, "are you and your pals here going to do something to cause me to drop this hammer?" He gestured his eyes toward the distant hill line. "The minute this rifle barks, the Apache are going to come to see what's left to pick over."

Burke looked off toward the Twisted Hills. "You figure they're still here?" he said.

"They've been here a hundred years or so," Sam said. "I've seen no sign of them leaving."

"I meant, right here, right now," Burke said.

"They locked onto the four of you the minute they saw you stirring up dust," Sam said. "Only fools ride abreast that way. It makes too wide a rise of dust."

"Hey, watch the name-calling, Jones," the man with the Montana-crowned Stetson warned. "Killing Dirty Tommy Mullins and the Argentinean doesn't cut you a width swath, far as I'm concerned."

Sam didn't answer. He looked back at Burke.

"Want to sit here and see if I'm right about the Apache?" he asked Burke.

Burke scratched his beard stubble as if in consideration.

"You brought me a horse, huh?" he asked.

The other men gave him a curious look. They couldn't believe he was falling for it.

Sam nodded.

"He's over there watering," he said.

"What about a gun?" Burke asked.

"No gun," Sam said. "I didn't trust you that much." He gestured at Burke's mount. "Now that I see you've already got yourself a horse, I'm keeping the one I brought as a spare."

"This man thinks we're idiots, Burke," the man with the Montana-crowned Stetson cut in. "He didn't come here thinking you were still here after all this time."

"Hush up, Montana. I know why he come here," said Burke without taking his eyes off of Sam. "He come here headed the same place we're headed. Am I right, Jones?"

Sam only nodded.

Burke took a deep breath. "Jones, this is Jarvis Finland, the Montana Kid," he said. "If you think Montana won't kill you, you'll be wrong starting off."

"*The* Montana Kid," Sam said, eyeing Finland up and down.

"One and the same," Finland said proudly.

"And this is Stanley Black," said Burke, gesturing toward the next gunman, a rat-faced young man with pinched cheeks and a crooked nose.

Sam only nodded.

"And this is—" Burke said, gesturing toward the third man.

"We met already," said the third man. He pushed his hat brim up and Sam recognized him as the gunman he had chased out of town the day he'd shot it out with Segert and his men. "I'm Boyd Childers," the third man said.

"Oh, that's right," said Burke. "I nearly forgot—you two have met." His sly grin told Sam that he hadn't forgotten a thing. "Boyd here told us how you and him stood each other to a truce after the gunfight. Said you watched him mount up and ride out of Agua Fría. Is that how you recall it, Jones?"

Sam recalled telling this man to leave town, not slow down and not look back. The man had raced away on foot, and had not even stopped long enough to mount his horse—left it standing at a hitch rail. He stared at Boyd Childers, letting the nervous-looking gunman wonder what he would reply. Childers looked embarrassed with Sam's eyes searching his.

"Yeah, that sounds about right," Sam said finally, letting Boyd Childers off the hook. He saw relief flood through the gunman.

Sam turned to Burke. "I figured when I saw you coming, you were headed out to find the three bags of gold I hid from Segert."

"You'd be right in thinking that," said Burke. "Would I be right, figuring you're headed the same place?"

Sam only stared at him. "Wherever I'm going, you'd also be right figuring I don't want any partners," Sam said bluntly. "How were you going to find the gold, anyway? Turn over every rock on the hillside?"

"Might have had to," said Burke. "But now that we're all here, let's talk about partnering up."

"Didn't you hear me, Clyde?" Sam said. "No partners." Yet even as he objected, he began working the idea around in his head. He still needed to find Madson and his men. Burke was part of the gang. "I figure with you riding for Madson, you'd be prone to letting him know about the gold, maybe even giving it up to him," he said.

Burke started to answer, but before he could, something sliced past his face. "What the . . . ?"

He looked around just as Childers let out a yelp and grasped an arrow shaft sticking from his shoulder. Another arrow thumped into Montana's saddlebags. His horse reared. As it touched down, he drew his Colt and fired wildly into the rocks above the water hole.

Stanley Black let out a sharp yelp and stiffened as an arrow sliced across his hat and left the front brim hanging down below his eyes.

"Injuns!" shouted Burke, gigging his horse forward, making for cover. Upon hearing Finland's gunfire, he jerked his own Colt from its holster on his hip.

"Don't shoot!" Sam yelled, but it did no good.

Montana fired wildly in three different directions. So did Burke. Stanley Black did the same as arrows streaked in, broke and bounced off rocks, sliced through mesquite and low cactus.

Sam ducked down, rifle in hand, and ran in a crouch toward his two watering horses. He got there just in time. A small, bent figure had taken the reins to the two horses and turned to lead them off to the rocky hillside. But this was no warrior, Sam realized at once. It was an ancient relic of a woman in a ragged checked dress and a straw skimmer hat. Upon seeing Sam rise up with his rifle, she stumbled and fell and let go of the horses' reins. With guns roaring behind him, Sam saw that the silence on the desert floor was broken.

Sam had brought his rifle to his shoulder. Yet upon seeing that it was an elderly woman instead of a warrior, he held his shot. He watched as her terrified face looked at him from thirty yards away. She stumbled to her feet, her toothless mouth agape, and scurried off out of sight.

An arrow slid across the ground at Sam's feet. He ducked and swung his rifle in the arrow's direction. Again, he held his shot, seeing a half dozen children racing away like young jackrabbits across stone and brush in the same direction as the old woman. They carried bows and arrows in hand.

Babies . . . , Sam told himself. But babies whose arrows could kill a man.

He released a tense breath and hurried to the two horses as they stood milling about where the old woman had turned them loose. Leading the two horses hurriedly back to the crest of rocks surrounding the water hole, Sam kept himself and the animals covered by a large boulder as he called down to Burke and the others.

"Hold your fire," he shouted. "It's only kids and old folks. They're gone." He stood in the ringing silence after the final shot was fired. Had there been any question of the Apache across the sand flats knowing they were here, the gunfire had answered it.

MORE GRITTY WESTERN ACTION FROM

USA TODAY BESTSELLING AUTHOR
RALPH COTTON

Available wherever books are sold or at
penguin.com

NOW AVAILABLE IN PAPERBACK

THE LAST OUTLAWS

The Lives and Legends of Butch Cassidy and the Sundance Kid

by Thom Hatch

Butch Cassidy and the Sundance Kid are two of the most celebrated figures of American lore. As leaders of the Wild Bunch, also known as the Hole-in-the-Wall Gang, they planned and executed the most daring bank and train robberies of the day, with an uprecedented professionalism.

The Last Outlaws brilliantly brings to life these thrilling, larger-than-life personalities like never before, placing the legend of Butch and Sundance in the context of a changing—and shrinking—American West, as the rise of 20th century technology brought an end to a remarkable era. Drawing on a wealth of fresh research, Thom Hatch pushes aside the myth and offers up a compelling, fresh look at these icons of the Wild West.

Available wherever books are sold or at
penguin.com

National bestselling author

RALPH COMPTON

"A writer in the tradition of Louis L'Amour and Zane Grey!" —*Huntsville Times*

**Available wherever books are sold or at
penguin.com**

S543